ADVANCE PRAISE FOR

Annapurna

"Meg Serino artfully layers past and present to explore how our unruly desires and betrayals can be as fatal as nature. Both an adventure story and an addictive exploration of more human mysteries."

— MICHELLE WILDGEN, Author of *Wine People*

"*Annapurna* carries some of the rare air of the Himalayas in its prose, a novel that's layered, large, and heady with the complex and overlapping emotions of desire, guilt, love, rage, and complicity. Meg Serino is a wonderful new writer; her debut novel is thrilling."

–LAUREN GROFF, Author of *The Vaster Wilds*

"Set against the mind-bending beauty of Nepal, a woman sets out with a group of trekkers to scatter the ashes of her onetime best friend, along the way confronting long buried secrets, startling truths, and herself. An immersive, gorgeous read I didn't want to end."

–CAROLINE LEAVITT, *New York Times* Bestselling Author of *Picture This* and *Days of Wonder*

ANNAPURNA

ANNAPURNA

MEG SERINO

A REGALO PRESS BOOK
ISBN: 979-8-88845-763-4
ISBN (eBook): 979-8-88845-764-1

Annapurna
© 2025 by Meg Serino
All Rights Reserved

Cover Design by Conroy Accord

Publishing Team:
Founder and Publisher – Gretchen Young
Editor—Adriana Senior
Editorial Assistant – Caitlyn Limbaugh
Managing Editor – Aleigha Koss
Production Manager – Kate Harris
Production Editor – Courtney Michaelson

This book, as well as any other Regalo Press publications, may be purchased in bulk quantities at a special discounted rate. Contact orders@regalopress.com for more information.

As part of the mission of Regalo Press, a donation is being made to Porters Welfare Program, as chosen by the author. Find out more about this organization at: https://keepnepal.org/program-category/porters-welfare-program

Regalo Press
New York • Nashville
regalopress.com

Published in the United States of America
1 2 3 4 5 6 7 8 9 10

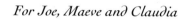

For Joe, Maeve and Claudia

"To love or have loved, that is enough. Ask
nothing further. There is no other pearl
to be found in the dark folds of life."

——Victor Hugo, *Les Misérables*

"But at times I wondered if I had not come
a long way only to find that what I really
sought was something I had left behind."

——Jon Krakauer, *Into Thin Air*

PART ONE

ONE

I sit alone, snow swirling around me. And there is sound to that, a hush to the wind as it spins the snow sideways, wetting my face, my hair, spitting bits of ice against my chest, against the tender skin of exposed neck. A soft patter, a whisper. But it's not innocent, this sound. If I stay here, in its lull and swoon, I will be dead in a matter of hours. Lost in Nepal, somewhere on the lower reaches of the Annapurna mountain range.

Frozen.

And yet, I'm already frozen. For the past twenty years, trying to forget, I have numbed myself in a sheath of ice, a welcome relief.

But I remember.

TWO

There is a photograph. Edges curled. Gloss smudged by too many thumbs. We are a motley lot, the seven of us, in various poses of staged togetherness. Mo's steady gaze at the camera, eyes unblinking. She glows, even in the faded Kodak color, fairy dust sparkling her skin. The sun shines from somewhere outside the four corners of the picture, igniting us, though Mo's face alone is unshadowed. She was twenty-two.

I used to look at it often. Several times a day in the beginning. And then, over time, less and less. Every week, maybe, a few times a month. Finally, after many years, I was able to put it away, tucked among old letters and dusty paper clips and hardened erasers in a box from post-college moves.

Until the day the parcel arrived. I examined the return address, scrawled with such boldness in black Sharpie: West Sussex, UK. My initial burble of excitement in seeing a box contracted a little, confused, then seized in my throat, knowing.

So they still lived there, in Bourne House, the very image of a British, ivy-clad home, though I never understood why a house had to have a name, like a child. Or a pet.

For several moments—maybe more—I stood in the kitchen, pressing the soft pads of my fingers into the box's sharp corners.

My son came in. At nine, Paul was small for his age, with a taffy voice and a bomb of blond curls. "Hey, Mama."

I placed the parcel on the kitchen table and turned just in time to brush my lips against his damp hair. It smelled of lake: the green chill of decay, the fresh slap of muck.

"Um, Mama?"

"Yes?" I never liked the name *Mom*. My husband, Graham, had attempted the whole *Mummy* thing, being British, but since we lived in a very un-British town in upstate New York, I went for *Mama* instead.

Graham had agreed. He had agreed to separate, too.

"Dill asked me to go sailing later, after lunch. Can I?" Paul opened the refrigerator and reached inside.

"Will his mom be there?"

Paul stepped from the fridge holding bread and mayonnaise and lettuce and a package of sliced turkey. "Yeah. He said she could drive me home after."

"Need a hand?" I said, eyeing the lettuce that was balanced atop the mayonnaise jar.

He plunked his load on the counter. "Nah, I got this." Taking a knife from the drawer, he began spreading mayo on a slice of bread.

"Hey." I filled a glass with water from a jug in the fridge, took a sip, and placed it on the counter in front of him. "I'm going to help Sienna down at the shop this afternoon. Maybe we could sail tomorrow?"

"Okay, yeah." He rubbed his nose with his shoulder, holding the knife midair. A mayo glop trembled against the blade, held, then slid onto Paul's knuckle. He licked it.

"Actually," I said, cursing myself, "Dad's got you this weekend. So maybe Monday?"

"Sure." He cut his sandwich in half, his mouth a quiet line.

I rose and put a chocolate cupcake on a plate from a covered platter near the sink. "Here, honey. For after." It wasn't a surprise; he'd made the cupcakes himself. But I wanted to do something for him, and this (sadly) was it.

I thought of his third birthday, how together he and I had made his cake: carrot with cream cheese frosting. I'd swaddled him in one of my aprons and sat him on the counter. Wooden spoon clutched in his dimpled hand. How he stirred and stirred, so serious, those little lips plumped. His cheeks pink-flushed. How he held the mixer, his small arm vibrating with the motor, watching the powdered sugar fly and cling to the sides of the bowl as if by magic.

And the magic stuck because this kid loved to bake. Shortbread (beloved by Graham) and chocolate-covered peanut butter bars (beloved by me) and apple crisp and peach pies, the thick sweet syrup bubbling from the top, and cupcakes, of all sorts (beloved by Paul), and oatmeal chocolate chip cookies and blondies with hazelnuts instead of walnuts (because I once said I preferred hazelnuts) and zucchini muffins in the summer and banana bread, anytime, and beloved by us all.

Paul finished his sandwich and rose to pour himself a glass of milk. I sat at the table. The parcel glowered at me from its perch.

"What's that?" Paul picked up the cupcake, pointed at the box.

"I don't know."

He took a bite. "Who's it from?" His mouth was full. He brushed a lock of hair from his cheek with the back of his hand. "Are you gonna open it?"

"Eventually."

"As in, *Eventually but not now?* Or *Eventually but not in front of you?*"

I laughed, and cupped his chin for a moment, gently. "Eventually as in don't talk with your mouth full."

He wiped his mouth with that same back-of-the-hand swipe.

"Ready to go?"

I got him a dry towel and filled a water bottle and hustled his sun-goldened, unhurried body to the car. Ignoring the silent command of the parcel on the kitchen table, sitting there so confident, so cocky, waiting for *eventually*.

Eventually was that night after Paul was in his room, lights out, asleep. After my second glass of cabernet. I had been a chardonnay drinker, but Graham liked cabernet and my taste in wine was recalibrated, along with a few other tastes and quirky Briticisms that I adopted, probably annoying to others, like the word *parcel*, for instance, when we say *package*, and the use of a *drying closet* instead of a dryer for laundry, which really does save money,

I might add, and brisk walks and *tinned* sardines (not canned) with toast for dinner. And tea. Lots of tea. I did not say *Wellies* for rain boots or *mac* for raincoat, or, thank God, use the term *biscuit* for cookie.

I sat at the kitchen table, my empty wine glass next to me, red wine marks, I was sure, at the corners of my mouth. Graham used to motion to me at dinner parties — discreetly, though, just silent quick nips with a finger near his own mouth — for me to wipe mine.

With the sharp edge of open scissors, I cut the parcel's taped middle with a fine and steady motion and pulled out a small wooden box. Inside was a Ziploc. A heavy-duty one, but a Ziploc nonetheless. And inside *that* were chalky bits of grit-like pebbles (like *bone*, I thought) and though I didn't open the bag I could feel its dense and life-less weight. The fragments shifted in the bag, reminding me of the coarse, dry sand down at the lake, and the little piles I always found trailing from Paul's flip-flops or in the pockets of his swim trunks.

A note was in the box.

Dear Olivia,

It's been a long while. I've meant to write you and Graham, but you know how that goes. Life has a way of muddying things up.

Here is the news: Mum finally passed, last month. Her cancer. She was quite herself to the end, ordering the nurses about, making us all feel rather incompetent. So. Now I'm trying to put things to right. Hence Mo's ashes. Mum refused to part with them while she was alive, but

ANNAPURNA

I'm selling the old place and can't see Mo's ashes boxed in storage somewhere. Plus, I always felt you should have them. You were her dearest friend. And you were there.

I trust you'll know what to do.

Best regards,
Hugh

I stood. Found the bottle of wine—it was right there, I didn't really have to go looking for it—and poured myself another glass. What did that mean, *you'll know what to do*? I most certainly did not know. It had been twenty years! And now Mo's brother, Hugh, who had kissed me once in some dark, crowded bar while on break from college, and who was not, I might add, a particularly good kisser, expected me to do the thing I supposedly knew. Plus, he *trusted* me.

I swallowed a large mouthful of wine.

The wooden box had glittery inlays of some kind. I looked at the bottom. *Made in Nepal.* Hah. Right. How perfect.

I picked up the cardboard box from the kitchen table to break it down for recycling. Something inside slid. I reached in.

Covered in brown paper, like that of a grocery bag, was Mo's journal. Its corners were cottony. I remembered packing it up, along with her clothes and trekking para-phernalia—that old kerchief and those hiking boots with the red laces she loved—and sending it to her parents.

And now Hugh had sent it to me.

For many hours that night I sat at the kitchen table, Mo's journal on my lap, watching the purply red of the wine catch the light, capture it, making it dance and twirl. A tiny flame, a fire. It glowed in my hand.

Mo had been that flame, except she wasn't something you could hold onto. Maybe if I'd known that twenty years ago things would be different now. Maybe she'd be alive. Maybe my marriage wouldn't be ruined, or Paul's life, our family, wrecked.

A cry caught in my throat and I gulped it back with the last swig of wine. Tossing the journal onto the table, I went into the hall and climbed the stairs to the attic. It wasn't a real staircase, just the foldaway kind that disappeared into the ceiling, narrow and rickety. I was slightly off-kilter, having jumped several times to grasp the rope to pull the stairs down and missing (possibly due to my lack of athletic grace or more probably due to the bottle of wine I'd consumed), but I finally reached the landing above and hoisted myself up.

It was hot and dry and smelled of dead mice.

Breathing through my mouth to avoid the stench of bloat and rot, I crawled on my hands and knees, bits of grit digging into the flesh of my palms, the bone of my kneecap, searching for what I had hidden.

Back in the kitchen, I sat at the table holding the photograph, debating whether to open a second bottle of wine. No. Tea. A proper cup of tea. Proper cup. Proper tea proper. Cup.

I shivered, though the night was warm. And an image of Mo appeared, spring semester, senior year of college, wearing a slip of a dress, white and shimmery, to a formal at her boyfriend's frat house. I hadn't wanted to go, done with the whole frat-party thing, but go I did, and it was fun (sort of) in the disgusting, sticky way formals at frat houses can be. Girls vomiting in the bathroom. The smell of sweating bodies and sour beer.

The party emptied outside into the cool night air, the stars bristling in the dark. Damp clothes chilled our skin. And Mo said, Let's make a fire. *A bonfire!* She must have been freezing in that hankie of hers. So someone cleared a space on the ground, surrounding it with bricks and cement blocks found I'm not sure where, and the whole party, all of us, were collecting broken-down cardboard liquor boxes, chucking in term papers and handouts and other classroom crap, until there it was, gorgeous and alive, snapping and skipping and darting to the sky, a fire dazzling and deathly all at once.

We cheered our success.

And then the wind sprang up and the smoke rose above and we drew in, and together, quiet now, our faces warm in the orange glow. Tiny fires reflected in the blacks of our pupils. Mo and I were separated by several people, all huddled together, bodies tucked in for warmth. But she stood, somehow, alone. Her spine was straight and she held her hands clasped in front of her, arms covering her breasts, almost as if she were praying. Her hair looked even more golden in the firelight and it streamed behind her in the wind. Her cheeks were smooth, her forehead, but the skin on her shoulders and arms was goosebumped. She looked brave and calm and she glittered.

Mo had always glittered. And she always knew just what to do.

Now, I wondered: What had Hugh meant? What was I supposed to do?

But even as I rose, unsteady, to fill the kettle with water, turn on the stove, to find a cup in the cupboard, *cup in the cupboard*, to sit once again, lift Mo's Ziploc between thumb and forefinger, and then wait for the water to boil, I knew.

THREE

"Well, what do *you* think?" I asked Graham. It was the next morning and he stood in the kitchen, hips resting against the counter, watching me make tea. Arms crossed in front of his chest, one ankle resting atop the other. He wore a faded red T-shirt and jeans and looked more like a mellow, aging ski instructor than an anthropology professor up for tenure. I handed him a mug. "I'd rather these were gin and tonics at the moment, but since you're driving, well." I shrugged.

"It's nine in the morning, Liv."

"Another good reason." But oh, how I wanted one. Hair of the dog. My head felt as if it were squeezed by a belt, bound too tight, compressed.

"Hugh wouldn't ask if it didn't matter," Graham said, accepting the tea with a nod. "Though it is quite an ask."

"Right. I mean, to go all the way back to Nepal?" I didn't know why, but I'd made it sound as if Hugh had specifically mentioned Nepal. Maybe I wished he had.

Maybe I wanted to go. But at the time, I didn't see it that way.

Graham sipped his tea. One of his best and most maddening qualities was his patience. Or was it a lack of curiosity? Sometimes I felt like one of his students, fumbling for an answer, unsure of what came out of my mouth but feeling the need to speak.

I took my tea to the opposite side of the kitchen and leaned against the stone wall above the fireplace. It was cool against my back and smelled of earth and smoke. The fireplace was one of the reasons I loved our house, and we sometimes roasted hot dogs for dinner there, the three of us. At least we used to.

"Want some eggs?" I asked, straightening again. "Or toast?" I started toward the fridge but Graham smiled, shook his head, looked down.

"Right. Okay." I stepped back awkwardly. And then, because Graham still wasn't saying anything, "I guess going back makes sense. I mean, the base camp is where she died, but it's also the place she loved most."

"Annapurna?"

"That's what she said. While we were there." Lying, it seemed, came more easily than I cared to admit. "That it's where she'd want her ashes scattered when she died." I watched Graham looking at me, his kind face. I felt scratchy and uncomfortable.

"So that sort of settles it," he said.

"No. Not really—"

"You don't want to go?"

"I'm not sure it's about want," I said. "It's about *can*. Can I afford it? Can I leave Paul for that long? Can I leave my job? Can I even physically get to the base camp and back?"

"Leave me where?" Paul said as he bumped by with his backpack. And then, seeing his father, "Are we gonna sail today?"

Graham's face broke into a smile. "Sure, if you like."

"Can we fish too? And Dill? I kind of told him he could come."

"Of course, if there's time. If not, we can all go tomorrow. We've got the whole weekend."

They could *all go tomorrow*. And they would. And it would be wonderful, I knew, Graham helping the boys hook the worms, helping them cast. Whistling, the way he did when he'd wash the dishes after I'd cook, scraping the pans of any stuck-on rice or sauce, his wrists soapy. So bright that sound, so buoyant. And I saw the lake, and the sunshine, felt the dry heated breeze, heard the clean pureness of his whistle, and it made me angry that I would miss it. Angry that it was my fault for missing it.

Graham placed his hands on Paul's shoulders, pulling him closer. "Have you emailed Hugh, then?"

"I don't know what to tell him."

"If it's about the cost, Liv, we can figure it out —"

"It just seems so impossible."

"Well, it's up to you." He seemed as if he was about to say something more but shook his head.

"What?"

"Nothing."

We looked at each other. His eyes were crinkled at the corners as if he was smiling but his irises were brown shattered glass.

Oh, but to kiss him.

"Right, well then, off with you two," I said. Busying myself getting Paul breakfast, putting the tea things in the sink. I turned to see them at the door and, walking quickly, kissed Paul on the top of his head. And then Graham bent his head toward mine, and, surprised, I lifted my chin, unsure, but grateful, too, and as he kissed first one cheek and then the other—friends, after all—we bumped noses, my lips cold, and I jerked back, mumbling *sorry*, red-faced, I knew, and Graham saying nothing, stepping away, hand on Paul's backpack, guiding him. My hand brushed against the soft cloth of Graham's shirt as he moved past me.

Fingertips tingling, I touched my cheek. And from the open door I watched them go.

And I remembered that terrible night when Graham had left, when we'd decided to separate. Me reaching for him, wanting him, wanting to know that he still loved me, wanting things to be the way they used to. "I can't stay here, Liv," he'd said, mouth grim. "Not now. Not so we can fuck things up forever." And I'd stood at the door then, too, watching. And I'd felt empty and relieved and filled with regret.

And worried that I was making another horrible mistake.

FOUR

I was in bed that night reading when the phone rang. It was Graham.

"Hey," I said. I was on "my" side of the bed, Graham's pillow smooth beside me, the top sheet folded over the duvet, undisturbed, yet disturbing. "You okay?"

"Were you sleeping?" His voice was low, almost a whisper, as if he didn't want to wake me.

"Reading." I plumped the pillows behind me. Trying not to remember how Graham used to come to bed after me, turning off the small reading lamp on my nightstand, taking the book gently from my hand and folding the corner of a page to save my place.

"Sorry," he said.

"No worries."

The lamp cast a yellowy glow on the white duvet. The room was otherwise black; I waited.

"There's just something I've been wanting to talk about, that I need to tell you, that I'd planned on telling you, today in fact, but then with your news, and with Paul right there, well—"

My heart thumped hard against the bone of my ribs. Had he found someone else? An image leapt in my head of Mo and Graham locked in an embrace—impossible (and ridiculous) now that she was dead—but real enough in the past.

I flung the image aside. What, then? Or who?

"I've had an offer. A tenured position. In Boulder."

And there it was. Not the worst thing he could have said, no, but not good either.

"Wow!" I hoped I sounded enthusiastic. "Congratulations! Tenure. Wow," I said again. "That's huge!"

"Thanks."

"But Boulder? I didn't know you wanted to move." *And so far away.*

"I didn't. It was a long shot. Thought I'd throw my hat in the ring and see what happened."

"But you were looking."

"I'm always looking. You know that. To your point, tenure is rather huge."

"Soooo—" How to ask? "Do you want it? I mean, are you going to take it?" I felt like I was whispering now, too, and I tried to make my voice sound competent and smooth.

"I don't know." He paused. "I want tenure, of course. And the idea of Boulder—the hiking, the skiing—a new life. The idea—"

And? What about as more than an idea? Something seemed to clutch at my throat. Because what if this separation—temporary, supposedly, a trial—was to become permanent? What if this pause in the movie of our marriage became the movie's end?

"When do you need to tell them?" I asked.

"A few weeks. I said I needed to discuss it with you."

I nodded, though he couldn't see me.

"But the move wouldn't be immediate," Graham said. "A year from now. Next summer."

I didn't know what to say. I kicked the duvet off and stood, feeling the rug's soft scratch of wool under my bare feet.

"I want you to come," he said. "You and Paul. I want us to move to Boulder as a family."

I opened my mouth. How could I go? But what if I didn't? What if *we* didn't, Paul and I. What if.

"It's up to you," he said. "You need to decide."

"Oh, Graham —"

"I know," he said. And again, softly, "I know."

What was it he knew? The only thing I knew was that I knew nothing. Nothing about whether we should go to Boulder, and nothing about this trip to Nepal, this whole wretched, horrible mess of Mo.

No. Don't even go there.

FIVE

There are lots of ways you can swallow a mouthful of bad memories. Of grief. Of something more than grief. You can stuff your face, eat until your stomach aches more than your heart. You can drink or drug yourself dumb, so the ache is anesthetized, numbed like your gums from Novocain. Or you can pick at yourself, like a scab, or go to therapy so someone else can do it. You can bury it, like a body, shrouded and encased and enveloped by the earth. Hoping that somehow it will disintegrate, dissolve; disappear into the mire and muck that surrounds it.

I guess I was in the last category, that of bury and hope. I thought of Mo only intermittently, sometimes never. Always with fondness, a patina of youthful amusement. Recently, however, and certainly after receiving the parcel, I had begun to squirm. Mo's journal lay like a powerful magnet in the drawer of the little table next to my bed, at once pulling and repelling me. So far, I'd resisted.

Now, as I sat at the computer after work the next day, searching my contacts for Hugh's email address, feeling not so successful in my bury-and-hope methodology, I found myself looking for several different addresses instead.

And thinking of Mo, dammit, of how it all began.

As a college graduation gift, Mo's grandmother had given her a trip. "My dear, *dear* Nana!" she'd sang, twirling around our dorm room, inches, it seemed, above the piles of clothes and boxes and half-packed suitcases that littered the floor, holding the letter, clutching it to her chest. "We can go trekking—to Nepal!"

"Nepal?" I said. "We?"

She stopped. Leaping onto my bed, where I sat watching her, half-amused, she reached for my hands, still holding the letter, pulling me toward her. "Yes! You *must* come! Nan says it's a trip for two—see?" She dropped one of my hands to show me the letter. "You *have* to come, Livy, I *need* you, you *must* come, please."

"I've never trekked before in my life." I waggled my foot, clad in white Tretorns. "Do these babies look like they can trek however many miles? How many miles is it?"

"You'll be brilliant!"

I raised my eyebrows, smiling, skeptical. "Brilliant may be a strong word."

"*Do* come. *Please*, Livy. It's an adventure of a lifetime! Really—when else will we have such a chance? How can you refuse?" Sparkles practically flew from her skin, the tips of her fingers, as she pressed her palms together as in prayer.

Who was I to refuse?

So that October, Mo and I joined a group trek to the base camp of Annapurna led by Nepalese guides. We met our fellow trekkers downstairs at the Yak and Yeti hotel in

Kathmandu the evening we arrived. *Trekkies*, I had whispered to Mo, laughing. I was so frazzled from the flights I thought everything was funny. She, on the other hand, looked beatific. Calm. Her golden hair hung down her back in a thick braid and she wore a flowy, gauzy skirt that still looked perfect even after thirty-two hours of travel.

My curly brown hair frizzed unevenly around my head, as it did whenever it was warm. Which surprised me. I'd thought it would be chilly.

A tall, thin man wearing glasses held out his hand, introducing himself as Joshi. He was older, thirtyish, with a narrow face and narrow front teeth, a musical lilt to his voice. He told us he was from New Delhi, on his annual pilgrimage to the Himalayas. His hand was dry and smooth. Two other men stepped forward, both from Michigan, both younger-looking than Joshi but older than Mo and me. They knew each other from home, they explained, as members of the same hiking club. Ben was soft-spoken, well-muscled, rangy—the way I'd imagined a climber would look. Rick wore a bright orange T-shirt with *Taco Bell* stretched across his hefty chest.

"Drinks anyone? Beer?" he boomed. His wide mouth opened and closed as if it were hinged, like a marionette. "Ladies?"

Mo and I caught each other's eyes. Ladies?

Joshi politely declined; we politely accepted.

"Ben?" Rick said. "I know you're a Bud man." And without waiting for an answer, Rick strode with purpose away from our little group, toward what I wasn't sure. There wasn't a bar in sight.

Our lead guide appeared and introduced himself. Rishi spoke to us about our itinerary, what to include in the duffels to be carried by the porters, what we needed in our own packs, and what to leave behind. I shifted from one foot to the other, testing my otherwise minimally tested hiking boots. Was I prepared? Could I do this? *Stop*, I told myself. *This is an adventure of a lifetime!*

After Rishi left, Rick returned, carrying four sweating cans of Star Beer in his beefy hands. "Guess there's no bar here." He was grinning. "Had to go down the street. But I wasn't going to let the gals down! No one goes thirsty on my watch." He distributed the beers, and we clinked cans, thanking him.

I tried to catch Mo's eyes again—this Rick was kind of a douche, even if he was being nice—but she was looking at Ben. Of course.

The next morning the five of us plus our two guides posed for a picture at the start of the trail. The same picture Joshi sent me several weeks after I returned home from London and Mo's memorial service. The picture that I'd hidden away, that over the years I'd allowed to gather dust, the one that I'd recently unearthed.

It was Joshi's home address I found first. Ben and Rick I found on Facebook, where for almost an hour I was sucked into the virtual world of their lives: smiling faces and crimson sunsets and jagged mountain peaks and quippy comments regarding various posts. Rick, I noticed, posted almost daily; Ben, rarely.

Surely it wouldn't hurt to ask? To put it out there, test the water, whatever. *Throw my hat in the ring*, as Graham had said. They probably wouldn't want to go anyway. Right? It was twenty years ago! And yes, of course, who could forget a girl's sudden death on a trek. But remembering was one thing. Wanting to haul yourself back to where it happened? Forget it. And even if they did want to go (which they wouldn't), I couldn't even think about it right now, not with the question of Boulder looming in the background. Or foreground.

Although the trek itself wouldn't be too long. Two weeks at most.

And, anyway, it might be fun to reconnect.

So I wrote to them, explaining that Hugh wanted us to go, all of us (okay, not exactly true, but to be fair, he *had* left it up to me, kind of dumped it in my lap, and going back to Nepal would be hard enough without having to trek with strangers), acknowledging the ridiculous expense, the bad timing (it would have to be winter, by the time a trip could be organized, but that would keep the cost down, too) making it difficult for any of us to go, but it was Mo's most cherished wish (this last I deleted, then added again at the last minute) and how could I say no? And no pressure, of course, which even I wondered if I meant, but if they could find a way to *join me in this journey to honor Mo* (yes too cheesy, but in the end, I kept it) Hugh would be forever grateful. And so would I. And though these were all things if not true were true-*ish*, and were so inconsequential, so tiny, who could blame me?

I pictured Mo, the swirl of her skirt as she turned, as if in slow motion, a carnival of color. A flash of white, her teeth, as her lips parted in a smile.

SIX

It would be a lie to say that I mailed Joshi his letter, messaged Ben and Rick, and then wiped clean from my mind any thought of them or Mo or Nepal or Hugh, for that matter, whom I hadn't actually emailed. A lie to say that I didn't check the mailbox or Facebook with renewed and nervous interest, despite the many times I told myself that it didn't matter what they said. Or if they replied.

Even so, a week later I was shocked to receive an email, though I'd included my email address, from Joshi. He'd never forgotten Mo, he wrote, *and I think often of the light that shone within her. I would be honored to accompany you on the journey to celebrate her spirit.* He included Ben and Rick's email addresses, with whom he occasionally corresponded.

Oh God, I thought. What had I done? Graham and I hadn't spoken again about Boulder. It was as if that conversation hadn't even happened (sort of). And now I'd made everything more complicated.

It was seven in the morning and I was still in bed, propped against pillows, staring at my laptop. I heard the creak of a floorboard, its sharp whine, and I looked up. Paul shuffled to the bed.

"Come on," I said, flipping back the poofy duvet so he could climb in.

I closed the computer and pushed it aside. Sunshine blared from behind the curtains, making me slide down and burrow under the sheets next to Paul, who lay on his belly, breathing deeply. His stale, sleepy breath. And I thought: *How could I leave?* This boy, my life. Only for a couple of weeks, yes, but to what end? It was pointless. Useless. Chasing I wasn't sure what (or running from something)—it didn't matter. I couldn't go. I wouldn't.

And I would think about Boulder. Later.

I showered and dressed, toasted and buttered a corn muffin for Paul and then drove him to the lake for his sailing lesson on my way to the village. It occurred to me, as I was opening the shop, straightening the jars of strawberry preserves and apple cider vinegar and moving a display of silver jewelry made by a reclusive and somewhat famous artist who lived in a neighboring village, that maybe I was wrong. Maybe emptying a Ziploc of Mo's ashes on Annapurna was not what Hugh had meant at all. Maybe, as usual, I was overthinking—or underthinking—or just missing the whole point.

But then two women walked in, and I smiled, murmured a greeting, and went behind the register to the piles of paperwork that cluttered an old pine desk so they could shop without some "helpful" soul (me) hovering. As it neared lunchtime, other shoppers trickled in, tourists mostly, touching the mouth-blown glassware, thumbing the hand-knit sweaters. I busied myself behind the desk, ringing up small purchases as they were brought over. And then I saw a boy about Paul's age with what appeared to be his older sister, both in flip-flops with sunburned noses and shoulders, waiting while their mother decided to buy some jam or olive oil. I watched, transfixed, as their father circled the boy and girl in his arms and moved them, as a unit, over to their mother, where they huddled around her, heads bent in, giggling and squirming and talking softly. Poking at each other. Laughing.

That laughter was like a punch to my heart.

We used to laugh like that, Graham and Paul and I. Laugh and laugh, until tears leaked from the corners of my eyes. I thought of the time we lay on our backs on the floor in front of the fire, my head resting on Graham's belly, Paul's on mine. And Paul said *Ha* and then I said *Ha Ha* and Graham *Ha Ha Ha* and so on and then suddenly our heads were bouncing against the other person's belly and all that *Ha-Ha-Ha*–ing bubbled into hilarity, the kind that made you curl up and gasp and say *stop*, even though looking back you wished it never would.

After Paul was in bed that night, I called Graham.

"You should go," I said after he picked up. "To Boulder, I mean." He was so good at that whole British, buttoned-up thing. But I knew my silence about his pending move was hurting him, and that was the last thing I wanted to do. I loved him still. "No matter what, we'll make it work. For Paul. Long distance or not, it won't matter." I wanted to cry.

"Or not?"

"Or not what?"

"Do you mean I'm to go on my own?"

It was a simple question, and he asked plainly, quietly.

"I just think this is too huge an opportunity to pass up. I mean, it's everything you've worked for. And who knows when another tenured position might become available. And in such an incredible location. It's not like it's in the swamps of Florida or in North Dakota or wherever; it's Colorado, and skiing, and all that fabulous hiking, and—"

"Right."

"Right! It just makes sense—"

"Is this what you want?" he asked. "Livy." He said my name like a question. Not begging, there was no force behind it, though I felt its desperate tug. Inside my name were a thousand questions, and grief, and all he wanted was an answer.

At some point during the night, or early morning, as light bled into the blackness of the room, I had an answer, though not to the question Graham had asked. I would go to Nepal. I needed to get away from what wasn't: away from Graham, who wasn't really my husband, away from a life that wasn't really ours. Away from Sienna and her strawberry preserves, her tall and slender presence, sleek-headed like a Doberman, saying coolly when I asked for time off, "The two weeks after Christmas are dead around here anyway. But your boys, what will they do?" I was about to say that Graham was hardly a boy, let alone mine, but she continued, "Of course they'll be fine, you know how boys are—they'll have fun—and you will too. New Year's in Nepal!"

Fun? No. I knew what lay ahead, though I hadn't looked at Mo's journal, could barely touch its cover. Inside would be her looping, lopey scrawl. We'd taken the same English classes in college, sharing notes and swapping books, her doodling all over *The Things They Carried* and *The Virgin Suicides*. No, I wouldn't be reading her journal anytime soon. And no, it wouldn't be fun.

But Graham would be more than happy to take Paul. They would have fun. I was deeply grateful; and yet I also felt a yellow twang of misery, despite my awareness that this was all my doing. Graham wouldn't be working over the college's Christmas break—which made my leaving possible—and they would have lots of time together. Time that wouldn't include me. And I knew I was petty and small, and I was ashamed.

As it was, it would be our first Christmas as a separated couple, separated now in time and space and not just because we weren't together. We *couldn't* be together, because I would be thousands of miles away! I was like a runaway teenager, desperate to flee, my tongue too twisted around itself to speak, even as I saw us all unraveling. My marriage, my family, unraveling.

Not that I would have said that; not in the softest of whispers, the tiniest of fonts.

Because I wasn't a teenager, obviously, and I wasn't running away. This was for Mo. And it would be an adventure! Yes, I was older; less nimble, less fit, perhaps, and with a greater sense of life's unexpected dangers. Not that a trek to the Annapurna Base Camp was dangerous, but I had a son now and I knew the risks of peanuts and fishhooks and biking on gravel. Paul still had a pinkish V-shaped scar on his chin from last summer. I remembered how the skin had flapped open when the PA at urgent care had cleaned it. I remembered how he'd cried.

SEVEN

O n the plane from Delhi to Kathmandu, the last of
three flights. We lifted off, in the air, weightless,
this two-hundred-ton machine. And such is the
beauty of travel: the possibility to deny what you know
to be true. To believe in the impossible. That it is possible to leave reality behind, at home, tucked away; that
it won't follow, attached to your heels by some invisible
thread. Peter Pan and his shadow. I wanted to believe. I
wanted to fly.

The plane roared through the sky.

In Kathmandu it was night and we descended in darkness prickled by thousands of airport lights and the city
beyond. Beyond that were the Himalayan Mountains.
Unseen, they were no less present. No less alive.

We waited to disembark and to pass through cus-
toms and to collect our luggage. On the first trek, packing was more like an amassing of repurposed clothes and
borrowed gear. We had a list of what to bring, but the
only new thing I could afford was a pair of hiking boots.

My school backpack, a sleeping bag from camp, and an extra headlamp from Mo plus a couple bottles of Evian water, to be refilled as necessary. I didn't even think about whether it was safe to drink the water.

This time, it took two months to pack. On the floor of my bedroom went fresh batteries, a headlamp, trekking poles, a first aid kit, and, yes, water purification tablets. Long underwear and wool socks and fleece sweaters and puffy jackets and a GORE-TEX raincoat and rain pants I'd found on sale. Plus, a CamelBak for water. Plus, toiletries. Plus, tampons. Mo and I had been lucky the first time around and didn't have to deal with the absurdity of changing tampons on the fly in the mountains. Not that we'd been prepared. But now I was stocked. Just in case. As I packed, I threw in a stack of sanitary pads and an abbreviated roll of duct tape. Just *Because*.

This time, I was ready. And all thanks to Graham, who'd offered our vacation savings to help pay for the trip. "You'd do the same for me," he'd said. And though I was unsure about many things I'd said or done—or was going to do—that much was true.

Now, one lone suitcase, red plastic with peeling stickers on its sides, circled round and round the luggage carousel. It tottered as the conveyor belt moved jerkily. But it stayed upright; it held on.

EIGHT

I lugged my bags outside the airport and found, with some difficulty, the driver sent by the hotel. In the car, the air was stale and reeked of artificial lemon. But I was here; I had made it. We juddered along roads pocked with holes, clogged with traffic. I rolled down the window and felt the cool breeze lift the curls from my forehead. Oh, but the dust! I had forgotten. Dust everywhere. Kicked up from the legions of motorbikes that *harummed* past, the vans crammed with bodies, the streets layered with dirt that couldn't absorb the rains when they came. Most people I saw walking and on motorbikes wore masks of some kind, surgical masks or scarves wrapped around the lower half of their faces or ones that looked like they were made of a thick, stretchy fabric. I didn't remember masks.

But I remembered Rick's face when I saw it, his hinged mouth, and I knew instantly I had made a mistake.

After I had written Hugh, finally, thanking him for the *opportunity for closure*, I emailed the others, glad Joshi would join me but wanting Ben and Rick too, clinging without reason to the idea of this group, this trip, that would somehow save me.

And *closure*? Really? What was happening to me? I hated that word.

Ben replied within the hour, apparently unaware that I had messaged him earlier on Facebook. I felt a wash of relief as I read his email, telling me he was glad I'd asked, that he was flattered, that he would be there to support me in any way he could. Rick's response, annoyingly, didn't come until almost three weeks later, as if to say, *see how busy and full my life is that I can't respond*, his many Facebook posts popping up on my newsfeed to prove it. Even then, he wouldn't commit. But I emailed him back, within seconds of reading his, my fingers typing away in oblivion: *She would have wanted us to be together. She loved you guys, she loved our group*. Which was laughable, really, and sounded too wrong, too ridiculous, even to me. *Please*, I said, *just think about it*.

And when he finally agreed, I was satisfied. I was pleased, in a grim sort of way.

"Liv," Rick said now, in that low but insistent way he had. He laughed (more like a bark) as if to punctuate my name, and his face was redder and larger but otherwise unchanged. He looked, wearing sneakers and polyester pants and a *Just Do It* Nike shirt, like the salesman he was. A salesman with a belly.

I was sitting in the lounge area of the hotel and I stood to hug him, because I thought I should.

"What're you drinking?" He motioned to my glass.

"Club soda."

"That's smart. Don't want to get dehydrated before you get into some altitude." He sat down heavily beside me. "I led a group on a climb in the Smokies, Clingmans Dome, not quite 7,000 feet, not high altitude, but still. Hard to catch your breath going up. Some of the ladies struggled, even though I warned them ahead of time. *Stay hydrated*, I said." He paused. "I might just have a beer, though."

Ladies. I pressed my fingertips against the cold glass. Beads of water hurtled down its sides.

I looked up and there was Ben. Graying hair, damp from a shower. Still trim. Still muscled. Wearing shorts and I could see the outline of his thighs, the elegant bulge of his calves. His shirt clung neatly to his shoulders. An aging mountaineer who in the last twenty years had climbed Mount Rainier and Denali and Mont Blanc. Not that he'd told me. It was all on social media.

We hugged. He smelled of soap, clean and sharp.

"You look great," Ben said to me. "I'm so glad to see you, to be doing this." He turned to include Rick. "With all of you. Though the circumstances, well —"

"Thanks," I said. "You too. I mean me too." Silently I cursed my awkward self.

We settled ourselves around the table. A young guy with a thin mustache appeared; Rick ordered a beer, Ben a mint tea.

"I mean, I know it's a lot." I thought of Graham. "It's a big ask. But I'm really grateful you decided to come."

"I didn't know her that well," Ben said. "But I think I understood Mo. The way she loved the mountains, how she saw herself. Her future. That was me. Is me. Although now, well, I don't know. Sometimes the way you see your-self has to change. Or should."

I didn't know what to say.

"I guess I just got her need to put herself in uncom-fortable situations, to find comfort in that, or peace, if that makes sense," Ben said. "To not think about anything else but that."

"Okay, yeah, well, that's not me," I said with a faint laugh.

"No judgment here," he said, and smiled in such a gen-uine way that it seemed more than just a flippant comment.

Their drinks arrived.

Rick swallowed half his beer and licked the foam from his upper lip. "I had to do quite a bit of juggling. Clear it with the wife. It wasn't easy."

"The weather won't be easy either," Ben said. "It's been snowing up there, pretty steadily."

"Has anyone seen Joshi?" My voice sounded high, falsely bright, even to me. *Fake it till you make it*, I thought. This was my big idea; I had gathered everyone, persuaded them to come (only later I'd use the word *forced*). I couldn't act like a daft cow, as Mo might've said. I couldn't call it a day. I would just have to *be a sport* and *carry on*. Stiff upper lip and all that.

My life as a British cliché.

"He's upstairs in his room," Rick said. "I told him to come down when he's ready."

"His daughter had a baby this year," Ben said.

"A grandfather!" I hadn't realized. "How old *is* he?"

"He trekked to Everest Base Camp last year," Rick said. "He'll be fine."

ANNAPURNA

"You know Joshi," Ben said. "It's more than a trek for him — and it will be for all of us, too, of course — but he sees it as a spiritual thing, to be in these mountains. He'll find a way."

I nodded. Took a sip of water. That's what it was for Mo, too, to be in the mountains. Maybe she wouldn't have said it like that, but you could tell. And just thinking of Mo made me think of her journal, and I knew I should start reading it that night. I would, not should.

I might.

I did. I sat on my bed, holding her journal, looking at the unused, still-tidy twin bed next to me. If Mo had been here, that bed wouldn't have been tidy. It would've been heaped with clothes, clean and dirty, wrappers from Snickers (swiped from me), her blue-and-white flowered kerchief. All of it, everywhere. And she'd sleep like that, tucked under and around the piles, her golden hair peeking from the dreck that claimed every bed, every room that was hers.

I opened her journal. Bits of dried marigold petals, dusty orange, fluttered to the ground.

October 21, 2003

We're here! The driver who met us gave us garlands of marigolds to wear round our necks — there are storefronts with masses of them everywhere — and they smell so strongly, so pungent, Liv couldn't bear it and gave hers to me. They are the color of orange juice, so bright they look fake. Copper and sunshine in one little flower!

Kathmandu is not at all what I expected. I guess I was thinking it would be more open, less built-up. Fewer bikes and bodies. I don't know why. We walked in the Thamel district near where the hotel is, the alleys all crowded with little shops selling figurines of Hindu gods and Tibetan singing bowls and climbing gear and cashmere sweaters and pashmina scarves. One sandwiched next to the other. Above the streets hang blue and white and red and green and yellow prayer flags, some tattered and faded, others new and bright and stiff, still curled, but all fluttering and swaying. Hundreds of them. Thousands! Everyone calling out, trying to interest us in whatever they're selling. And yes, of course, I am interested! I want it all!

No sleep on the plane so I'm knackered. But no matter. Tomorrow we start. Nan, how I wish you could be here! You're the only one who understands, really, aside from maybe Hugh and of course Liv. But she doesn't care much for all this and Nanny I know you would. Even here, among all this noise and confusion and dust, you can see mountains off in the distance, hanging there in the sky almost, waiting. It's like everyone who's here is connected in some way to those mountains.

Even me.

Even you, and you're not here. But I have the kerchief you wore climbing and Nan I'm going to wear it every day! And when things get hard — IF they get hard — I will think of you. You are with me. I know you had to convince Mum this was a good idea, or at least not a bad one, and I can't thank you enough. I don't know how she got to be so posh and proper about etiquette and all that, given her very own mum climbed Mont Blanc. Chalk and cheese, as you say, the two of you. And the Matterhorn! I think of that picture of you at the summit, wearing those horrid men's knickers. Nanny, you are my hero.

Livy's snoring so I can't sleep. I hope we won't go mad being together constantly. She's so neat and tidy and I'm, well, not. If anything, I'll probably annoy her. We met the other members of our group and the guide, Rishi. He looks so young — too young to be leading a trek I would think — with a mouth full of square white teeth. One of the other trekkers, Ben, is smashing though. He is such a man. Kind of like those old photos you showed me of French climbers from the 1950s — that rugged sinewy thing. I could tell by the way Liv kept curling a finger round a lock of hair that she liked him too. Or maybe not — she's loyal as a dog. Would never cheat, or even let her eyes wander. Maybe because Graham's her first boyfriend? I never saw her with anyone else. Hugh said she attacked him one night in the bathroom of a pub while we were visiting him at uni, ages ago, before she met Graham. Hah! I asked her at the time if she fancied Hugh, and she just got all blushy and defensive, saying he had been all over her. Not that I'd mind, but I can't see it. For one, Hugh goes for blond girls with big boobs. Sorry. But Liv? Even with her blue, bluer, bluest eyes, she's not that!

I closed her journal firmly. *Well.* All those exclamation points reminded me of how Mo spoke, with a whispered enthusiasm that seemed to come from a place other than her throat, a place deeper and lighter all at once. She'd never mentioned Hugh's side of the story, and it pained me to think of them talking about me and laughing. So maybe I'd remembered it wrong, maybe I *had* made the first move. So what?

Also, while yes, I considered myself loyal, the likeness to a dog struck me as not quite complementary. Was that how she saw me, lapping at her heels? Was that who I was?

I lay awake that night, like Mo had, images of that first trek flashing through my mind. Rishi and the porters, all of them. Her journal. Mo sitting outside, wearing that blue-and-white kerchief, chewing on the end of a pen, looking out, down across the rice paddies, her face to the sun. Writing, it seemed, about all of us. About her grandmother.

It had all started with Nan. It had ended with her, too.

Mo had spent her formative years hoofing it halfway through Britain and beyond with her grandmother, who was not, as one might suppose, the soft and delicate sort who drank endless cups of tea in her garden. No, Mo's grandmother was quite the perky thing, and sturdy, and they hiked together from the time Mo was small. Mo and I had hiked a few trails in the Presidential Range in New Hampshire and climbed Mount Washington the summer after sophomore year. She'd assured me I would love Annapurna, and though love seemed a strong word to me, I thought I might at least like it. Annapurna, she told me, killed one of every three climbers who reached the summit, the deadliest mountain in the world, including

ANNAPURNA

Everest. But we wouldn't be attempting to summit, she laughed, *obviously*, so those statistics wouldn't apply to us.

We started that Annapurna trek without fear, without doubts, the way you do when you're young. Ears perked and noses twitching, a couple of bunnies happy to go forth and hop.

There would be no hopping this time.

NINE

At six the next morning we stuffed ourselves into a rusting van for the airport, my body twined with exhaustion. Sagar, our head guide, squished in next to me. His smell, though we had only met last night at the welcome dinner, was instantly familiar. That oniony bite of body odor. I breathed through my mouth.

The driver swerved through the narrow streets and I clutched my backpack between my knees, gripping the seat in front of me so I didn't fall into Sagar's lap. He seemed nice enough, not particularly chatty, solemn maybe, but I wasn't feeling chatty either. I had texted Paul that morning, telling him that cell service would be poor or nonexistent as I headed into the mountains. I would be thinking of him. I thought of him now.

Before I left, Paul and I had gone to the farm and selected a pre-cut Christmas tree and had it tied to the roof of our car. We decorated it in the living room with chains of red and green paper loops and clay angels we had made years ago, their silvery-white paint flaking on our fingertips as we hung them. The house smelled of pine and the comfort of woodsmoke and yeast from baking bread. We rolled cookie dough in cinnamon sugar and then ate them, too hot, straight from the oven. And after an early dinner of spaghetti and meatballs (Paul's favorite) and fresh bread, he was off to his father's. I walked him from the car and stood in the doorway of Graham's rented lake house, barely winterized, hugging Paul for perhaps too long. The light shone from behind Graham, darkening his features so that he appeared mysterious and foreboding in a way he never was.

I wanted to stay there, hugging Paul, smelling his unwashed, silky hair, but I was afraid I'd start blubbering, which would be confusing in front of Graham, at least for me, and I was already confused. All I wanted was to gather my boy in my arms like a baby and return to the warmth of our own home, its warped wood floors scattered with pine needles like sprinkles on ice cream that crunch sweetly between your teeth.

I wanted that sweetness. I wanted to stay.

Abruptly I turned, sucking back the tears. "You have fun, okay?"

Paul wrapped his arms around me once more and squeezed. "Is it dangerous?" he asked. I pressed his head against my chest, felt his breath dampen my down coat.

"No. But it'll be cold, that's for sure. Colder than here, probably, at least at base camp."

"I don't want anything bad to happen to you."

"Hundreds of people do this trek all the time."

"But why do you have to?" he said. "Didn't you do it already?"

"This is different," I said. "This time it's for someone else."

He squeezed me again.

"I love you," I called after him, as he slipped into the
goldening light of Graham's house.

"Love you too!" And was gone.

"Got your kit together?" Graham asked. "All set?"

I nodded. "Thanks for doing this." I could see my
breath, tiny puffs of white. "I just mean, it's very understanding of you. And generous."

"Maybe it's what you need."

"Well, it's for Mo, this trip, I'm doing this for Mo."

"She's dead, you know," Graham pointed out, in that
flat pragmatic way of his that wasn't meant to be unkind
but stung nonetheless.

"Of course," I said. "It's for us—all of us who were
there—but for Hugh too, to do this in her honor."

"Right."

"It's what she would've wanted."

"And what do you want?"

I opened my mouth to answer, but nothing came out.
What *did* I want? We stood there, looking at each other.
Words hung in the air, thousands of them, like stars,
weighted and delicate and straining and useless. And then
Paul called from inside and Graham turned, stepping
back into the house, hand on the doorknob. I could see
him smile as he faced me in the darkness. "It'll be brilliant," he said. "Happy Christmas."

That night, before I went to bed, I walked through the
house, turning down thermostats, checking windows and
faucets, feeling the shift and warp of the smooth wood

under my bare feet. Outside, the wind shuddered the
bones of the house and I could hear the creak and swish
of trees, the scratch of branches against the windows. I
bent over my large roller-duffel and dug around, finding
and tossing the fleece-lined slippers I had packed, along
with two extra books, two bags of Kind chocolate gra-
nola, a large hairbrush for post-shower detangling, a pair
of fleece pants for cold nights at the teahouses where we'd
be sleeping, three extra pairs of socks, a whistle, and six
packs of hand warmers, the kind you put in your mittens
when skiing. These last I worried I'd regret—my fingers
were always so cold—but they were bulky and relatively
heavy and would have to go.

From far off I could hear the lonely sound of a dog
barking. Over and over, a sharp echo in the black of
the night.

It *would* be a good trip, I told myself. A brilliant one.

We bounced along in the van. My backpack slumped
against Sagar's legs and I retrieved it, apologizing. I could
hear Rick yammer on about some hike he'd led along the
Appalachian Trail. Ben listened politely, nodding and
smiling where appropriate. He was a nice man. Married, I
knew, again from Facebook, with two boys and two stores
that sold running shoes and gear. I pictured him talking to
a customer about their feet, their running gait, and imagined him nodding and smiling, nodding and smiling, with
that same respect and gracious courtesy.

In line at the airport, I tried to let the drone of Rick's
voice flow over me, but my throat prickled with the urge

to tell him to just please shut up. Which was probably not a good way to start the trip. A brilliant trip.

"Remember last time?" Rick turned to me. "When Mo forgot her passport? We almost missed the plane. I thought, *What are these gals doing?*" His jaw swung open and shut as he spoke. He laughed, turning to look now at Ben, at Joshi, hoping for that group laugh, that camaraderie he probably bathed in at sales conventions.

Joshi, grayer and thinner and possibly taller than he was twenty years ago, offered only a smile. "I remember that as well," he said. "I was so worried, thinking she might not be able to join us."

"Thank God for Rishi," I said. He'd thought to use a xeroxed copy of her passport, which we were all told to carry, and was somehow able to convince the airport authorities to accept that in lieu of the real thing. I'd been more relieved than Mo, who seemed satisfied knowing that her passport was safe in her remaining luggage back at the hotel. Without Mo, I wouldn't have gone.

"Hey, check out the sausage fest at three o'clock." Rick lowered his head but directed us with his eyes—was he trying to be discreet?—to a corner where two young men stood hugging. It wasn't your typical American bro-hug, that *manly* thump on the back while shaking hands, but a full-on, arms around waists, chins resting on shoulders kind of hug. Eyes closed. Deep with breaths. Beautiful. Loving. And then a kiss.

Rick made a sound like a guffaw, or a snort, sharp and loud, and I could feel my face flush hot. I stepped away from him, behind Ben, who shook his head. "You're ridiculous," he said.

Rick shrugged. "Hey, just calling it as I see it."

"Maybe you don't see so clearly," I said, more to myself than Rick, wondering why he was there.

Because you invited him.

The line moved slowly.

After we checked in, we moved to another line for security and then to a waiting area that was small and crowded and smelled of frying oil and burnt coffee. I had thought because it was winter the airport would be emptier somehow, that without the crush of trekkers in the spring and fall it would be a more solitary trip. We herded our bags and backpacks through the lines and onto the plane. It was a twenty-minute flight to Pokhara, and the rattle of propellers, or wheels maybe, it was hard to tell, twisted me into a damp and clammy tangle. I clasped my hands in my lap and kept my eyes trained on the seatback in front of me.

Twenty minutes.

The young man sitting next to me smelled, not unpleasantly, of aftershave or deodorant, woodsy, like the cedar chips I put in sweaters to repel moths. He gestured for me to look out the window. Mountains, pointed and knife-like, pierced a canopy of clouds. Distant and altogether too present, they waited.

There are times when you realize that you've made a mistake but you're too far in to turn back. When you've lied, maybe, one tiny lie and then another, one after the other, packing it on, until you feel trapped inside an ever-growing snowball and you're not even sure which way is up or down or how to get out because you're so wrapped up in it you can barely move. And you know it's wrong, or you should tell the truth — it's the only way out — but you don't. You can't. Despite the consequences. I hoped this wasn't one of those times.

TEN

From the airport we drove for an hour and a half, bumping and weaving our way to Naya Pul, where we met our porters and our assistant guide, Naba. It was greener there, the dusty road flanked on either side by small-treed mountains and, in the distance, terraced paddy fields. Beyond that was fog. We had lunch on the slanted wooden porch of a little convenience store painted bright blue: dal bhat and rice and huge bottles of water. The guides served us and then sat with the porters to eat.

Before we set off, we all made a pilgrimage to the toilet, which was a hole in the wooden floor of a narrow hut out back.

"My wife wouldn't dare go in there," Rick said to me when I returned. "It doesn't bother you?"

I shrugged. "I'm just glad I remembered toilet paper." I waved the roll in the air and returned it to my backpack, pulling out some hand sanitizer.

Sagar stood next to me, his backpack on, waiting. "We all have a headlamp?" he said. "We are going late and it is dark early this time of year." He spoke softly, but without concern. As if he were asking a group of children if they had brought bathing suits on a beach outing.

I felt a bubble of hilarity forming in my throat. No one else, I knew, would find it funny, hiking in the dark, and neither did I. "I hadn't realized," I said to Joshi. "Did you? I thought these headlamps were only for emergencies."

"We may not need them," Joshi said. "There are still many hours of light." He looked at the sky. "And see? The sun is shining. It is beautiful."

I looked up. The sun was bright and the sky clear and very blue.

"A picture?" Ben gestured with his camera for us all to stand together. There was some awkward rearranging of bodies, discussion about who should take the picture, until Sagar spoke to a wiry man who seemed to be the shop's cook and cashier. Ben showed him what button to push and we all huddled together, Sagar and Naba and the three porters included. We smiled. I was standing next to Rick, and the cook/cashier motioned for me to move closer. I inched toward him, my lips stretched grimly over my teeth. Rick burped and the smell of his lunch hovered in the air between us. Smile.

The picture taken, we hoisted our packs and set off down the dirt road, which initially was lined with shops selling onions and garlic and small potatoes heaped in plastic bins and packages of instant noodles and cream biscuits and salted crisps. Cans of Coke and boxes of corn-flakes. Sunscreen and trekking poles. Oreos. When did it get so touristy? It wasn't how I remembered it; maybe I just hadn't noticed.

ANNAPURNA

For the first hour or so, that was the trail, this pitted, rock-strewn road over which motorbikes and trucks and vans traveled, kicking up mouthfuls of dust, making us dive and scramble to avoid being hit. By the time I saw the trailhead and the steep climb that awaited us, I was almost relieved. Almost.

Near-vertical steps wound, seeming without end, to the heavens. The steps were made of rock that twisted through rice paddies and mountain villages as a means of travel and trade. Going to school or going to work in the fields or going to borrow a cup of sugar or sorghum or millet, it was these steps and paths that the villagers used. And horses and cattle and goats. And trekkers.

I hung back with Joshi, unsure of how I'd fare going up, content to listen to his voice dip and twirl as he spoke with Naba. Like a flute. Like a sparrow.

Up ahead, Rick fell behind Ben, whose steady stride and mellow rhythm I enjoyed watching. This was easy for him. Along the road, I had noticed, he would stop occasionally to take a picture with his large Canon camera that swung across his shoulder and onto his hip. He was quiet, and seemed pleased to be there, in all that dust, and as we ascended into clearer air I wondered what he thought about.

This is what I was thinking: *Left right left right left right left right in out breathe step left right left right breathe left breathe right in out in out left right left right left right left right left right breathe in breathe out breathe in breathe out in out in out left right left right left right left right left right left right left right left right left right.*

61

Sometimes, as the trail got harder, as I struggled to control what felt like uncontrollable panting, I'd picture Paul standing alongside, cheering me on as if I was running in a race, clapping and hollering and pumping his fist, his blond curls bouncing as he jumped up and down. Go, *Mama*, I heard him shout. *You can do it!*

At its steepest, I moved at a slow but steady pace. Step by step without pause. Joshi fell behind me, and so did Rick, whose weight in bone and girth must have made it harder to climb. Ben, ahead of me, stopped to take a picture of fluffy white clouds heaving across a vast blue sky over the snow-smothered mountains in the distance.

"What'd you do with all those pictures you took last time?" I said when I caught up. The trail had flattened, and then went down sharply, so I was able to breathe normally now, and speak.

"Not much," he said. "I guess I just like to take them. I have stacks at home, though now of course I download them all onto my computer." He motioned with his head. "Is this how you remembered it?"

I looked down and off to the right, where the mountain dropped away. "I'm not sure what I remember. What do you notice at twenty-two?" I shifted my pack higher on my back. "I think I was annoyed by how much I was sweating, how uncomfortable I was. Isn't that awful?"

Ben laughed. "I remember how crowded the trail was," he said. "This is incredible; we have it all to ourselves."

And we did. It was warm and green but not so warm that I was sweating. We were still low enough that there wasn't any snow along the narrow trail, but everywhere, soaring above, was the blistering blue-gray-white of mountains. Sharply toothed, they bit into the tender sky. Shadows carpeted their jagged edges, cascaded down their rollicking sides. Everything felt bigger, magnified, but somehow smaller, too. The green of the trees greener. At my feet, piles of yak dung littered the rocky path, and it wouldn't be long, I knew, before my boot landed in one. And it was only us, for as far as I could see, plus Sagar and our three porters ahead. Every porter carried one or two blue duffels, each weighing at least fifty pounds, by a single strap wrapped around their foreheads. How did they do that? And so fast? I felt guilty and grateful and somewhat pathetic.

"And how good it felt, just to be here," Ben continued. "No pressure, no stress. I think about it all the time. It was kind of *it* for me."

"But don't you do real climbs? Like Denali?" I mentally clapped my hand over my mouth. Dammit, that was info gleaned from social media stalking. "I mean, this trek must've been just a blip for you."

"This *was* real. It was as real as it gets," he said. "Maybe I didn't know that at the time, but when I look back, I don't know—"

Rick came up behind us. "This reminds me of a trip I once led in the Smokies. It was off-season, December, just like this. Sixty degrees at the bottom and negative twenty on top. It was intense."

"Wow." I was impressed. "Were you prepared? With all the right gear and stuff?"

"Well, *I* was, and I had distributed a packing list, of course, but some people didn't pay attention, I guess, so we had to turn back."

"Oh," I said. "So you didn't actually get to the top?" So rude, I knew, but I couldn't help it.

"As the leader, I had to make the decision to go down." His voice was knotted with self-importance. You could hear it tighten, like a rope.

"Of course," I said, nodding, looking sideways at Ben. "Smart decision."

Ben, unaware, or maybe just a better, nicer person than I, said nothing.

The trail started climbing again and conversation, at least for me, ceased. Ahead, Sagar and Ben spoke, mostly Ben asking questions about the different villages that we passed, the rice paddies and fields and shrines that we saw. From time to time we stopped, to reassemble our group or to catch our breath or, for me, to pee. This, finally, was the biggest difference between the two treks, other than Mo not being present. I had to pee all the time. Did I not drink water twenty years ago? I tried to remember, as I stood over the toilet hole, holding my breath against the smell, holding my pants away from the stream, crouched, my thighs trembling. I had three liters of water in my CamelBak and to lighten the load, not to mention I was thirsty, I drank constantly.

We continued going up. Up and up and up and up. The sun was thinning, its light less yellow, and I could feel a shiver in the air. When would we arrive at our teahouse?

Before dark? As it was, there was so much loose rock and scree on the trail it was all I could do not to slip or lose my footing. But with only the light of a headlamp?

What had I done? I looked hard at the trail, at the clouds and sky above. I wanted an answer, and there was none.

ELEVEN

We reached our teahouse in Ghandruk six hours after we began, just as the mountains purpled against a lavender sky. The small teahouse was made of stone and painted white and built into the mountain with rooms running along its side and up above. Each room had two or more wooden cots or bunk beds, a bare lightbulb hanging from the ceiling, and gray clay walls. Some painted bright pink. Some scrawled with trekkers' graffiti.

It was very cold. From my pack I pulled out a fleece top and a PrimaLoft jacket and put them on. Plus a wool hat. We sat down in white plastic chairs around a square, wooden table, the only diners in the small common area that evening, all of us similarly bundled. In the center of the room was what looked like a wood stove—squat and black with a central chimney—but burned yak dung instead of wood.

Sagar served us tea. Milk tea for Joshi, mint for Ben and me, a Coke for Rick.

And Mo? Masala chai. I almost asked for some, just to smell its cinnamon heat, but knew I'd never drink it. I didn't care for it, but Mo had loved its sweetness.

I warmed my hands around my stained, plastic mug and then held it aloft.

"I just want to say thank you," I said, gesturing to each of them. "For being here, for doing this, all together, for Mo. She would have loved it."

"Here, here," Rick said, raising his glass. "To Mo."

"To Mo," we all echoed.

"This must be hard for you," Ben said.

I sipped my tea too quickly, burning my tongue.

"I just mean," he continued, "you must miss her."

"I do." Tongue on fire. Eyes brimming. "But I'm so grateful to you guys for coming. Thank you, really. It's everything." I looked at Rick when I said this, as if to prove I could. But I meant it. I wanted them there—all of them—their comfort maybe, their presence. If nothing else, they were a distraction.

"Have you thought of how you would like to honor her?" Joshi said. "Where you will have her memorial?"

Sagar came in carrying plates of food. I looked at my omelet and boiled potatoes, and suddenly wasn't hungry.

Her memorial?

"I have her ashes," I said, sheepish. "And I thought we'd scatter them, at base camp, at sunrise maybe? But that's about it." I realized I should have brought some kind of marker maybe, a plaque of some sort. I should have prepared something to say, a little speech or poem or quote from some famous mountaineer.

Joshi spooned a bit of dhal onto his rice. "I think that will be beautiful," he said. He sang. "Sunrise. It will be as if her spirit is rising with the sun."

"That's lovely," I said, warmed by the thought. By the image of Mo, rising from the earth, from the gray rubble of her ashes, into the light of the sun's rays.

After dinner I went back to my room. I had it all to myself, unusual in teahouses that, during peak season, crammed in as many beds and bodies as possible. Mo and I had often shared a room with at least two other women, and though I was glad of the privacy now, I wished for the solace of another person's company, the comfort of not being alone.

I organized my clothes for the next day, readied my pack and duffel, my empty CamelBak that would need refilling in the morning. Exhausted, I sat on the edge of the cot. It was only eight o'clock, if that, and my whole body ached. I'd made it through the first day, sure, but my left Achilles burned and I knew I'd be sore tomorrow. Full body sore, but up to see the sunrise and then another seven or eight hours of trekking? How? I thought of Paul. It was ten hours and forty-five minutes earlier at home. Was he eating breakfast? Lunch? I lay back, worrying that Graham would feed him donuts and hot dogs and potato chips and frozen pizzas. As if that was the worst that could happen.

Rolling over, I pulled Mo's journal from my duffel, shimmied into my sleeping bag, and turned on my headlamp.

ANNAPURNA

October 22, 2003

Nan! First day and it's over too soon. Saw the Annapurnas peep through the clouds. And Machhapuchhre, called Fishtail, its peak fanning out fin-like, glistening the way rainbowed scales do in the sun. Rishi says that no one's climbed it, it's too sacred. And it feels sacred here. I want to stay! Just spend my days hiking in all this glory and godliness. God must be here Nana! There is a green you can taste, it's so fresh, with that endless blue above. A different light moves and breathes and brightens everything. The people who live in these mountains seem to have little, but it's a different kind of little than you see in London or New York City or anywhere I can think of really. Chickens run about and there are bins and bins of some kind of corn and rice spread outside to dry. Women with babies strapped to their chests or hips wash and hang laundry. I know you would tell me I'm being too romantic but it looks so idyllic! It is just this: LIFE.

I think of Maurice Herzog and the first climb of Annapurna, of any 8,000-meter peak, and I try to imagine it, aiming to summit before the monsoon hit, breaking trails in all that snow, even finding a trail to the mountain itself! Creating them! What must that have been like?

I've made friends with one of the porters, Tika. He's not a Sherpa, though. Rishi explained that even though people use the word "sherpa" to mean a job, like a porter, Sherpa is actually an ethnicity, people who live in the mountains in the east, closer to Everest. Maybe you knew that? I thought I'd be able to see Everest from here, but I guess we're too far west. In any case, we don't much walk with the porters, as they leave before us, but last night I saw Tika sitting outside with his tea and I sat down with him for a chat. He's just learning English and he likes to practice. He's rather funny, too, laughing when he mispronounces words, and with that smooth skin of his, those enormous eyes, well, it's lovely to sit with him.

Poor Liv in the heat can't quite keep up, but she never complains. Just keeps licking the sweat above her upper lip, retying her bandana, trying to keep the hair off her face. Those curls! Gorgeous, yes, but I wonder why she doesn't pull her hair back, or braid it, like I do.

Mostly I walk with Ben. He's so easy to talk to. I feel like I've known him forever. You'd like him, Nan; he's read all those books you gave me about climbers and Everest and he gave me the names of a bunch of ones I haven't read. He's always pointing out some animal—we saw monkeys swinging and jumping in the trees!—or the children as they pass us on the way to school, so smart in their navy uniforms, asking for sweets. Ben said that was sort of sad, that lots of trekkers must go by, and Rishi did pull from his pocket handfuls of brightly wrapped sweets called White Rabbits, which made me think of how you used to read Alice in Wonderland to me, and we stopped to watch their little fingers unwrap and pop them into their mouths. Thank you, they say in English, and off they go, picking their way across streams, balancing on rocks or bridges made of felled trees, keeping their feet dry, their smiles wide.

ANNAPURNA

Sometimes I feel beastly spending all this time with Ben, but Livy doesn't seem to mind. She's good like that. Rick is usually up ahead with Rishi, thank God, as he is annoying and the worst kind of American, but Joshi goes at his own pace, sometimes talking with Tika in Hindi, I think, and sometimes just in silence. We all catch up at lunch. I am ravenous, I can't seem to eat enough, but Livy just nibbles at her soup or noodles and winds up eating a Snickers. We all tease her, Rick especially, though I'd wager he'd be the first to snatch it from her hands. I hug her and say it's all in fun and then she offers me a bite, which I accept, because I love Snickers too.

Even with the chatter on the trail, the horses and cattle, the passing villagers with enormous baskets on their backs, strapped across their foreheads, even old women, their tiny bodies bent, there is a silence here. It is huge, among the mountains. As if it's waiting to swallow us whole.

I, for one, want to be swallowed.

Livy doesn't seem to mind. And I hadn't minded. Or had I? What I hadn't done was think about it. Or if I had, I'd also done my bury-and-hope thing.

I lay on my cot, my sleeping bag cocooned around me, the circle of light from my headlamp friendless and alone. I turned it off and the blackness in the room seemed to seep into my sleeping bag.

I had been *good like that*, I thought. Until I wasn't.

TWELVE

I woke to what felt like a slap from my alarm at four-
thirty the next morning. I hadn't thought I'd slept, so
consumed with memories of Mo and then missing Paul
and wondering what it meant that I missed Graham, too.

For a second, in the dark, I didn't know where I was.
And then the body ache, the cold.

I shuffled outside to see the sun rise with the others;
we clutched our phones and cameras, shivering. Fog hung
low and dense and I was irritated I'd lost a precious hour
of sleep for nothing. I hugged myself and hopped around,
pretending to be hopeful. *To not mind.*

But then Ben pointed to the sky. A blaze of bronze at
Fishtail's edges, ignited, like a smoldering piece of paper.
Its peak was drenched in gold. And then the sun flattened,
as if bored, spreading its more muted light down the sides
of the holy beast. Taking our cue, we turned and went
inside the common area, where it was warmer.

I sat down. My quads and glutes—every single muscle—felt as if they'd been pummeled by hundreds of tiny

fists. Muscles I didn't even know I had, something in my shoulder, across my back even. And today we would ascend almost 2,300 feet, and then descend about 1,600. That was the thing about this trek—it wasn't straight up to a summit, straight down—you went up for a while, down for a while, up and so on to base camp. And those down parts, easier in terms of breathing, didn't otherwise offer a bit of comfort as you knew you'd have to make up all those lost feet in elevation.

When it arrived, I swallowed my porridge, even though I wasn't hungry. Mo had eaten her porridge with little puddles of whole milk on top. With spoonfuls of sugar. Of honey. And her tiny waist, her slender legs. It was an insult, I'd thought, to those of us who ate their porridge made with water. Who had to do sit-ups. Not that I did them, but still.

Joshi came in, worry creasing the corners of his mouth. "I am afraid I cannot go on."

"What?" I said. We stopped eating.

"My boot." He lifted a foot. The heel of his boot flapped loose, like a wagging tongue. "I cannot walk like this."

Ben stood. "I've got duct tape," he said. "I bet we can make it work."

"I have some too," I said.

We both went to our packs and dug through, unloading the contents into small piles on the floor. Out went my hand sanitizer, my toilet paper roll, my Ziploc of tampons and pads (which I shoved behind my pack), my emergency first-aid kit, an extra fleece, raincoat and rain pants, a wool hat, gloves, headlamp, water purifying tablets, and finally, at the bottom (of course), the duct tape. I noticed as I tossed my belongings in a heap that Ben was much more methodical; each piece of extra clothing was rolled tightly and secured with a rubber band into a neat bundle, with rain gear coming out first and the heavier items last. Mo, for all her sloppiness, her apparent disorganization and sloth, had also packed like this.

Joshi removed his boot and sat down to eat his breakfast of tea and toast and two hard-boiled eggs. Seated cross-legged on the floor, Ben wound duct tape across the top of the boot to the bottom and heel, wrapping it round and round, using mine when his was gone.

He looked up at me. "I can save you some," he offered.

"Oh no, it's okay. Go ahead."

His strong hands, how competent and sure he was. Graham was like that, always fixing things—and fixing them well, too—it was something I knew I lacked, this ability to be skillful. To be capable. For me, changing a lightbulb was an accomplishment.

Joshi tried on his duct-taped boot, taking several experimental laps around the little room. He pressed his hands together in front of his chest. "Thank you," he said first to Ben, then to me. "I think it will work very well."

Rick looked up from his plate heaped with eggs, toast, and some kind of pancake. "I've got some duct tape too, if you need it."

Sagar came in as we were gathering our gear. "Ready?"

We stood in a group, backpacks on.

"The porters already go," he said. "Everyone has water?" He looked at us, his round face dusky, his brown eyes unreadable. "We are all fit, yes? I worry yesterday, with our slow start, but today I know we are fine."

"Why were you worried?" I said lightly. "Didn't think we'd make it?"

"We need to be quick," he said. "It is good here, but snowing above and snow is avalanches. There are many this season already."

I looked at Ben. "Avalanches?" I felt that strange urge to giggle.

"We go first thing, when it is cold," Sagar said to me. "Quickly, while we can."

But *quickly* wasn't happening. The trail led vertically up a steep series of steps and within minutes I was out of breath.

I had just begun, and I struggled, and I tried to think of Mo, to channel her graceful movement in the mountains, to step with ease and confidence. And delight.

Suddenly the weight of all I was carrying seemed unendurable. Unbearable. And there was nothing much in my pack, but there was everything, too. Panic settled on my shoulders, making them strain with the additional load. What was I doing? Why did I think this was a good idea, returning here, to this place where I never belonged? Why would I want to remember? When I had tried so hard to forget.

All I could hear was the sound of my breath. An ocean of breath. Rolling in, rolling out. Roaring.

And then behind me, quick steps, a trot.

A dog pushed past, his tawny fur burred, his paws tapping along the stones. And I thought how Mo loved dogs—all animals, mammals, cats and whales and horses and sheep—but dogs especially, and on our trek she had befriended one, or it had befriended her, following her for a solid day up the mountain.

At school she had smuggled a lost dog into our dorm room, begging me to allow him to stay, her hands clasped under her chin, telling me I could name him, that I was so good with names (which I wasn't, or at least never having named anything, who would know) and the dog, so long-eared and short-legged, with such a serious expression, stood nobly beside her, waiting, already loving her, I was sure. So I said *Yes. Of course.* And she leapt a little, and hugged me to her, and I didn't mind having the dog (which turned out to be for only a few days) or that she had named him Johnny (as in Cash) or that I woke early to walk him. It made me happy to make her happy. It was so easy.

Now the dog stopped and turned to look at me.

Okay, I thought. *Okay.* Here I am and there's no place to go but up. I lowered my head, fixed my eyes on the step directly in front of me, readjusted the weight on my shoulders. *Go.*

I went. Step by step. By step.

There was the click and scratch of my trekking poles on stone. A breeze rustled the shrubs and stubby trees that dotted the side of the mountain.

The dog waited as I approached, and then trotted ahead.

We stopped for lunch at a teahouse several hours later.

"Tomorrow," Sagar said when Joshi appeared with Naba over the lip of the ledge where we sat, "we do not stop for lunch. We walk straight through."

"Really?" I said. It wasn't that I didn't think I could go without a meal—it was hard for me to eat in the mountains, after so much exertion maybe, the altitude—but I was worried about the lack of a significant rest. A chance to sit down.

"Joshi, how's your boot?" Ben said, and then, to me, more quietly, "You'll be okay. By tomorrow, you'll be jogging up the trail."

"Hah," I said. "Sure."

He put an arm around me and squeezed gently. I pictured him with his boys, a supportive dad.

Joshi sat down hard. "It is holding," he said, but he was out of breath, and pale.

"Do you want some water?" I asked. "Some tea? We haven't ordered yet."

He shook his head. "I am okay." The word sounded as if it were two, *o-kay*. "I am just going to rest for a moment."

The wind picked up, snatching at my short-sleeved shirt, chilling my bare skin. I turned to look for my fleece, and there was the dog, sitting several yards away, looking but not looking at me. Waiting.

That night I sat in bed, staring into the darkness. Mo's journal on my lap. There was a rustling outside—footsteps?—and I held my breath, listening. I thought of the coyotes at home and of the lost dogs that Mo had loved and I imagined the one from today still out there, foraging for food or warmth, a bed, a body.

I felt the cold earth under his paws.

October 23, 2003

A lovely, lovely dog has been with us all day. I've named him Dal. There are lots of dogs here, some better cared for than others. This evening it's raining and we sit in the teahouse common area, warm and dry, and I worry about poor Dal. Livy keeps telling me that he looked well-fed, his coat wasn't dirty or matted, but I can't help it. What if he's lost or can't get down the mountain to his home? What if he gets hurt, or starves? I asked Rishi to give him some food and he promised he would, but I can see Dal sitting there in the rain, and I'm not allowed to bring him in, and I'm heartbroken.

What will become of him?

Later:

It's black outside and I can hear the rain bucketing on the roof, without end. Just pouring its heart out. I went looking for Dal on the way back to our room, but I couldn't find him, not anywhere.

I looked up from Mo's journal. How crazy. For a brief moment I wondered if the dog I saw today could be the same one. But no, no, of course not. A dog over twenty years old? But what if the dog was *Mo*? It was such a weird thought, and one so spookily Mo, that I turned to look over my shoulder, as if she could be there too. *Stop,* I told myself. *You're a grown woman. You're a mother. Get it together.*

I refocused my headlamp on the journal and continued to read.

Nan, I'm so worried. And freezing. But Liv's so good, she's given me her extra pair of thermals to sleep in and dry socks and a Snickers. This girl loves her Snickers. She's always complaining about her weight but really, she has a smashing figure and the tiniest ankles imaginable. Snickers are dear here, very expensive to buy if you can find them, so the fact that she broke into her stash for me is quite nice.

You've only met her once, but Nan, you'd love Livy. In a way, she reminds me of you. Not all outdoorsy, or sporty, but game. She was the one who went sledding with me on trays we nicked from the school cafeteria. And took me to hospital when I slammed into the tree. And spoke to the dean of students on my behalf to avoid the nonsense of involving Mum and Dad.

When we get back—if I go back, I do so long to stay!—Livy and I shall come for a proper visit. A really long one so you can know her. I'm certain you will love her.

In the morning, before it was light, I lay in bed, thinking of that day in college. What idiots we were—taking those brown plastic trays from the cafeteria, stoned out of our minds, thinking it was genius to tray down the hill into the village, not realizing, not even contemplating, the many potential hazards that existed, not the least of which were trees, the actual and greatest danger, but the road itself, which wound perilously close to our intended goal, the village below.

I pictured her, poised at the top of the hill, knees at her chin, all crunched up on the tray. And then she was flying down the hill, her mouth open in pure delight, hair streaming wildly behind, laughing—I could hear her laughing until the minute she wasn't—and I was laughing too. Until I saw that she was headed straight for a tree. And I was running, even before she hit, running and waving my arms and shouting at her to bail, to fall into the safe cush of snow, and maybe she didn't see or maybe she was too high or maybe she didn't care, but she didn't. And she crashed.

A cracked clavicle and a chipped tooth were the worst of her injuries.

I thought, at the time, she was lucky. That some special angel watched over her. That she'd remain untouched, unscathed by adversity or misfortune.

But, of course, I was wrong.

THIRTEEN

The sound of a man spitting. I must have fallen back asleep, but that sound. The gathering of mucous, that angry scrape and smack. A flat *thwack*, like a dog urinating, marking his spot. On the trail, at the teahouses, it was that sound I remembered, but had wanted to forget.

Sitting up, I found the clothes that I had laid out the night before and pulled them into the warmth of my sleeping bag. I pressed my shirt and pants between my knees, feeling the cold leech through my long underwear into my skin. Hurriedly, I dressed, and then headed outside with my toothbrush and water bottle to brush, swish, and spit at the tiny sink. When I returned, I chucked back into my duffel the two pomegranate-blueberry-pistachio Kind bars I had planned to eat. So much for antioxidants. I'd buy a couple of Snickers.

Today we were headed from Chhomrong to Bamboo and the trail, bless its heart, started with a descent instead of an upward slog. I knew we'd eventually be going up and up and up, but for now I was able to gaze easily at the white mountains ahead of us, growing closer every day, and the abruptly terraced cliffs that surrounded us, tiers of green and then darker green, tidy and manicured and magical in their immaculate order.

Ben was right. Maybe I wasn't jogging along the trail, but I knew it was going to be okay. I was still sore, especially my Achilles, which rubbed against the back of my boot, but I was more at ease, less prone to feeling the crush of hysteria. I hadn't been insane to plan this trip; it was more than okay, it was good.

Wet rocks and clumps of mud sludged under my feet. The chilled morning air warmed in the yellow sun.

We crossed a long, swaying suspension bridge. The sound of rushing water swirled around my knees, my chest, making me dizzy. Eyes wide and fixed on the other side, I felt the wooden slats move under my feet, felt the pitch and roll, the free swing of its arms. Ahead, Ben stopped to take a picture, and when I caught up, laughing with relief on the other side, we walked together as the trail began to climb steeply through a forest thick with rhododendrons on our right; on our left, several small waterfalls tumbled down stone cliffs, wetting the path, making tiny rivers around the clutter of rocks and scree, forcing me to keep my eyes focused on the trail once again.

"So how old's your son?" Ben asked.

"Nine." A wave of longing. "What about yours?"

"Sixteen and eighteen. I'm a few steps ahead of you in that department." Ben adjusted his camera as it bounced against his hip. "My oldest boy's a freshman."

"Ugh, what's that like, when they go off to college?"

"I was devastated," Ben said. "My wife and I both. For a while it seemed that we'd stay forever curled up on the couch together, under blankets, not moving."

I tried to picture this.

"But then, you know, you get used to it. And it brings up other stuff, kids leaving. The whole empty-nest thing. Suddenly your life isn't stuffed to the gills, trying to juggle work with getting your kids to their soccer games or track meets or their friends' houses, or just getting to *watch* your kid's track meet, or getting everyone to have dinner together, to play a game of Scrabble. Time was always so precious," he said. "And now, well, it's still precious, but in a different way."

"Oh God, I'm sorry," I said. "Taking you away from your family! It's not an ideal time of year —"

"Not at all," Ben said. "James is off skiing with his buddies. The two of us'll go in the spring. And every summer the family spends a week in a cabin up in the Oregon mountains. No running water. Just a wood stove, fishing all day, massive stars at night."

"Wow," I said. "That sounds pretty incredible." To Mo, maybe.

"But this, well, I've thought about you. I mean, what happened. With Mo. And this was more important. Coming here."

Of course. No one could forget Mo, once she'd cast her spell. Who wouldn't be haunted?

"What about you?" he said. "Where's —?"

"Paul? He's with his dad." I'd received a text from him that morning, telling me that the lake had finally frozen and the whole town was out on the ice, skating.

I thought of him now, chapped lips, his nose tipped with red. He'd made cream scones for after, Graham's favorite, and I promised him we'd make apple cider donuts when I got back, something he'd been begging me to do. *Cool*, he'd texted. And I felt good, knowing he was happy. Almost good.

"I'm separated," I told Ben, immediately regretting it. Why tell him? He hadn't asked. "But he's a great father," I rushed on. "And he and Paul are very close."

I could feel Ben nodding and smiling next to me. He stopped to take a picture of the mountains just ahead of us. Shining silver in the sun. The air smelled suddenly of snow, frozen metal. I waited, watching him, drinking from my CamelBak. When he was finished, he turned to me.

"Marriage is tough," he said. "Complicated." He returned the camera slowly to its case, resting it on his hip. "I'm sorry that happened."

"Thanks."

We began to walk again.

"But it sounds like you guys are good?"

"*He's* good," I said. "Kind. And smart. I'm not sure— we don't know, we're trying to figure it out—what we'll do. In the future, I mean." *Why* in God's name was I telling him all this?

And why, really, were we separated? I loved Graham. Loved him still. But things had gotten weird; confusing. *You're angry all the time*, he'd say. *No matter what I do, you're mad.* And he was right, and I couldn't explain why, and he was hurt, and I was silent. And I missed him, and us, even when we were together. Did he miss me?

"It's hard when you've been together for a long time," Ben said. "When did you guys meet?"

"I was in London with Mo our junior year of college. He was a friend of her brother's. So, of course, we're all weirdly connected. But also, very different. He's just a very good guy."

"And you're not?" Ben said, smiling. "Good, I mean."

"I'm decently good," I said, though I wondered whether it was true. "But not as good as Graham."

"You seem incredibly good—a caring mother, a loyal friend. I mean, look at what you're doing now! And someone who appreciates and respects her husband, even going through difficult times—"

"Easy for you to say, you barely know me," I said. He had no idea. "But what about you? When did you meet your wife?"

"High school sweethearts," he said. "We were fifteen."

"My God," I said. "You were babies."

"We've done a lot of growing up," he said. "Though not always together."

"I guess that's inevitable. I mean, people change. Or at least, that's the hope."

"I've changed." He said this in a different tone, quieter, and with less levity. "Fifteen is very young."

I wasn't sure how to respond.

We'd been walking side by side, but now the trail narrowed as it rose and Ben stepped back to let me go ahead.

"Oh no, you go first," I said. "You're faster. I don't want to hold you up."

"Don't worry so much," he said. "Please." He waved me on with his trekking pole, which we all, save Rick and the guides, were using.

I shook my head, refusing, but he shook his right back at me, as if I were a stubborn child.

Finally, he relented. "I'm glad I came," he said, as if wanting to confirm that fact. "I hope you are too."

And then he turned, leading the way up the rocky pitch.

All we could hear was our breath and the tapping of our trekking poles against the stones as we climbed.

I hadn't noticed, but the dog was long gone.

For what seemed like hours we continued up. I tried to focus on anything other than the up. The relentless up. And how loudly I was breathing, and how hard. Like, if I could eat anything right now, what would that be? French fries, maybe. With ketchup. *Chips*, Graham would say. Or a toasted bagel, dripping with butter. No, smeared with cream cheese. Or no, a lovely charcuterie plate: a wedge of Manchego, some prosciutto, some red grapes—the kind Paul likes—definitely some blue cheese, Stilton, for Graham, with a sliced pear—and I caught myself.

But then I let myself think about Graham. We'd known each other for so long. Not as long as Ben and his wife, no, but what did that matter? We'd shared so much. When we first met, it was at a luncheon following the funeral of Mo's cousin, Leslie Darren Stockton III, whom everyone called Darren. He was a year older than Hugh. All was very hush-hush about how he'd died. Mo had never even mentioned him. When I saw his picture, I understood why (at least regarding Mo's lack of interest): not good-looking. Anyway, she dragged me along, claiming she Refused to Attend Such a Heinous Event without her best friend. I was pleased; the words *best friend* made me shimmy, if only to myself.

Darren's funeral and service were rigidly orchestrated, tight-lipped and straight-spined. Dark suits and black dresses and hats for the women. I had never worn a hat, other than a baseball cap or a wool hat in winter and hadn't known that such was expected of me. Mo's mother lent me a smart black number with an inch of veil. Perched atop my curls, it felt awkward, and I worried that it would slip off and I'd crush it.

And then there was Graham.

Holding a glass of scotch, I guessed by the color, standing by the bar at the luncheon. He wore a navy blazer and gray slacks, a white shirt, and there was a lightness about him that came not from his non-black clothes but from somewhere else. Somewhere inside.

Golden-blond hair, like Mo.

But the way he stood—in the middle of the spin but apart from it too, as if the eddies and currents happening around him had nothing to do with him—that was different. With Mo, she was the center; the magnetizing pull around which other people revolved. Graham was a presence, to be sure, but his own. He was an observer, not the observed.

I walked over to the bar. "Is that scotch?" I asked him.

"Bourbon." He held the glass out to me.

I shook my head. Immediately I touched the hat to make sure it wasn't askew. "Not my jam, but thanks."

"What would you like, then?" He signaled to the bartender, an extremely short man with a nose like a small, waxy potato.

"Tequila, please." And then, quickly, "No. White wine. A glass of chardonnay. I can't get trashed at a funeral luncheon."

"I would say that's the best time to get trashed."

I glanced around. All those hats. "Somehow I don't think so."

"Shall we leave, then?"

"Now?"

"Do you *want* to stay?"

"Not really."

"Then why?" He put his glass down on the glossy, dark wood of the bar.

"Because I should?"

"Is that a question?"

"No," I said. "We should. I should." I took my wine from the square white napkin where the bartender had placed it.

"Later, then?" he said. "After? Can I take you somewhere for a tequila or two?" He smiled and I saw that he had a dimple in one cheek. Blond curls and a dimple. Cupid. Sweet. He introduced himself and I told him my name and he nodded as if he had heard of me, though I might've been mistaken, and we shook hands formally.

After the meal of medallions of veal with puddles of whitish sauce, asparagus and new potatoes (which I didn't eat) and chocolate mousse served in tiny chocolate cups drizzled with raspberry sauce (which I did), I noticed Graham watching me from across the room and he cocked his head in the direction of the door.

I turned to tell Mo, to ask her if it was okay to leave. She was looking at Graham, and I remembered thinking, *Shit, he'd been motioning to* her. I asked (super casually), Oh, do you know him? And she said, A bit, and winked at him, a rather large wink, and he jerked his thumb toward the door, trying to be subtle but also very clearly directed at me. Mo elbowed my elbow. Go on, she said. He's brilliant, you'll love him.

And I did.

But before I left, I caught Mo looking hard at Graham. Did he look back? Did something pass between them? It was difficult to remember. Memories in general were difficult. Parsing out the truth of the past—what really happened—from what was true in the present. Or were present truths all just grand rationalizations, justifications to make us feel better about the past?

When did the past matter? Or matter too much?

FOURTEEN

We reached a small plateau and found Sagar, Rick, and the porters waiting. Rick was breathing hard, a slick of sweat on his broad, red face.

"All okay?" Sagar said. "We rest here, wait for Joshi and Naba."

I leaned against one of the stone walls that appeared along the trail, offering a place for trekkers to rest their packs or for villagers, their baskets, strapped across their shoulders and forehead, loaded with wood and kindling.

I took a Snickers from my pocket, bit into it and chewed. Best. Thing. Ever.

Joshi arrived and we started gathering our packs to move on. He looked so somber behind his smile. "Do you need to rest a little?" I said. "Want me to wait?"

"Oh no. Please, you go on." His voice was soft but still with its music. "I will stay here, just for a moment, if that is okay with Naba." He said this last as a question, which Naba answered by nodding and saying something I couldn't understand.

"Are you sure?" I looked at both of them.

"Yes, please. I will see you at Bamboo." Joshi took off his pack and lowered it to the ground. Slowly, facing the wall, he placed his hands against it and began stretching his calves, one leg then the other.

The others had left, Rick with the porters, as he seemed to like being in front. Ever the leader. Ben followed Sagar; I could hear their voices though I couldn't see them as the trail climbed steeply ahead.

I began to walk, feeling good, that Snickers just galloping through my blood, giving an extra giddyup to my step, feeling, in fact, better than I had in a long time.

And then I had to pee. My eyes scanned either side of the path. On the left, a straight wall of rock. On the right, a sheer drop; a few low bushes clung to the flinty earth. I kept walking, the urge to pee rising in me with a jiggling worry. As Graham used to say, it felt like *my back teeth were swimming*.

He would, if he were here, help me find a place to go. He was like that.

But he wasn't here; we were separated. And now, quite immediately, I needed to pee. The pack's strap around my waist pressed into my belly, making my bladder feel fuller, ready to explode, like a balloon cinched in the middle.

I wrestled the pack off and, not bothering to find toilet paper (drip dry would do), I started down to my right, keeping low, holding on to whatever I could find as I made my way behind a thin and scraggly bush. With one hand, I grasped its branches and with the other I tore at my pants, pulling them down and to the side as I squatted as the hot stream hit my leg, which I moved away, or tried to, pulling at my pants, relief coursing through my body, even as the flow splattered everywhere, on me, and I stepped back and then suddenly I was no longer grasping a branch but air, falling backward, landing hard and bare-bottomed, tangled in my pants, rolling, without a sound or breath but in silence, the whole world crashing inside my head as I thought, *This is it, this is how I'm going to die.*

And then I smacked into something with branches, and I grabbed it.

And stopped.

Shaking, I held on. Scrabbled to my knees. And crawled, ass to the wind. Caked in dust, covered in pee, scratched and bruised all over, I pulled up my underwear, my pants, and stood.

My left knee throbbed. Tears filled my eyes. Now what? What if I couldn't walk anymore? What if I had to go down, a failure once again, go home and tell my son, my not-quite-husband, *Well, it was all for nothing. The cost, the effort. Why? Oh, I fell assbackward while peeing and screwed up my knee.* It wasn't even a real injury—frostbite or altitude sickness—just my own stupidity.

And then I heard that spitting sound and started to laugh. Not a funny *Ha, Ha* kind of laugh, but that weird hysterical thing that happened to me at the most inappropriate times.

Naba peered over the ledge.

"All okay?" he said, looking uncertain. What must he have thought, seeing a crazy American, laughing.

"I'll live," I said. "I think."

Calmer now, my little fit near its end, I limped up to join him and Joshi, both of whom looked similarly concerned.

I returned to my pack, forgoing hand sanitizer and pulling out a wool hat instead. I was cold. The wet places on my pants clung to my legs. I shivered.

"Are you hurt?" Joshi said. It was obvious, then, that I had fallen. I put my less-damp leg in front of the other, hoping he wouldn't notice the darker spots.

I hoisted my pack. "I'm not the steadiest person, I guess," I said, trying to sound less bruised than I felt. "But onward." I gestured with my pole, the way Ben had, earlier.

We reached the teahouse in Bamboo by midafternoon. Ben and Rick were sitting inside the common area, waiting for us. The porters were there too, and they were all playing cards together around the one large table surrounded by benches. It smelled of unwashed bodies and smoke from the stove. But it was lively and cheerful, and I was glad.

Joshi and I sat down, both of us quiet, and Naba walked around the table to join the others in cards. The porters were laughing, thundering their approval at Rick's exuberance as he slapped down cards, all of them hooting, all but Ben, who laughed along pleasantly enough but refrained from the shouts and guffaws. It was fascinating, Rick's acceptance by these young porters, when to me he seemed nothing but a buffoon. *A baboon*, I thought evilly.

When they finished, we ate. I was famished and slurped up my soup and boiled potatoes and white rice and fried eggs with barely a breath in between.

"What happened to you this afternoon?" Rick said. He speared a forkful of noodles into the cavern of his mouth. "We thought we lost you."

I glanced at Joshi. "I had a little tussle with the mountain, taking a bathroom break."

Joshi held his cup of milk tea, his legs crossed, and smiled. "I believe she won," he said.

I smiled back, grateful, not at all sure if that was true. My knee still throbbed and I cupped it under the table with my hand, as if that could soothe it.

"How's the boot?" Ben asked Joshi.

"I am afraid the heel is starting to come loose again." Joshi's thin face was heavy. "I will ask if there is something stronger here, some type of glue, perhaps. Otherwise I am not sure I can go on."

"Do we have any more duct tape?" I asked. "Rick, didn't you say you had some?"

"Yeah, but it sounds like duct tape won't do the trick—"

"Thank you," Joshi said. "But I will ask now. Before it gets too late." He rose, excusing himself.

There was nothing to do then but go back to my room, organize myself for the following day, and read. I washed my hands and face with soap and icy water from the sink outside and changed into the long underwear I slept in. There was a huge purple bruise blossoming on the side of my knee and I pressed it to see how much it hurt. It hurt. I tugged on a pair of fleece pants, a fleece top, and a PrimaLoft jacket, pulling its hood over the wool hat that I still wore. I unrolled my sleeping bag and sat on top with my left leg stretched out.

The cot across from me yawned empty and accusing. I didn't want to read Mo's journal, not the entry I knew must be next, but I'd do it anyway.

If I couldn't do that, why had I bothered to come?

October 24

I don't know how to write this, or to whom.

You are gone.

A message from Mum, awaiting our arrival in Bamboo.

A fall in the tub, a broken hip. Complications.

And you are gone.

A BROKEN HIP. A broken hip? In the tub?

I can't believe it. I can't believe it. How is it possible.

You, who made the mountains everything to me. Gone.

Later:

Everything is wrong. I won't go back to my room. I can't. I ran out while Liv went to the loo and now it's dark out and I'm sitting with Tika in the common area, where the porters sleep on the benches and floors, even on the table. I didn't know. They're all looking at me, wondering what I'm doing here I'm sure but I don't care. I don't care!

After Rishi gave me the news, there was another message from Mum: I should stay on the trek and not come home, you would have wanted it so. I just sat on my bed and cried. I know, I know, I know, you never permitted any blubbering about, and certainly not for you, not ever. But I couldn't help it, sitting there, wearing your kerchief, as it was, and Liv came in, saying, Let's go for a walk, just to the little hill above, and I shook my head, but it was early still, we had made good time, and she pulled me up and shoved my feet in my boots and dragged me up the hill, where we sat looking at the green below, sloping down and away, and the black shadows of white mountains above, and the blue of sky.

We didn't say anything, we didn't need to. Liv understood what you meant to me. What you mean.

And then we heard voices, low laughter really, and the smell of skunky smoke, and we both looked at each other and I might have smiled if I weren't so sad. But Liv smiled.

You want to? she asked.

I shook my head, saying, I don't think so.

But again she didn't listen, and I let her pull me up, and we walked down a little crest of tufted grass and there was Tika and another porter, Amrit I think his name is, smoking a joint. Tika held it between his thumb and forefinger, tucked under his palm, not hiding it exactly but cupping it so it wasn't obvious. As if the smell and the twist of smoke weren't enough.

Liv gestured with her eyes to Tika that we knew what was up and he offered me the joint and we sat and I shrugged at Liv and took a hit and then passed it to her. Neither of us was really surprised, you could see marijuana plants growing alongside the teahouses, lush and tall as if they were sunflowers just waiting to bloom.

The four of us smoked together for a while, Tika and Amrit talking and laughing and Liv and I exchanging glances. I knew Liv wanted to cheer me up but if anything, I just felt worse. I sat there, watching my body watch the others, watching the clouds darken the sky, watching the light change, growing dim and blue, the hills below turning a deeper, darker blue, ink.

We finished the joint and then rose and headed back to the teahouse, Liv and I waving our thanks.

And then.

I lay on my cot and cried. My face to the wall.

And then Liv sat down next to me, touched my shoulder, told me it would be okay. And then I turned over, and she lay down next to me and hugged me. Just a long, beautiful hug. Holding me like she knew me, which she does, or at least I thought she did. You were never a hugger, but you knew me anyway. And Liv is a hugger. She just wrapped her arms around me and pulled me in and I felt better. And maybe it was the joint, and maybe it wasn't. But I felt comfort then. I felt love.

And then, I don't know, it was like the air changed in there or something, like someone was stirring it with a giant spoon and we were caught in the swirl, going round and round, because Liv brushed her cheek against mine and with the softest, lightest of touches, a fairy's eyelash of a flutter, she kissed my lips.

And I drew back, for a moment.

And then nothing mattered but that feeling, that comfort mixed with something else, and I closed my eyes and let her kiss me again. And again.

And again.

And we both were breathing hard. I must admit it. Everything became more urgent. Our breath, into each other's mouths. There was bright orange behind my eyelids, a pinwheel of color. I felt it in my chest, in the beat of my heart, and then our bodies were moving, together, against each other, and everything was falling open, and I felt myself, God, I felt myself getting wet and then Liv's hand moved down to my breast, her cold hand against the goose-bumped skin of my nipple, and she was squeezing, but lightly, and then I felt her mouth, electric, her tongue…

…and I froze.

It was like those dreams when you're falling and you wake with a sudden jolt in your bed.

ANNAPURNA

I came hurtling back to my cot in a teahouse in Bamboo and the fact that you were dead.

And me, horrified, staring with my eyes wide open at Liv, poor Livy, who looked as horrified and ashamed as I.

I'm sorry, she started saying, and I said, Liv, I don't want...I'm not like this, and she said, No, no, I don't even know what happened, maybe it was the weed, and you were so sad, and I said, Yes, of course, the weed, for sure, and we both got up and she went to the loo and I grabbed my pack and ran to the common room.

Because Nana, I must be honest now, and I know you won't ever read this, but it wasn't the weed. Or it wasn't only the weed. And it wasn't me just being sad. There was something else, something I saw in Livy's eyes, a hunger. Her blue eyes always seemed so clear to me. So forthright. So plainspoken. It was one of the reasons we got on so well.

But now I wonder. There's a world behind that blue I don't know.

I closed the journal and closed my eyes. My forthright eyes. I'm pretty sure I groaned out loud. The shame of it all. From that moment on, that one moment, it all went wrong.

I remembered thinking: I was just as shocked as she. After all, I'd been the one to kiss her.

It was more than a kiss.

Not much more.

It meant more.

It meant nothing, two best friends, we loved each other, of course. Two best friends.

Of course.

And I remembered her saying: *Liv, I don't want...I'm not like this*.

And me? Was I *like this*? Did I want this? Had I wanted Mo?

I remembered, after, wanting only one thing: to make things normal. To go back to our laughter and chatter and inside jokes and Mo strewing her shit everywhere and twirling and pleading for one thing or another and the everyday (normal) crap of being friends. Best friends. I had wanted that. Desperately.

But wants change. If being a mother had taught me anything, it had taught me that. Everything changes. Just when you think you know what's what, you find out you know nothing.

I thought how earlier in the day Ben had said he was glad he'd come, that he hoped I was too. And I knew now that I wasn't. How I most definitely, one hundred percent, was not.

FIFTEEN

ðing.

The phone. I sat up, sending Mo's journal flying from the bed. I lunged to the windowsill where my cell lay charging, legs tangled in my sleeping bag, arms outstretched, hooking the cord around my icy pinky as I tumbled off the bed, the phone and portable charger slung in the air like a boomerang, like a nunchuck flung from the hand of some cool-as-shit ninja flipping in the air only to land with the nimble precision of a cat, except I wasn't, and I didn't, and I landed in a heap on the floor instead.

Unhurt though. Graceless, maybe. Okay *fine*, a klutz, or, as Graham might say, but not referring to me, a clod. As Mo might have said.

I looked at the silent, unused cot next to me, the tidy piles of clothes for today laid atop my duffel.

Mo would have laughed. At one point, at least, she would have laughed.

I scrabbled out of the sleeping bag and located my phone, lying face down on the hard stone floor, its glass face shattered.

Fuck.

I could still read my message though, a day-old text that somehow had come through. It was from Graham.

Sorry to bother. Paul's down with flu. Not to worry but thought you might want to know. Hope all is well. Carry on.

Carry on?

Hastily, I texted a reply, asking for news about Paul, how he was feeling, sending him my love. To Paul, that was.

But there wasn't service anymore, or maybe it was my phone, and when the text didn't go through I got dressed, rolled up my sleeping bag, packed up my duffel, and headed outside.

Snow sparkled the ground in the morning sun. A hard glitter, making a *crch crch crch* sound as I hustled to breakfast, late. My left knee felt stiff and sore, but otherwise, I was relieved to note, my bare-assed tumble from yesterday hadn't done much damage.

Sagar was standing inside the doorway between the common area and the kitchen, waiting for the cook to hand him plates.

"I'm sorry," I said. "But is there a way to get a message to someone in the States? Or to receive one? I'm not getting any service, or not much, I'm not even sure if my phone is working —"

Sagar stood, his hand outstretched, silent.

"My son is sick," I went on, "and he's with my, well, he's with his father, but of course," I tried to laugh, "I'm worried. I can't help it."

"Yes." Sagar nodded. "Would you like some breakfast?"

"Oh. Okay," I said. "Great. Yes. Thank you."

I gave him a message, which would be relayed to his company's headquarters in Kathmandu and then to Graham, and ordered breakfast. Coffee, which I needed but always somehow tasted of ashes, plus porridge and two hard-boiled eggs.

Joshi was speaking when I slid onto the bench next to Ben. "Now that there is snow, and there will be, most likely, all the way to base camp, I cannot risk going farther. The heel has come loose again, and even with more tape it will not stay fast. Yesterday, it was affecting how I walked. I was very slow."

"Speed isn't important," Ben said. "But safety is. You weren't able to get some kind of glue?"

Joshi shook his head. "All of these mountain villages this time of year have few supplies."

"But are you sure?" I asked. "Have you spoken to Sagar?"

Just then Sagar placed a bowl of hard-boiled eggs in front of Joshi and a plate of toast and a cup of tea, disappearing into the kitchen doorway once again.

"Yes," Joshi said. He picked up an egg from the bowl and held it out to me. "Would you like one?"

"Oh no, thank you," I said. "I ordered some as well."

"So what will you do?" Ben asked.

"I will wait here," Joshi said. "You will be back in three days."

Sagar returned with more plates, placing them on the table in a direct and simple manner. "Do you have everything?" he asked us.

We said yes, and thank you, except Rick, who nodded with a mouth full of pancake.

"Good." Sagar straightened. "We hear there is deep snow above. At Deurali we ask about avalanches."

I looked up from my coffee, the taste of bitter ash stuck in my throat. Rick kept on chewing; Ben frowned as if in contemplation.

"Bring warm layer in your pack," Sagar said. "And we walk through lunch again. Yes?" He looked around the table.

I wondered if I should buy more Snickers.

"Will you be okay?" Ben asked Joshi. "Three days in the mountains can feel like a long time."

"Satish will be fine," Rick said, referring, apparently, to Joshi. He chewed a last bite of pancake, swallowed. "Isn't that so?"

"Yes," Joshi said. "I will meditate." He looked calm, certain. Maybe it was a relief. "When do I get the chance to meditate in the mountains for three days? It will be perfect for me. Please, do not worry."

"We'll miss you," I said.

"I will be with you in spirit," he said. "And when you return, you will tell me all about it, so I can see it then."

Joshi was outside when we left. Smiling, hands clasped in front of him, his skinny front teeth and oval glasses giving him a wise, rabbity look. After breakfast, he had knocked at the door to my room, apologizing when I opened it.

"No worries," I said. "You're not interrupting. I'm just trying to find my mittens." I was pulling things out of my duffel, several pairs of socks, my toiletry bag, the book I had brought, though hadn't yet cracked: *The Snow Leopard* by Peter Matthiessen, one of Graham's. He'd suggested I bring it.

"I want to give this to you," Joshi said.

I turned. In his palm sat a tiny wooden figure of a man's fat-bellied body with an elephant's head. It was dark brown with a worn luster, beloved like a pair of old leather gloves.

"It is Ganesh." Joshi took my hand and placed the Ganesh inside. "My mother gave him to me when I was quite young, when I first started climbing in the mountains. I carry it with me always, every time I travel."

"Oh, Joshi—"

"He is the Hindu god of good fortune, the remover of obstacles. He embodies the ability within all of us to overcome whatever is impeding our success, our journey." Joshi stood in the doorway, his glasses reflecting the white light from outside. "He has kept me safe, this gift from my mother, and now I will give it to you."

"Oh no, Joshi, seriously, I couldn't—" I opened my mouth to say more; it was too dear a gift.

"You will return him to me when you come back."

"Thank you." I closed both hands around the Ganesh. "I'll take good care of him."

"Perhaps he will help you, during Mo's memorial, deciding what to say," Joshi said.

"Perhaps he will," I said, reaching up to hug Joshi.

He patted my back stiffly, turned, and stepped out the door.

I opened my hand and looked at the little elephant man lying in my palm. And then closed my fist and held him to my chest. A safe journey. Mo's memorial. And Paul.

Now as the trail rocketed upward through a bamboo forest, dark and cold, slippery with snow, all thoughts of Ganesh were gone and it was back to *left right left right left right keep going left right breathe left right left right don't look up left right left right left right.*

I passed Rick, who struggled on the steeper sections, despite his evident desire to be in the lead. Who said, "Looking good, Livyest," as I huffed by, which was generous, I suppose, but also, I might add, annoying as hell, because the only person who called me *Livyest*, ever, was Mo.

I grunted my thanks and carried on, as she would say (and as Graham had, in fact, said), thinking of how in college we would hold our shots of tequila aloft, Mo shouting, To the Livyest of them all! and me chorusing, To *Mo*-velous! and then we'd clink the little glasses together, thinking we were clever, the two of us, swallowing the burn, sucking on limes and shuddering.

And yes, I remembered now, she called me Livyest on the trek, at least those first few days, while we were jumping across streams or brushing our teeth or peeling our boiled potatoes. But that, of course, ended, and I shoved the thought aside as the forest opened up and the sun shone whitely and the snow flashed its welcome in tinsel and sequins.

SIXTEEN

I caught up to Sagar. Ahead, Ben had walked a few steps off the trail to take some pictures of the glacial river below. It churned over rocks, unfurling from the side of the mountain through the valley like a milk-green ribbon. Looking down, I was shocked to see how high we were already.

"All okay?" Sagar said. We stood together, watching Ben watch the river through his lens.

"I can't believe how much I don't remember about the trail. Maybe it's all the snow."

"There will be more snow this afternoon," Sagar said.

"There will?" The sky was blue, and cloudless. The sun a glowy orb. "It doesn't look like it."

"The weather today is for snow."

I wasn't sure who to believe: the sky or the prediction.

"Was Naba with Rick?" he said.

"He was when I saw him," I said. "Are we waiting? Do I have time to find a bathroom?"

"Yes." Sagar pointed to a large boulder up ahead and to the left.

I climbed up to the boulder. It was dusted with snow, and slippery, and I worried about the few extra steps uphill as my knee was starting to throb. It tugged at me, the way a child tugs at your pant leg, demanding and insistent.

When I returned, Ben was talking to Sagar.

"Our guide was named Rishi," he was saying. "Rishi Ram Bhantana? Liv, is that right?"

"I think so." I busied myself in my pack. Looking for God knows what.

"And Tika, I remember him. He was one of the porters. Do you know either of them?" he asked Sagar. "Is it a small enough industry that everyone knows each other? I remember Tika wore those rubber water slides the whole way up, with socks even. I couldn't get over it."

"I know of Rishi," Sagar said. "We are from the same Gorkha region. But Tika?" He shook his head.

"He didn't make it," Ben said. "I wonder what happened to him."

"He was hurt?" Sagar asked.

"No," Ben said. "There was an incident, one night, at base camp actually, and —"

I bent forward, my head practically inside my pack.

"—and he left. Or just disappeared. We never knew what happened to him, even when we got back to Kathmandu."

Sagar scratched his chin, his face expressionless.

"There were lots of stories, of course, that he was involved in some way, but we never heard. He always seemed like a sweet kid to me."

"Is that Rick?" I said loudly. "I think I hear him." I abandoned my pack to backtrack down the trail, and sure enough, bless him, Rick's marionette face appeared alongside Naba, who was carrying Rick's pack in addition to his own. While whistling. A twiddling tune, unhurried, but vibrant too, uplifting. Which made me think of Graham, and home. And Paul.

"Are you okay to go?" Sagar said.

An ache rose in my chest and I stomped it down, hard. We readied our packs, Ben returning his camera to its case, as Naba and Rick approached. We greeted them both, though Rick wasn't saying much, while Sagar told Naba to meet us farther up the trail.

And *up the trail* it was, up a rocky ravine, scrambling, my knee barking, my open-mouthed breath so loud it seemed to echo from the stone that surrounded us. I was sweating somehow, despite the cold, and without a shower these last few days I was bound to start smelling like one of the porters. I already did. It occurred to me that I didn't care.

The air was clear and sharp. Sometimes as I climbed, I entered a warm patch, like when you're swimming and feel the sudden balm of sun-soaked water. And then that freshness again, the chill, against your face and neck.

It was endless, this up, and I tried to remember how it felt the first time. The trail was more crowded then; you could see colorful backpacks bobbing ahead. Waves of chatter in foreign languages floated past; the mountains seemed more alive, friendlier. More welcoming. As if we were part of a living and breathing being that wanted us there, wanted to feel our feet as we climbed. Now I wasn't too sure.

Using my trekking poles to hoist myself up, I reached a rock platform. There was a huge overhang, making sort of a cave. Ben and Sagar were waiting there, along with a Korean couple and their guide. The guide spoke to Sagar as the couple sat on a ledge inside the relatively dry cave. Panting a little, I watched the Korean woman reach into her pack and pull out a lipstick, which she applied while looking straight at me. Straight through me.

Fire-engine red. A perfect pucker at ten thousand feet. I smiled at her.

She did not smile back, which felt awkward. Nor did the man, clad in a smart, black ensemble — matching jacket and pants — black sunglasses, a black knit hat.

Ben motioned to me to share his seat on the edge of a boulder. I rested my pack as I leaned against it, easing my shoulders.

"I'm sorry," Ben said. "I didn't mean to bring up bad memories. Earlier, that is. Talking about Mo, the trek."

"But isn't that the point?" I said, trying for lightness. "We're here to honor Mo, and that means, of course, to think about her. To think about what happened. And to talk about it." I drank deeply from my CamelBak.

"It's hard to accept uncertainty, of not knowing what happened," Ben said. "To Mo. But also with Tika. It's like, if you just *knew*, then it'd be okay. You'd know how to feel, how to behave. And yet, I'm not sure that's always true." He pulled out his camera and trained it on the trail that dropped below, closer to the river. "I haven't been good with that unsettled feeling. It's one of the reasons I came back."

"To find out what happened?" I tried to sound casual, curious.

"Not exactly," he said. "I mean, of course I'd like to know, but for me it was more. It's that feeling of not knowing what's up ahead. The risk, maybe, or the fear. I don't know. Sometimes I think that safety just lures you in and you choose what you know, again and again, until it feels like you have no choice."

I nodded, as if I understood, which I did. Kind of. The relative safety of telling a lie—yes, you could get found out—but telling the truth?—a guaranteed risk. The risk of the unknown. "Well, I think the Tika part is pretty settled, no?" I said, hoping that was true. "At least, whatever happened, he must've been involved. No one saw him after the night Mo disappeared—I mean, after she—" I couldn't finish.

Ben moved his camera away from his face and looked at me. The whites of his eyes seemed very white. "I wonder what he's made of his life. If he's even alive."

"I try not to think about him," I said truthfully. "I've tried not to think about any of it, for twenty years. And now look at me, here I am, wondering what I'm doing on some random mountain while my son's home with the flu." I felt tears start to loosen my throat. My nose began to run.

"He'll be fine," Ben said. "Both my boys have had the flu—and he's with his dad—"

"I know, I know," I said, straightening a little on my stone seat. "It could be worse. I'm just being my stupid self."

"You're not stupid—" He reached a gloved hand to my face, as if to wipe away a tear. Sagar came over to us and Ben lowered his hand, touching my shoulder and then gently my arm; it lingered there a moment before he let it drop. He seemed to want to say more, but maybe I imagined this.

"I spoke to the guide," Sagar said. "They come from base camp. Ahead, we cross a glacier, is a big avalanche track. He said there is one avalanche, maybe more, since they come on their way up, two days ago. They just cross back, we can do it, but we must go fast." His voice was matter-of-fact.

I looked at Ben, eyebrows raised, and he looked at Sagar.

"Shouldn't we wait for Rick and Naba?" he said. "So they know?"

"We wait," Sagar said. And then to me, maybe because I was shivering, "Are you warm enough?"

But I wasn't cold.

The Koreans and their guide rose and headed down, without a word, even between them, and we sat in our cave and waited.

I contemplated breaking into my last Snickers.

The blue sky turned white. And then deepened, darkening to a flat gray without the outline of a single, separate cloud. There was movement, though, behind the flatness. You could feel it.

"You were right, Sagar," I said. "Snow."

"Soon," he said. And then he stood. Rick and Naba appeared from below.

"Sit," I said to Rick, feeling bad for him, even as I was disgusted by his red, sweating face. His neon yellow jacket. Why wear such a color if you're as wide as a house?

I was such a bitch, and I knew it.

Ben and I both shifted to make room.

"Drink some water," Sagar said to Rick. "Then we go." He said something to Naba in Nepali.

Naba turned to Rick and handed him a hard candy in a bright wrapper, urging him to take it, and to drink. And then to all of us, Naba held out his open palm full of candies; I took one. White Rabbits, those candies that Rishi used to give the schoolchildren along the trail. The Pied Piper of Nepal.

I unwrapped it and popped it in my mouth. Coconut.

Rick mopped his face with the back of his hand. "We go?" he asked Sagar. He spoke in abbreviated sentences to the guides and porters, a trumpeting sort of pidgin, and any mercy for him I might have felt fled.

We gathered our belongings and started down to the glacier. Rick set out first, his strangled ascent—mere moments ago—already forgotten. Forgotten too that he'd needed Naba to hump his pack for him. Once again, I could hear the drone of Rick's voice from ahead as he chatted with Sagar, who seemed (shockingly) to enjoy his company. His two-worded sentences. So placid, so reserved, Sagar now was laughing along with Rick, his hands gesticulating in the air that as a rule were linked by his thumbs to the shoulder straps of his pack.

The snowy path was narrow and descended abruptly toward the glacier below. I tried to follow the tracks, holding on to rocks and boulders, their slippery surface of little use. Naba was behind, in position, I imagined (I hoped) to scoop me up if I fell. If I didn't stop myself first by smashing into Ben, who was directly below me.

As we neared the glacier, I could hear a rushing sound. Water. I stopped.

All I could see was snow-covered rubble, hunks and heaps of it, with dark gray, like chunks of cement, poking through. This was the glacier? I remembered from the first trek a large, undulating expanse of pulverized rock, wet with gaping holes. A pulse of water, maybe. A vibration. You could fall in those holes, I remembered thinking, but at least then I could see where they were. Now, they were covered in snow. And where there wasn't water there was worse: nothing. A crevasse that might drop a hundred, two hundred feet. Or more.

"Is it safe?" I asked Naba, who had stopped behind me. As if he could answer such a question.

He nodded, though I wasn't at all sure he understood, because he just pointed me forward, motioning to keep moving. Sagar and Rick had begun to climb up the other side of the glacier, up, up, and away.

I began to pick my way across, noting Ben's trajectory, holding my breath but only metaphorically, because I think, in fact, I was breathing pretty hard, huffing and puffing, every muscle tensed, focused as a unit on not slipping, not falling, not stepping on unstable snow, a foot plunging down into what I could now see was water, through gaps in the glacier, gushing below the surface, making the entire experience of choosing where to step a step into the unknown. And what is the unknown but a bottomless chasm of fear?

A snowflake landed on my eyelash.

Oh please, I prayed not to anyone in particular, *please not now.*

I blinked it away.

Snow began to fall from the huge white sky.

Please.

Ben, now, was on the other side. He turned and watched me, calling out words of encouragement as if I were one of his boys, running track or something. "You've got this, Liv, come on!"

Mouth open, breathing, a snowflake caught in my throat and I coughed.

"WAY TO GO!"

Please.

I snagged the toe of my boot on some ice, and I stumbled forward, grabbing the air, but then arms out, poles dangling, I steadied myself—

"YESSSS ALMOST THERE!"

And then I *was* there, finally, giddy with relief, trying to scramble up the other side.

When I reached the group waiting for me, Naba in tow, Sagar nodded.

Ben said, "Nicely done."

Rick said, "You're quite a gal, Livyest."

It began to snow harder.

We were now above the tree line and I could see more of the valley and the river below and the sheer rock-face cliffs above. Swirls of frozen waterfalls clung to their sides, their crooked fingers clutching the walls in a death grip. I lowered my eyes, trying to ignore the fat flakes coming down, the white—all that white—as we climbed steadily to Deurali.

SEVENTEEN

The common area at the teahouse in Deurali was larger than those lower down the mountain, as it was cold here even in the spring and fall and most trekkers wanted to stay inside after they arrived.

The wind was bitter, howling. I had changed in my tiny room, layering up in wool and synthetics and down. Dry socks. Sitting in the common room, I still wore mittens as I held my phone, blank and useless. My hair was damp from sweat and snow and I tucked it under my hat, hoping it would dry from body heat. I missed the crowded warmth of the regular trekking season. I missed Paul.

The porters trickled in, gathering around one corner of the large rectangular table. Someone produced a deck of cards and when Rick stepped inside the porters greeted him loudly and Rick hooted his response, his mouth pursed, presumably, like a monkey's. He sat down and began to play.

I kept looking at my phone, jiggling it, clasping it in my mittened hands to warm it, hoping, somehow, it would show a sign of life. Of Paul.

Sagar came in and I jumped up. "Any news?"

"Yes." He handed me a piece of folded paper. "Narayan in Kathmandu spoke to your husband." Written in black ink, in someone's block lettering, it said: PAUL IN HOSPITAL. HE OK. CARRY ON.

"Is that all he said? Is that it?"

"Is the message. What Narayan told when he called here."

"Can I call him? Narayan? Or Graham? Can I call the States from here?"

Sagar shook his head.

Ben, who had sat down next to Rick but wasn't playing cards, swung his legs over the bench and faced me. "Use my phone," he said. "I'm not sure about the service, but it's worth a try."

"Really?" I felt my whole body warm. "Thank you."

He handed me his phone as Sagar moved behind the seated porters to watch their game.

"Is it, what time will it be?" I asked as I dialed.

"Very early," Ben said. "We're ahead almost ten hours, I think."

Graham picked up on the third ring and I walked rapidly away from the group toward the windows, where it was quieter.

"How is he?" I asked.

There was static and a garbling of words.

"What?" I looked at the phone. One bar of service. "Can you say that again?" I felt like I was shouting.

Another underwater gurgle. And then, "...a tough one...best care...just to keep an eye, standard..."

"Wait, *what*?" I looked at the phone again, as if by see-ing it I could magically make it have better, clearer ser-vice. "Paul is in the hospital?"

"...pneumonia..."

"Wait, he has *pneumonia*?" I started pacing in tight lit-tle circles. "Okay, I'm coming home. I can't stay here. Can I talk to him? Is he right there?"

Suddenly I could hear. "Yes," Graham said. "But he's sleeping."

The crackle of static. And then, "...handle it...doc-tor...fine and you don't...guilty over...fair to him."

"But I'm his mother," I said, not entirely sure of what Graham was saying. "I should be there."

And then the line went dead.

I stared at the phone.

"Sagar," I said, as I walked over, returning the phone to Ben, thanking him, "I need to go back. Home. My son is sick—"

"Too dark now," he said, pointing to the windows that did, indeed, reveal a blackness beyond. "Tomorrow is a few hours to Machhapuchhre base camp. In the morning you can call for a helicopter to take you to Pokhara."

"Okay," I said, relieved. "And from there I can fly to Kathmandu, and then home? Is that the best way?"

"Yes." Sagar didn't offer any sympathy or concern. His role was that of guide: to provide for our safe passage and propose solutions when problems arose.

And I had a problem.

But I wasn't going to leave tonight, in the dark. That much I knew.

Across the table, Rick looked up from his game. "Hey, Livy, want to play?"

I sat but shook my head.

"I could teach you," he said. "It's easy."

I knew he was being kind, that this was his way, perhaps, which softened me toward him. But only a little.

"Okay," I said. "Thanks."

Ben joined too. Right away I realized that the men were betting.

"I don't want to take their money," I whispered to Ben.

"Who says you're going to win?" He elbowed me, trying to get me to laugh. "It's only a few pennies, and it's worth it to them." And as if to prove his point, the porters slapped their cards down with a flourish, with a satisfied smack and wallops and hoots, even when they lost.

We added our rupees to the pile in the center and then the dealer threw down a card in front of each of us, to the shouts and back-slapping of the group. And on it went, until a person got the highest combination of cards, or pairs, some mountain iteration of poker.

I won once and lost twice, and then Ben and I stopped playing and just watched, talking quietly about my leaving the next day. He understood, he said, but encouraged me to use his phone the next morning, to call or text Graham for updates before I made any decisions.

"Who knows," Ben said. "Paul might be on the rebound. Kids bounce back pretty quick."

"Or bounce in the wrong direction."

"Bouncing makes you stronger, no matter what direction you go."

"But what if—" I bit my lower lip as if trying to block the words from coming—"what if you can't bounce? You try and you can't. Zero bounce."

"That's a bounce, too," he said. "There's always a bounce. Even when you think there's not."

What was he saying? It didn't occur to me that maybe we were talking about different things. That would come later.

My hands were clasped, resting on the table. He reached out, as if to take them in his, and then seemed to change his mind, scratching his head instead. "Just promise me you'll call before you decide anything," he said.

"I'll reimburse you," I said. "If my phone isn't working. I have a bunch of calls."

"Do what you need. Whatever feels right."

"Nothing feels right."

The afternoon passed slowly.

We ate our dinner and wondered how Joshi was doing and I wondered, too, about Paul. Afterward, Rick tried to get us to play another game of cards but Ben went to get his book and I went back to my room to get ready for the next day. Made all my little preparatory piles of snacks and clothing. Unrolled my sleeping bag. Shuffled around the room, picking things up, putting them down. Repacking.

Outside again, I used the bathroom and then circled the hut looking for a sink, somewhere to brush my teeth.

"I couldn't find it either." It was Ben.

"No sink?"

"Let's go over here." He motioned to an open, grassy space to the side of the hut.

We both wore headlamps and the bright beams bobbed along as we walked. There was a rushing sound: the river. We didn't speak.

Ben stopped and put some toothpaste on his toothbrush and started brushing his teeth. I did the same. We stood by the river without seeing it; the sound pressed against us; the thick black night. Above, an endless spangle of stars.

He offered me some water to rinse—I had forgotten mine (of course)—and there was something tethering us then, I could feel it; intensely, oddly intimate. Swooshing and spitting next to this man who wasn't my husband. In the dark, under the stars.

The rushing sound grew louder, filling my ears. I looked up. A cold wind blew. And it was just this: the air all around and the toothbrush in my hand and the ground beneath our feet. The blank, unseeable night. The nothingness and the everything.

EIGHTEEN

When I returned to my room, I read Mo's journal. I thought maybe I'd finish it since I was going home the next day, but I could barely manage the one entry.

Home the next day. Something eased in me, and not just because I'd be seeing Paul.

October 25

Everything is wrong. Not here, in this place. I want to be here, these roaring mountains a comfort, their size; everywhere, massive without need for explanation, without need of anything. So complete. Uncomplicated.

Just not with Liv.

Today she is everywhere. Suddenly, I feel her breath on the back of my neck. Or her footsteps along the trail, her toes grasping at my heels. What is this? What is happening? Why did she come here? For this? For me?

I ate breakfast and left with the porters before Liv was up. Rishi asked me if I wanted to wait for the others but I was ready to go. He told me to wait at Machhapuchhre Base Camp where we'd all have tea together. As if that was a good thing.

The porters chat a bit among themselves as they walk, and I try to ask Tika about other treks, other mountains, but I don't think he quite understands. Mostly he nods and laughs, says a few words I can't catch.

And so I walk in silence. Thinking. I won't go home when this is over, I know that now, I must continue. I won't be able to afford a proper guided trek, but if I'm careful, I can make what little I have last in these mountain villages. And then, who knows? I'm going to lead the life maybe you wanted to, Nana. There's nothing here but sight and sound. Nothing more than putting one foot in front of the next.

I want to see the green turn to gold. Turn to brown turn to gray. I want to see the earth smothered in white. My breath, clouds of white. The silver of mountains edged against blue. And nothing else. Colors and heat and the blankness of cold. And breath.

I want to keep walking.

I want to feel the wind.

I want to talk to you.

I sit outside at Machhapuchhre with my masala chai and watch fluffs of clouds flash across the sky. And think, this is what matters. And you taught me that, Nan. All those walks in the countryside when I was small. Never holding my hand, not once. Just telling me Chin Up if I fell. Which I did, remember?

I hope you are somewhere remembering.

The time I tumbled over, somersaulted, and lay there on my back, all of five, my lips quivering, that pause before one cries, and you peered over me, saying, Well done, that! Now up you go! and up I went. And then later, the summer I turned nine, when we hiked up Snowdon, staying at the Pen-Y-Gwryd Hotel, where Hillary and Tenzing trained for Everest. I remember sitting in front of the fire when we were through, shaking with wet and cold from the rain, drinking hot chocolate and feeling rather sorry for myself, despite the summit, when you pointed out Sir Hillary's mug on the mantel, inscribed with his name. You handed me a blanket and sat next to me, telling me the story of his Everest adventure. We sat there for hours as you talked and I watched the fire and listened to your voice soar and dip, first about Everest and then other mountains, ones you climbed. I followed you everywhere. Mount Fuji in Japan and Mount Olympus in Greece and Mount Kenya and Machu Picchu and trekking in New Zealand.

And now here I am, in Nepal.

Mum would say What Utter Nonsense and that you've filled my head with rubbish. But Mum doesn't know what it's like, and she isn't here. You are.

When the rest of the group arrives and sits down, it's all Liv's eyes pulling at me. She sits next to me, of course, orders tea, her voice high and strained, not the low gravel that I used to think—I must admit—was rather sexy. Strong. Now she laughs, again too high, and I don't know why she can't act normal, why she has to make a bigger deal of this than it already is. It is awkward. And ridiculous. And I don't know why any of this had to happen.

It's ruined.

And I just want it to be over.

We gather our things and I go to the loo. When I open the door, there's Liv, waiting for me.

Can we talk? she asks and I say, trying to be normal, Of course, and she says, Will you wait? and for the life of me, I don't want to, I want to start walking, but I tell her I will and when she comes out of the loo she says, I just want you to know how sorry I am, it just happened, it was one of those things, but please don't think, you know, that this is how I am or what I want so you don't have to worry and let's forget about the whole thing.

Yeah RIGHT.

And I say Of course and No worries and Really it's no big deal. And maybe these things do Just Happen but suddenly I feel sorry for her and I can't bear feeling sorry for anyone and I can't seem to look at her in the same way.

But I smile and walk along the trail with her until I can pull ahead, chatting with Ben, until it's only him and me. In the distance, the peaks of the Annapurnas are visible through the clouds, circling us almost, but nothing, no one else. For the first time the trail is empty. We enter what's like the basin of a Greek amphitheater, mountains ringing the center as if it were a stage and we the actors on it.

Ben walks in front, and I stare at his back. His T-shirt clings to his shoulders, his tanned arms. His short hair sticks up wildly from his head, as if blown in too many directions by the wind. As if he'd just rolled out of bed. I imagine what he looks like under that T-shirt. Muscled, I am thinking. Taut.

And suddenly, the clouds part. For the first time the wholeness of the mountains appears, and they are flawless. And I think, What about Ben? He's smart and kind and loves the mountains. Like I do. Like Nan. And okay, a bit older than me but who cares? I picture us behind some enormous boulder, our packs sliding from our shoulders, the taste of him. What would he taste like?

Not Snickers.

Sorry. I know I sound like a bloody dolt. All hippie-dippy bullshit and sentimental rot. Even so. I'm going to talk to Ben and see if he'll come with me, on our own, or with Tika as well if he's not booked with another trek. We can go north to Mustang or continue on the Annapurna Circuit, or find some other trail to follow.

Oh man, yes, here we go: Mo and her merry men. Her many merry men. Who often weren't that merry.

I wriggled deeper into my sleeping bag and turned off my headlamp. Blackness. Heavy. Airless. I could see nothing.

But I could think. In all that blackness, I could remember, without even trying, without even wanting to. I remembered when I first saw Mo. She'd been standing in a frat house, the floors sticky, music thumping and slurred, surrounded by guys offering her red plastic Solo cups filled with tepid, foamy beer. She swung her hair as she talked (it was doubtful anyone could hear what she was saying) and tilted her head back as she laughed and generally glowed in every direction and the guys stood in her circle, in her thrall, her thrill, as if they were a pack of pups bewitched by a slab of raw meat. We were freshman. Someone thrust a cup in my hand and I took a sip. Tepid and foamy. A thick-necked football player with hair fringing his forehead was shouting something in my ear. I nodded and laughed, having no idea what he said, when suddenly some other guy came flying at me, jostling my elbow, which knocked the cup right out of my hand, sending my tepid foam hurtling onto Mo. Who stood there, her mouth a little "o" of surprise, beer sopping the front of her white shirt so you could see the blue of her bra — a turquoisey color, the color of the sea in Greece maybe, where it turned out Mo had been with her grandmother — and then the guy with the thick neck and bangs started fighting the guy who bumped me, whose friends started fighting the other guy's friends, and Mo dropped her Solo cup and grabbed my hand and we ran.

When we reached her dorm, I was panting. "Come with me while I change," she said, and pulled me into her room. With a precise English accent, she spoke. Dainty. She told me how she came to the States *for university*, so that she might learn, in addition to her classes, something *about life*. She talked in italics. In exclamation points. With so much yearning and emphasis it was easy to be captivated just by listening to her speak.

And she didn't stop speaking. She spun about the room, tossing one shirt after another onto her bed where I sat. And I listened. The room was a double, much like the ones we would share in the years to come: two desks, two bureaus, two beds. Her desk, I was to learn, was the one littered with gum wrappers and used tissues, half-empty cans of Fresca, tiny pots of pink lip gloss with their lids missing, clumps of dust and hole-punched paper circles and pencil shavings. Scarves. Stacks of textbooks and binders.

I plucked a tie-dyed T-shirt from the pile, the same Greek-sea color as her bra, and held it out to her.

"LOVE!" she said, as if she was seeing it for the first time. "It's *perfect*!" She put it on, and of course it *was* perfect, and then bent over her desk, opening drawers, pulling out a package of pens, a mascara. "Aha!" she said, putting a half-smoked joint to her lips. She lit it with a neon-orange lighter, inhaled, then handed it to me. "We can go back to the party after."

But we didn't. We sat on her bed and smoked. She opened a bottle of white wine—her roommate's, she said, who wouldn't mind—and without cups just passed the bottle back and forth, drinking and smoking and cracking up, for hours, until we forgot about the party, or didn't care, sprawled among the piles of clothes, finding a pack of cigarettes and smoking those, too, stealing beers from the fridge in the communal kitchen, just not giving a shit about anyone or anything. I always remembered that night in slo-mo: us running from the kitchen, clutching the beer cans cold against our bellies, her turning to look at me, a strand of hair across her open, laughing mouth, devilishly free in a way I never was, without worry, and I envied her and loved her. Maybe even then.

It was so easy, her ease. She shone her light and it landed on me and I was happy.

She told me that she wanted to be a writer—a journalist, perhaps—and travel the world and not just travel but *live* in different countries (!) and *meet* different people (!) and she had so many *and*s attached to what she hoped to do or see or accomplish it made up for the fact that I had none. I had no idea what I wanted to do. Or be. So along I went with Mo to English classes, to read short stories and Russian authors and Faulkner and Virginia Woolf and poetry by Yeats and Whitman and plays by Ibsen and Beckett and Pinter. I choked out timid tales in our creative writing classes, thinly painted and watery. While Mo—it was like she used acrylics—colored hers in bold and vivid strokes, the way she talked. The way she thought. Up there in the stratosphere. Splattering onto the ground.

The same way she was with men. Boys, really. Always in some vibrant swirl, telling herself some story. How this one was so passionate or intelligent or fascinating, *so* brilliant, *so* charming. Until he wasn't, and she was disappointed. So disappointed that she could no longer stand the sight of his face, the sound of his voice. The way he chewed his food or brushed his teeth or cleared his throat. On and on it went. And the guys kept coming, sniffing around, lapping at her heels until he was let go.

Story in tow, rope in hand, she lassoed the next. And the next.

And did that include Ben?

NINETEEN

When Ben walked into breakfast the next morning I was already seated, drinking the nasty coffee, a list of telephone numbers from Sagar at my elbow.

Ben held out his phone. "Charged and ready to go."

"Thanks." Somehow I was finding it hard to look at him.

"Let me know if I can help in some way," he said.

I smiled. "You already have." Thinking: *Is that what you said to Mo when she told you what happened? Did she tell you?* What did he know?

Naba brought my porridge but I left the table to make my calls, first to check on Paul, who was awake and able to talk but still in the hospital. "I'm good," Paul said. "Really, Mama, I'd feel bad if you came home. I'll be fine." He coughed.

"I know you'll be fine, honey, of course," I said. "But believe me, I *want* to come home." The hospital hadn't discharged him, and the sound of his thin, high voice, so far away (too far away), I couldn't bear it. Graham, to his credit, assured me that he was being honest; there was no need to worry, or for me to return. But I worried anyway. There was a wrench in his voice, and a crumple. He was worried too.

Next I called Narayan in Kathmandu—no answer—and then the helicopter service. I could figure out flights once I was off the mountain in Pokhara.

"You know about weather?" the voice on the other end said, cool and dry. Another day at work. "If weather is bad we not go."

I looked outside. Fog hung low and dense, obscuring the sky. But it wasn't snowing.

"And the cost?" I said. "I have insurance—I know it covers helicopter evacuation—how does that work?"

"Insurance is different for everyone. But it is for injured person who cannot trek."

Of course. And I wasn't injured.

The voice continued, "Your trekking company will pay cash deposit and you pay after. You call your insurance."

"How much is it?"

He told me and I closed my eyes. How foolish I was! Did I really think I could just call a helicopter and *poof*, it would appear, oh so free and easy? The cost was huge. It would affect not just me but Graham too. I knew he'd want to help. And I didn't want to put him in that position. He was already doing—he had already done—so much.

But.

We scheduled a time for the early afternoon (the only available time, anyway) and I hung up and returned to breakfast, where Rick now sat as well.

Sagar was speaking. "And after a snowfall such as this one, last night, it is possible. There is a report of an avalanche early this morning. Which may be good for us."

"What's happening?" I sat down, put a spoon into my congealing porridge. When I lifted it, it made a soft, wet *thuk* sound.

"It might be too risky to go," Ben said, "given all the snow yesterday and last night."

"Wait, *what*?" I put my spoon down. "I just arranged for a helicopter. It's only a couple hours from here, right?" I turned to Sagar. "Is that true?"

Sagar nodded in that imperturbable way of his. "Yes. You cannot see it from here, but Annapurna South sends down avalanches into this valley."

"But what does that mean?" I asked. "Is it impossible to go? Or just risky?"

"It is possible," Sagar said. "We go early, and no sun, and already an avalanche. The snow might be stable. But it is risky."

"Okay then." I turned back to my solidified porridge, to my cold coffee. I took a bite and a sip and swallowed the lot down. "I'm ready whenever you are."

Ben said to Sagar, "Is that what you advise, then? For us to continue?"

"I'm going," I said. "I have to go." I needed to go. Today. There was panic behind that need: I knew I couldn't face what I had set out to do. What I had claimed I wanted to do, dragging scores of people along with me. All I felt was a reprieve, a deliverance. A need (an excuse) to go home.

"But at what cost?" Ben asked. "You won't be doing your son any favor if you get hurt."

"If Sagar said we shouldn't go, I wouldn't," I said. "But that's not what he's saying." I turned again to Sagar. "Right? You're just letting us know the risks."

"But what do you usually do in these circumstances?" Ben asked Sagar. "Is there a protocol? Do you wait a day, maybe, see if the conditions change?"

"We wait if it is snowing now," Sagar said. "But it is up to you. Some clients go in these conditions, some clients they go back."

"Or wait?" Ben said.

Sagar shrugged. "Not so much. Unless it is snowing. Day to day from now on things will be the same."

I took another bite of porridge and pushed it away. "Well, I think I should go. It's not getting any better."

Rick, who'd been eating his fried eggs and thick slabs of toast with a steady, rhythmic movement of his jaw, circular almost, a clichéd cow chewing its cud, glanced up from his plate and swallowed. He really did remind me of a cow, with that big head of his, his wide mouth.

"I'll go," he said. He looked around with an even smile. "I'm ready."

"Ben?" I asked. I handed him his phone. "No pressure. You need to do what feels right to you, what makes you comfortable." And I meant that, knowing that I didn't want to be responsible for anyone's choices. Not this time.

Ben pocketed his phone. After a pause he said, "I'm game." And stood.

Game. I remembered the words Mo used to describe me to her grandmother. And I was *game.* Eager to participate, to go along. For all of Mo's adventures, her ideas and dreams that spouted endlessly from that golden head of hers. But now, this was me making the choice—one of the few times in twenty years, aside from the separation from Graham, which was really more his idea than mine—and it felt new and not that comfortable but it felt right, too, and that's what mattered.

"Are you sure?" I said. "Seriously, this isn't some major thing."

"It is to me."

"Mo would understand," I said.

"Mo would go." He stood.

And I knew he was right.

At first, the trail climbed gently through what must have been a riverbed, though covered in snow it was hard to know for sure. What I wanted to know, for sure, was that there wouldn't be an avalanche. My eyes were focused on the path ahead but my ears were all up around everywhere, levitating and flapping, trying to pick up but hoping, praying that I wouldn't, the low rumble, the whoosh or crash or whatever an avalanche might sound like as it surged down the valley. The fog had lifted but the sky was a hard slab of granite; the air smelled brittle, of snow. As the trail steepened, I was glad of it, instead of my usual dread and loathing. It felt safer to be moving up and away from the lower and more vulnerable depths. I was even more glad that I wouldn't have to retrace my steps down that skating rink of a surface. That I would avoid sliding into the path of an avalanche, that I wouldn't have to slip and cling my way to an uncertain and possibly calamitous end. And then I felt guilty, too, because what about Ben and (even) Rick? And the expense of the helicopter was so great. But it was for Paul.

Wasn't it?

I dug my trekking poles into the frozen trail. It was narrow here, barely two feet wide. Up, and up. Ahead, the path widened, descending to a bridge of felled logs, slick with snow. My stomach a clenched fist, I inched my way across. Toe by toe, thighs pressed together, arms spread wide for balance. With each weighted step I could hear a creak, a slow tear of tissue, as if the very fibers of the wood were separating. I had the crazy urge to close my eyes, pretend I was elsewhere, anywhere else. I tried to imagine Paul, as I had the first day of the trek, clapping from the other side, cheering me on as I made my way.

When I got there, it was just Ben and Sagar who greeted me.

I couldn't see Rick; he was behind with Naba, but I could hear his low monotone in the otherwise snow-stifled silence.

With a quick nod, Sagar turned and headed up the trail. Stone steps humped with snow rose precipitously and I worried that a misplaced foot—or an unbalanced one— would send me careening down. Bouncing and slamming, I pictured it, thinking of my fall when I was peeing just a few days earlier, and felt the jagged edges of rocks and debris, the wrench and scrape, the damage, despite their now gentle appearance under mounds of snow.

TWENTY

A nd finally, Machhapuchhre.

Up ahead, I could see the dot of a teahouse and a wide-open space, flattish, that seemed suitable for a helicopter to land. But what did I know? I could only hope.

The ascent was gentler here, the view unobstructed. Mountains soared from every direction, from the sides of the valley to the sky, weightless in their crush. I entered the valley and turned toward the Annapurnas. They towered, shoulder to shoulder, guarding all the white and blue beyond. Had I even noticed them on the first trek? It was shocking, their enormity. I felt very small.

I followed Ben to the teahouse. It looked dark and empty. Closed.

"Is no one here?" I asked Sagar. He was waiting outside the low, blue-roofed building, thumbs hooked under the shoulder straps of his pack.

He shook his head.

"So what does that mean?" I asked. "Will the helicopter be able to come?" Worry flickered in my chest.

"We will go to ABC," he said, meaning Annapurna Base Camp. "It is close. Just a few more hours, maybe less, and we will call from there."

"But where will the helicopter land?" I asked. "Back down here?" I was thinking of all the wasted time, up and down, my tired legs trying to hoof it like a person half my age. And failing.

"It will land at ABC. And then fly to Kathmandu."

"Wait, I thought I had to fly to Pokhara?"

Sagar looked down the valley and I turned. Rick and Naba were coming toward us, Naba once again carrying Rick's pack. Rick's face was a red beacon against so much white. He didn't look up.

I turned back to Sagar. "What if they're on their way and I'm not here? Will we get to ABC in time, before they leave?" I was getting frustrated. How had these plans gotten so screwed up? Didn't Sagar know the teahouse would be closed and we couldn't call the helicopter from here? And why hadn't anyone told me about flying straight to Kathmandu?

Liv, I told myself. *This is just the way it is. Shut the fuck up.*

"We will call from ABC," Sagar said.

Ben had taken out his camera and was snapping away at the scenery, spectacular, I knew, but I no longer cared. He lowered his camera. "Are we getting ready to leave?"

"I think we should," I said, directing my answer to Sagar. "Or at least I should."

Sagar motioned to wait a moment as Rick approached us.

"I think this pace is all wrong," Rick said, as if he were a disgruntled grandpa complaining about a chosen restaurant or a fishing spot. "We go so fast we can't enjoy anything. I want to enjoy things."

"I'm sorry," I said. "Today is probably my fault—"

"Every day," he cut me off. "It's like a race for no reason."

"In the afternoons the clouds come," Sagar explained. "And bad weather." He motioned to Rick to drink. "All okay?" he said. "Headache?" At over 12,000 feet, we were breathing in only 40 percent of the oxygen at sea level.

Rick shook his head and grunted at Sagar. "Lead on, Chief."

Ugh. Chief.

But *Chief* didn't seem to mind and off he went, presumably on the trail. Which wasn't immediately discernible, given the fresh snow. Sagar walked as he always did: head level, hands lightly clasping the straps of his pack, efficient, unhurried steps. We trudged single file, spreading out so that I followed Ben, with Rick and Naba once again falling farther behind.

Ben walked with long easy strides, relaxed, but deliberate too, thoughtful. He hadn't talked much this morning and I wondered if he was thinking of Mo, of her golden hair, and whether she had talked to him and what she might have said. *Liv pounced on me in my saddest, most vulnerable moment.* Or *Liv's been waiting to shag me for the past four years.* Or *Don't ever leave me alone with her.*

I wondered whether we would have time to honor her in some way before I left.

I wondered about Paul.

Suddenly, in the sky, as if it were hovering, I could see just the tip of Annapurna—one of the Annapurnas, I had no idea which—and for a moment it hung there, reflecting some hidden sun, on a bed of clouds that cloaked its flanks. It was just a golden peak, floating. A castle from some Disney animation, suspended as if by magic.

And then, just as suddenly, it was gone.

A cold wind blew. And with it, snow.

I tried to hurry, to walk faster, but my legs were tired and my knee ached and the cold dry air felt tight in my throat. And I had to pee. But I wasn't going to stop, because stopping meant taking off my pack and mittens and undoing my pants and the layers and heaving things down and out of the way and then up and reorganizing and there was no way I was going to waste all that time. I could hold it in; I would have to, goddammit, and *carry on* and pee when I got there.

Because that helicopter had to come today, it had to make it, it had to bring me down, away from here, back home to Paul and to everything that mattered.

Mo was dead, as Graham had pointed out; this could hardly matter to her.

The flakes started coming down hard now, fat and white, and I thought how the word *blanketed* was so often used to describe snow and how perfect, in fact, it was. The ground was blanketed. I was blanketed. Ben's pack, ahead of me, his shoulders and hat, all had a *blanket* of snow snuggling him in.

Could a helicopter fly through a blanket?

TWENTY-ONE

After a slow and solid push, maybe another two or three or hours—without a watch or working phone I was in a netherworld of timelessness—we saw the welcome sign to Annapurna Base Camp: NAMASTE, it read. AMAZING ANNAPURNA BASE CAMP HEARTLY WELCOME TO ALL EXTERNAL AND INTERNAL TREKKERS. Prayer flags were strung between the sign's wooden poles and behind and up a hill were four squat buildings *blanketed* in snow.

Ben stopped at the sign. I knew he'd want a picture, but all I wanted was to find a bathroom and a phone to call for the helicopter.

"Want me to take one?" I pointed at his camera.

"If you don't mind." He pulled the camera from around his shoulder and held it to his face, adjusting the settings. "Here," he said, handing it to me. "It should be okay if you stay where you are."

He stomped through drifts of snow up to his thighs, turning to face me once he reached the sign.

He smiled.

Click.

We both heard it at the same time. I know because I was lowering the camera from my face but then froze, and we locked eyes. A deep roar rose from the earth, shaking it, loosening the layers of snow so they ran like water through my legs.

The violence of it struck me. How sound alone could enter your bones.

The air seemed to vibrate with sound. The soles of my feet and my fingertips and my skin, my skin, the scream everywhere, all in a rush, rumbling, clouds of snow wetting my face. It was very loud and there was movement and everything was happening but it wasn't.

And then, abruptly, it stopped, and there was silence.

I made my way to Ben, jelly-legged, holding his camera out in front of me, shaking. When I reached him, I took his arm and hugged it. "Oh my God I thought that was it."

He put his arms around me, around my pack. "I know. I was waiting to be buried." His hold tightened. We didn't move.

"Where was it? Did you see it?" I pulled away, still trembling, and we both looked around.

"There?" Ben pointed. Above us and to the right, billows of white hung in the air, like giant cotton balls, barely visible through the falling snow.

"Let's get out of here," I said. And suddenly my need to pee came flooding back. And my desperate need to reach Paul. To speak to him. "We'll get more pictures later."

We tramped (gingerly) through the snow and onto the trail Sagar had made to the teahouse, and safety. The steps were slippery. At the top, at the entrance to the common area, Sagar was waiting.

"Bathroom?" I asked, breathless.

When I returned, Ben was with Sagar inside the common area. It was warm, with that familiar smell of body odor and fumes from the yak-dung burner. The porters were there, spread out on the padded benches in various stages of half-sleep.

"Congratulations," Sagar said.

"What?" I said. "Oh. Right." I had forgotten that most trekkers to base camp felt elated when they arrived; although a small achievement, it was an achievement nonetheless. "Thanks."

Ben turned to me and I hugged him. "Congratulations," I said.

"You too."

When I pulled away, I saw his eyes looked wet.

Tears? Were those for Mo?

Mo, who had led me here not once but twice. Mo, with all her dreams and ideas and stories and promises. It occurred to me how much of our friendship had been based on that alone. How obvious it seemed now.

I sat down on a bench and took off my mittens, pulled out my phone. Dead and dead and dead and dead. "Is there a phone I can use?" I asked Sagar.

"Here," Ben offered. "The service goes in and out, but at least it exists."

"No helicopter today," Sagar said, in that matter-of-fact way he had. As if he were saying *No pancakes today*.

"Oh God," I said, accepting Ben's phone, thanking him. "Did you speak to them? Was there some kind of message?"

"No flying in this weather. Not even in emergency."

"Well this *is* an emergency," I said.

"You don't know that—" Ben began.

"But it could be," I said. "It could be and I wouldn't know, because I'm here, and I shouldn't be. I should be at home—" Tears gathered in my throat, making my voice high and sharp. "Why did I even come? Why did I think this was a good idea? How could I have been so stupid—" And then I felt worse than stupid, I hated myself, whining and complaining like a bratty child. I had come here on my own; it was my choice.

"You're not stupid," Ben said—he seemed to be saying that a lot lately—"You're a mother who's far away from her son who's sick. Of course you're upset. Text him. Or call. See how he's doing. He might be better."

I wiped my nose with my mitten, pig that I was, and nodded.

Sniffing, I called Graham.

"Graham?" I said when he answered. *Graham Graham Graham.* "How is he?"

"I've been trying to get a message to you—"

The phone went dead.

I stared at it. Dialed the number again.

The cell service gods were elsewhere, or playing a twisted game, or hell-bent on punishing me, but I walked around that common area, holding the phone up, trying to get a signal, my eyes fixed on those little lines indicating service, a mountain unto themselves, disappearing,

appearing, but nothing and nothing and nothing. And I dialed again. And again. And I was pacing, back and forth, and in circles, and I shook the phone, hoping to knock some service into it, and then a text appeared.

Liv?

YES.

And then…nothing. More of nothing. Where was he? Why wasn't he responding?

Paul on the mend. Home today.

I started crying.

Oh thank God. What does doc say?

Pneumonia but Paul quite well.

Tell him I love him.

He loves you too.

At ABC and snowing. Unsure about helicopter today.

No need.

I want to come home.

There was a pause. I watched the cursor flash on the screen.

And then: *What does that mean?*

What did he think it meant?

To Paul. Right? I wanted to go home to Paul. Did Graham think I meant to him?

I don't know.

And suddenly I didn't know. I thought of Graham's words on Christmas, when we said goodbye—*and what do you want?*—and I wondered if that's what he meant then. Did I want him. Did I want to move to Boulder. And did I?

Graham had moved to the States for me. He never hesitated. He was "chuffed" about it, telling me (repeatedly) not to worry.

And I didn't worry. Or, at least, I wasn't consumed with worry. Just the normal things, the life things, laundry and baby and money stuff.

Until Hugh came for a visit, not quite a year ago, to meet Paul and "have a catch-up." When he arrived, there was much back-slapping and glasses of scotch and hiking in the sodden woods, the tree limbs bare, their trunks black with wet. Everything damp and gray and bleak.

Mostly I stayed in the house, fretting, baking bread and lemon bars and oatmeal cookies. I was in a baking frenzy. My insides crackled so, I couldn't keep my hands still. Just seeing Hugh brought back Mo.

On Hugh's last night, after a long dinner, Paul excused himself and the three of us remained at the table, powering through bottle after bottle of wine. I felt fine, finally. Or better than fine. Relaxed. Lovely. The wine had loosened the squeeze in my lungs and I could breathe in, unfettered. *So* fine.

Graham went to the living room to start a fire, and I rose, unsteady, to clear away the dishes. Hugh helped, stacking them at the table and bringing them to the sink where I had stationed myself, sloshing away (sloshed) in water and suds.

"It's remarkable, really," Hugh said.

"What is?"

"We're all here like this. What would Mo think?" He handed me the wineglasses, changed his mind, and returned them to the table. Lifting an empty wine bottle, then another, he found one not decimated, and filled the glasses.

"I think," I said, not thinking very well, "she'd think it was lovely."

"Lovely," he repeated.

"Yes. She would want to be here. She would love it."

"A jolly bit awkward, perhaps."

I felt my face flush. All that wine, to my face. "Awkward?" I said.

"Or maybe not, knowing her. She wasn't one to get hung up on old flings."

I was a fling?

"I'm sorry," I said. "I'm not following you."

"Graham," he slurred in my ear. I could smell the sourness of his breath. "She and Graham. Like bunnies, they were."

"Bunnies. Ah." I smiled, but inside I could feel my dinner—roast chicken, asparagus, new potatoes sautéed with butter, that bread, those goddamn oatmeal cookies— working its way up my throat. "Right."

"You knew, didn't you?" he said, and then, most likely seeing my face, stepped back. "Sorry. It was ages ago. One summer, was all. Back in uni. It was nothing to either of them. Really." He put his hand across his heart. "I swear."

"No worries." I laughed, still ill.

He put his arms around me. And I stood there, hands in soapy water.

Betrayed.

"Why does it matter?" Graham said the next morning, after Hugh had left. We were both nursing headaches— way too much wine—trying to organize ourselves to take Paul skiing. There were only a few weeks left in the season, and we had promised.

"Why didn't you ever tell me?" I wrestled ski boots out of the closet. "I mean, she was my best friend."

"She was your best friend, yes," he said. "But I didn't know you at the time. It had nothing to do with you. *Has* nothing to do with you. It was a shag."

"*A* shag?"

"Yes."

"A single, solitary shag."

"Yes."

"Why did Hugh say you were like bunnies?"

Graham made a face, dismissive. "Hugh was hammered."

"You told me about other girlfriends. Why not her?"

"Why is it so important to you?"

"Why can't you answer me?"

He was holding a cooler packed with our lunches; he put it down. I was hunched in the closet, pulling out neck gaiters and mittens, helmets and goggles.

"I'm sorry." He wrapped his arms around me from behind, nuzzling my neck.

I was stone.

"I don't know why I never mentioned it. Guess it felt odd, knowing you were such good mates."

"It feels odder that you never told me."

"She never talked about me, sounds like. Same difference."

I shook my head. Thinking back, what had she said about her summer escapades with men? There was always some guy, some story. Who could keep them straight?

He let go of me. "It meant nothing to either of us. Okay?"

One of Paul's mittens fell to the floor; I bent to retrieve it.

"Liv?"

"Yep."

"It was twenty years ago, at least. It's not relevant to us, to our lives."

He was right, of course. Except being right didn't always matter as much as being wronged.

And I felt wronged, though I couldn't have explained why exactly. It wasn't just because Graham hadn't told me (why *hadn't* he told me?); it was something else, too. I felt it. There was something more. Something he wasn't saying. What was it? Plus, he had fucked her—shagged her—had been inside of her, and I couldn't admit it then, but maybe I'd wanted to know her that way, and I was jealous. And I hated myself for that, which made me hate Graham, who I knew had done nothing wrong. I knew that.

Her heat, her innermost curves, the wet and dry of her. Maybe he made her moan when she came. Her eyes closed. Maybe she had loved it. Maybe he had too.

Somehow, and it made no sense, but I felt cheated. By both of them.

After that, whenever I looked at Graham, it felt tainted, this thing between us, our connection, our love, our marriage, everything. When he reached for me in the morning, scooting my hips back to tuck himself behind me, pressing, urgent, I could just imagine the faint smile on his face, and what I wanted to do—not the obvious, the natural—was slap that smile away, catapult myself to the other side of the bed, get into the shower, and scrub myself clean.

Over the next few months, that year, I watched his smile turn to hurt turn to anger. Or not anger, but resignation. Sometimes, as month after sexless month passed, I wondered if he'd found someone else, someone on the side. And every so often I would lie back in bed, feeling guilty, go through the motions of heavy breathing and little sounds, clutching his back, moving my hips. But we continued to drift, he and I, until we were two souls clinging to separate life rafts. I wanted to reach out, to save us, but couldn't.

"I'll come back," he said when he left. "But you'll have to ask."

And I stood there, silent and helpless, and watched him go.

Now I looked down at the phone in my palm.

Take this time, Graham had texted.

Did he mean take *your* time? As in: Don't worry about killing yourself to get back here because all is well? Or did he mean something else, as in: Take this time to figure your shit out because you're killing me? You're killing us?

I chose the former. *Thank you.*

Happy New Year.

It was New Year's? *Happy New Year! Will keep you posted.* And then: *xo*. I deleted it. Again: *xo*, delete, *xo*.

Delete.

Holding the phone out in front of me again, I searched for service, turning slowly around the small room, careful not to bump into the porters splayed out on the benches. How could I justify the cost of a helicopter, now that Paul was better? Where was the emergency? Insurance wasn't going to cover it, no matter how I might try to spin it.

I tried to readjust my head, the one that already was on a helicopter, on a plane back to New York, to our little village, the flat expanse of lake, the shop with its silver jewelry and strawberry preserves, our snug house, the fireplace that smelled even in summer of wood smoke and comfort, to Paul. To Graham?

And to Boulder.

TWENTY-TWO

Fine. Fine! I would stay. The relief I had felt at leaving now turned to surrender.

It was only a few more days on the mountain, and it made zero sense to turn around now, to pay a massive chunk of money to go back when I'd already come so far and paid so much, and Paul would be okay. And it would be fine.

Through the steamy windows I could see the snow coming down hard, slanted sideways by the wind. Tomorrow, hopefully, would be clear in the morning. We could climb to watch the sunrise and scatter Mo's ashes and say something and think of her. Remember. Because that's what we'd come to do. All of us. For Mo.

And then those wily cell phone gods must have waved their little wands because suddenly there was service, and I called the helicopter company and canceled before I could change my mind.

"Paul's okay, thank God," I said to Ben as I handed him his phone. "You were right."

"You must be so relieved."

"Beyond." I sat down next to him, unzipping my jacket. As warm as it was in there, it wasn't warm enough to take it off.

"I'm glad." He reached for my wrist and squeezed it. "So you're staying?"

"Happy New Year's," I said, as if I were Vanna White on *Wheel of Fortune* announcing the prize. "Or at least I think it's still New Year's here. It is at home."

"Happy New Year's."

"Do you make resolutions?" I asked.

"Nah. For me it's just a reminder to be here, wherever I am," he said. "Sounds sappy—" he laughed a little laugh "—but to be grateful. Right? You don't know what's coming next. What about you. Resolutions?"

"Not so much." But I did. My resolutions seemed silly even before Ben told me his: lose five pounds or stop nagging Paul to pick up his wet towel from the bathroom floor or do twenty-five sit-ups every morning or (finally) learn Spanish or read a poem every night before I went to bed. And like all resolutions (or at least mine), they never happened. Maybe I was done with resolutions. "Are you having tea?" I asked. "Did Rick get here yet?"

"I haven't seen him." He opened his mouth, as if he was about to say something else, then closed it. He closed his eyes, too.

"Are you okay?"

He opened his eyes. "Just a little headache."

"Altitude?"

"Yep. Probably."

"Do you have Advil? I've got some in my pack," I said.

"I'm okay."

But he looked pale. The creases around his eyes seemed deeper, his skin leeched of color. Like a faded photograph.

"Are you sure?" I asked. "What about some tea?"

I went over to the back corner where there was a doorway. Behind was a stove with large pots and, on the floor, bags of potatoes. There was a thin man with a broad face and narrow shoulders squatting on the floor. He didn't speak English. I gestured to him for tea, bowing my head in thanks, and asked for some popcorn by flicking my fingers in little bursts and flashes.

He must have understood because a few minutes later he carried it all out to us on a round metal tray.

We sipped our tea. A slow spread of glow. I took off my hat.

We devoured the popcorn. I went back and asked the cook for more. Ben's color had returned, but he was quiet, and I wondered what he was thinking about. And whom.

Rick came in, kitted out in the down coat that the trekking company loaned to all of their clients, even in the warmer months. His hood was up and he was wearing his headlamp, a gigantic thing, more suitable for a Boy Scout leader on an overnight in a park campground than a week in the mountains. He looked like an astronaut, all packed in and puffed up, arms hanging stiffly from his sides.

I couldn't help it. I laughed.

"Wow," I said, trying (not trying) to compose myself. "You sure look prepared."

Rick, to his credit, ignored me. "I took the first room," he said to Ben. "We can share but we don't have to. Naba was saying they don't expect anyone else."

"Then I think I'll go it alone tonight," Ben said. "I could use the rest."

"It's my snoring, isn't it?" Rick boomed, coming alive, unzipping his parka, laughing. "The wife's always complaining about it. She's got these green foam earplugs that stick out from her ears, make her look like Shrek."

More popcorn arrived and Rick, with his paw, scooped up a handful before the cook, who seemed even thinner next to Rick, could set it on the table.

"It seems that it's New Year's," I said. "So, Happy Happy." I wanted, despite my evil self, to be nice.

"Uh hunh," Rick grunted, chewing. A piece of popcorn fell from his mouth to the floor. "It was Sagar's back at Chhomrong."

"New Year's?"

"For the Gurung community. *Tamu Lhosar*. Would've been a big thing at Ghandruk, drinking and dancing."

"I wonder how Joshi's doing," Ben said. "I've been thinking of him."

"Me too," I said. Which wasn't entirely true. "I'm sure he's wishing he could be here."

"Satish's meditating in the mountains," Rick said. "He's happy."

"Why do you keep calling him Satish?" I said.

"It's his name."

"But he introduced himself as Joshi; we've always called him Joshi."

"That's his last name," Rick said. "And I don't like calling friends by their last name."

Well.

"I wish he could've been here," Ben said.

"I know what you mean," I said. The room was dimly lit and damp despite the blowing heater. Without other trekkers seated around the one long table, the crowds of porters squeezed along the benches by the windows, it felt lonely, haunting. Sometimes the absence of bodies made them more present. "For tomorrow, too," I said.

"We'll see him tomorrow," Rick pointed out. "Back at Bamboo. We go all the way down. About eight hours. Eight thousand vertical feet."

"I meant at Mo's memorial," I said.

"So what are you thinking?" Ben asked.

"Well, I don't know. Maybe we get up early, say three thirty? Is that too early? We could climb to watch the sunrise, scatter her ashes over the glacier. What do you think?" I was really asking Ben. Rick was busy chewing his popcorn cud. He gave a low grunt of approval anyway.

"I like it," Ben said. "But more importantly, I think Mo would've liked it." He held a kernel of popcorn between his thumb and forefinger. He looked at it as he spoke. "She really was a special girl. Lit up inside. And just part of the mountains. Or at least that's how it seemed, how she wanted to be—not that I knew her well, of course—but maybe it's the life she'd have chosen. Why it's so fitting we're doing this. That we're here." He looked up at me then, his eyes full of knowing.

He knew.

I nodded. Stiffly. "That's what Hugh said when he sent me her ashes." What he meant. Probably. "It's what she wanted." I drew my cup of tea into my palms. Its warmth was gone. "Her mother, though—she came from a very uptight background. Very proper. Boarding school. Very big over there." Graham had also gone to boarding school—called, confusingly, public school in England instead of private—and much of his etiquette and discipline, he claimed, came from there. "It was Mo's grandmother who took her climbing every summer."

"And didn't her grandmother die while we were on our trek?" Ben said. "I think I remember that."

"Mo was devastated," I said.

"I remember that, too," he said.

TWENTY-THREE

We ate dinner early.

I told Sagar of our plans and we walked outside and he pointed to where we should go. He offered to come with us, which was generous, I thought, but might feel strange, given he never knew Mo. And unnecessary, as I could see our route from where we stood. It had stopped snowing. There were no stars yet, just gauzy clouds moving fast against the purpling sky. The light was silver, the air sharp. He showed me the direction of the glacier and the best place to watch the sunrise. "Be back at seven," he said, "and pack tonight. The porters will leave before you come back."

"If we go before four, will that give us enough time? If we stay up there a bit?"

Sagar assured me it was, that it was a short distance, that we'd see the buildings of base camp the whole way.

I filled my water bottle with boiling water used to make tea and hurried to my lonely room. Curling into my icy sleeping bag, the hot water bottle tucked into my belly, I thought of how annoying it had been to have other women share our room the last time, how much I had wanted to have some privacy, with Mo. Now, I had so much privacy I thought I might scream. Anything, anything, to get out of my head. Anyone.

Is that how Mo had felt? Wanting to get away from me, who'd wanted to talk, to make things normal somehow, my guilt and insecurity and unhappiness causing Mo to retreat further, and me to try harder and—

Just then, it occurred to me that I didn't have any way of waking up—I slept so lightly I usually heard the porters outside—but we'd be leaving before they even awoke. Damn. Maybe I could just lie there all night and not sleep?

But no. Tomorrow was going to be one long-ass day and the more sleep I could get, the better.

I dragged myself out of my sleeping bag and into the frigid air. Pulling on my borrowed down parka that matched Rick's, I clomped in my untied boots and long underwear and stood outside Ben's room.

I hesitated. I knocked.

"Ben?" I said in a loud whisper. "Are you awake?"

I couldn't hear anything from inside. I hugged the parka around me and moved closer to the door. Should I knock again? Forget the whole thing? And then the door opened. Ben was in his long underwear too, hair sticking straight up, eyes squinting.

"Oh, I'm sorry," I said. "I woke you, didn't I? I'm so sorry," I said again.

"It's okay."

"I just—I don't have a phone—and I was wondering, I don't think I'll wake up on my own, would you mind? Just knocking on my door when you get up?"

"Of course," he said. "No problem."

I apologized again, thanking him, and went back to my room.

Except I didn't. Because suddenly I felt a warm hand circle my cold wrist.

He pulled me inside and shut the door.

"Ben—"

He closed his eyes. He lowered his chin. Not like he was going to kiss me, not exactly, but more like he was thinking. Or praying. Was he religious?

We stood together, his hand still circling my wrist. There was no sound but our breath. The black, frosty air was still.

Ben opened his eyes. We stared at each other. He touched my cheek.

"Your wife—"

"I know."

More breath, more stillness.

And then he took my hands in his, his hands warm and dry, rough, different from Graham's, calloused—*Graham*. "Wait," I said. "We can't do this."

"Livy, I—" he stopped. Nodded to himself. "I know what you're saying. But for me, this is it. I've been wanting this, needing it maybe, I don't know." He pressed my hands to his chest. "Wanting you, this whole thing, everything." I could hear a catch in his voice, like he was about to cry.

Wanting me? And he raised my hands to his lips and kissed them. He kissed my knuckles and I wanted my knuckles to be my lips and I suddenly wanted *him*, very badly.

I thought: *This is going to happen.* Somehow, this *was* happening. How was this happening?

And then I thought: *WAIT. Graham. You love Graham.* And then two little Livs were floating inside my head, chatting with each other, or rather arguing, one stirring the pot, saying, *Yes but you're separated, you're not together*, and the other, more reasonable, saying, *No but you don't feel separated and Ben is married and he has a wife and two boys whom he loves — you know he loves them — so what are you doing?* And then Pot Stirrer demanding, *What about Mo? She obviously told him you were some mad queer just waiting to rip her pants off so why would Ben want you? And what about her? What did he do with her?* Then Reasonable Liv replying calmly, *You are beyond Mo and what she did or didn't do. She's dead, remember?*

And then Ben's mouth was on mine and I stopped thinking. Or maybe it was caring. Looking back, that was it: I didn't care.

Later, and very deeply, I would care.

But then? We kissed. And for many moments it was only us, in the darkness, kissing, standing in the bare room.

"I'm sorry," I broke away. "I just don't understand —"

"I wanted you, Liv. All those years ago."

I made a face, as if he'd just told me the earth was flat. Or that the moon was made of green cheese.

"I still want you. I've thought of you —"

"What?" I almost started laughing. "What about Mo? She was beautiful! And she was just like you!" It was too preposterous.

"Maybe she was beautiful," he said slowly. "To you."

I shivered.

"Are you cold?" He pulled me into him. My cheek pressed against the soft scratch of wool. He smelled musty and warm and stale and sweet. Slightly mildewed. I lifted my head to look at him. The back of his neck, when I reached up to touch it, was cool and dry; his hair, bristly. With my thumbs I smoothed it from his temples.

He hugged me tighter then, and my hands dropped to his waist, wrapping my arms around him.

And then I could feel him, hard, against the soft of my belly.

And maybe it was the mountain air or the spin of Nepal or the relief that we had made it, that Paul was okay, that we were far away. Maybe it was the feeling of freedom, of not caring, of not needing to worry or wonder or believe. Maybe it was simple desire. But when Ben leaned down again, kissing me, pulling me onto his cot, his calloused hands, there I was. Kicking off my boots. Pulling off my long underwear. Hot and wet and then he was in me.

And I was free. I was free.

Except that freedom vanished pretty fucking quickly. It's one of those ephemeral things, hard to hold on to like water or sand. Slips right through your fingers.

As soon as I shuffled back to my room, I started worrying: What had I done? And to Ben's wife! What about

Graham? And oh *God* what about Mo? Had she gone to his room too? They were the first to arrive at base camp and had climbed together, alone, those last hours from Machhapuchhre. And then what?

Clearly, Reasonable Liv had fled the premises and all that was left was Pot Stirrer. I wanted to know.

Turning on my headlamp, I felt around in my duffel for Mo's journal. I wasn't tired, just cold, and I snugged back into my sleeping bag and around my water bottle, yanking her journal, itself freezing, into the damp warmth. Drawing my knees up, I hugged myself, my forehead pressed against Mo's journal. A tiny ball.

After some moments — not because I wanted to, no, but because now I needed to, I needed to know — I pulled out Mo's journal and opened it. A photograph fluttered out.

It was a picture of Mo and her grandmother. Mo had taped it, always, to the wall of whatever dorm room she'd (we'd) lived in. Except for fall semester junior year, when she'd gone to Ireland to study poetry, taking that picture and her sparkle and fizz, leaving me with a dimmer, duller light. While she was gone, she trekked from Chamonix to Zermatt along the Haute Route — 111 miles — and another trail of the same distance crossing Corsica on the GR20. And I? I went to class. I went to the library. I went out, to fraternity parties, to bars. I did my laundry and made my bed and ate my dinner. Finished my homework. Worked at the co-op.

I'd wiped the corners of my mouth with a napkin while she tossed hers in the air.

But I hadn't been bitter; I was lonely.

ANNAPURNA

I'd missed Mo, and though I received the occasional postcard with pictures of fluffy sheep on hills swathed in green or pints of Guinness sloshing onto a glossy wood bar, I doubted she thought of me much. By Christmas I had saved enough money to visit her at home on our break. When I first met Hugh and the rest of her family, my mouth ached with the effort to laugh at the appropriate time, to say the appropriate thing. On the surface there seemed to be a bounty of good-natured banter, a steady flow of witticisms and barbs. But just below, stretched thin, was some strict code, some sharp-edged line that could not be crossed.

Mo's mother, when I first arrived, showed me my cream-colored room with its heavy brocade curtains and many-pillowed bed. She pointed to a stack of white towels as we stepped into the adjoining bathroom. "You might want a bath before tea."

"Maybe she'd like a rest," Mo said, who stood shoulder-to-shoulder in the small bathroom between her mother and me.

"I'm sure she'd like a wash at least," her mother said lightly. Smiling. "If not a bath."

"Baths are so overrated," Mo said, matching her mother's light tone. "Sitting in one's own muck."

"One's muck is of one's own making." Her mother's smile tightened. "Which I suggest you see to." Still, though, she smiled.

"Oh, a bath sounds perfect," I said. Though the tub wasn't entirely inviting: cramped and narrow, with separate spigots for hot and cold water. And the bathroom was freezing. "I love baths."

"Don't feel forced," Mo said. "Mum has a way of making her wants your wants. But we *adore* her!" This last she sang, a hard trill, and she squeezed her mother's arm for emphasis.

Her mother frowned, though she was still smiling, which made me wonder what that was like, to do both at the same time, maybe like patting your head and rubbing your belly. There was a lot going on there. "Don't make me cross," she said to Mo. "And keep your adoration to yourself."

Mo's mouth clenched in a smile of its own and for the first time I saw her silenced, and small.

Mo's grandmother had been kind. She wore no makeup whatsoever, not even lipstick, and her skin was deeply creased, as if she'd been napping on a disorderly bed. Her wavy white hair was pulled into a bun at the back of her head. A single pearl studded each neat ear. Her clothes were practical and warm—a navy wool cardigan over a white wool turtleneck with brown wool trousers—and she drank scotch (or bourbon) from a glass with a single cube of ice in it. I had been handed one as well, and, not knowing what to do, I tried, unsuccessfully, to drink it. "Not to worry, dear," she'd said, probably noticing my not-so-subtle shudder. She took the glass from my cold hand and told me to get what I liked. "Life's too short to bugger about," she said in her clipped British accent.

And I knew immediately why Mo loved her so.

Now I held the photograph close to examine it. Tape was folded over the corners. Mo looked about twelve or thirteen, her long hair in a ponytail, braces on her teeth. Whoever said the British didn't care about teeth had never met Mo's family. Big, strong teeth, white and smooth, as if they brushed them with sand or salt. Both Mo and her grandmother were wearing hiking boots and packs and smiling at the camera with confident ease. They were on some summit somewhere. You could see wisps of clouds in the background.

As I tucked the photo back into Mo's journal, I noticed some faded writing on the back. *To my own Momo Herzog,* it said. *Find your Annapurnas,* It was signed simply, *Nana.*

I repositioned my water bottle—barely warm now—so I could turn on my side.

I flipped through the pages of Mo's journal and, though half of it remained blank, I found the final pages of writing. At the top of the page there were two paragraphs, a continuation of the previous entry maybe, one I hadn't noticed. So caught up in my memories of Mo, of the night we'd met, of what might have happened with Ben, I hadn't even turned the page.

Funny how Ben reminds me of Graham. Maybe it's why we get on so well. Right when I met Ben, I felt I knew him. His overall goodness. His thoughtful way of looking at the world, of appreciating what's in front of him. So much like Graham. And Graham—what a shag he was!—all that quiet energy had to go somewhere, I guess. Two summers ago, after sophomore year, Hugh and Graham always hanging about, drinking, and the heat. Torpid heat, even at night. Out on the patio by the greenhouse, fireflies, the moon flushed with light. A trickling sound from the fountain. Hugh pouring scotch or handing out beers or fixing gin-and-tonics for the girls that would appear and disappear, fireflies themselves, all our palms wet from the sweating, beaded glass of whatever we were drinking. And yes, we. Because suddenly that summer, I was there too, Hugh's little sister. I'm not sure what he knew about Graham and me—I never said a word, and I don't think Graham did either—and it was just sex anyway. Marvelous sex. Outside sometimes, the cool of the earth against my back. Behind the greenhouse and its windows shining black in the darkness. Our clothes twisted, bits of grass in my hair.

I wonder if Liv sees the similarity? Of course I could never ask, could never tell her about Graham. After she met him I remember her asking—oh so nonchalantly—if I'd ever been with him. She pretended she didn't care, as if sloppy seconds didn't matter. Poor Liv! If she only knew. But I couldn't do that to her, she'd never survive the heartbreak. Once Graham's letters started arriving, the celebrated long-distance phone calls, the plans to meet or visit in the upcoming weeks or months, what could I do? On holiday at home he came to our annual Christmas tea—which in this case also meant drinks—we kissed each other's cheeks hello in the friendliest of ways. I liked that about him. No drama, no complications. It almost made me like him, and not just in a friendly way. I whispered to him, Let's not say anything to Liv, all right? And he frowned, I'm not sure why—was it too late? Graham struck me as a very honest person—but then he nodded. I would have known if it was too late, anyway. Liv would never be able to keep that from me. Poor, poor Liv.

Poor Liv? Poor *poor* Liv? For a moment I was twenty again, sucked into Mo's thrall, newly devastated by her judgment, by her superiority, her contemptuous gaze that was so easily (and shockingly) trained on me.

And then I thought: *Really?* I mean, who did she think is? Or rather, was? Little Miss Spare the Poor Underling from the Knowledge That She Is Sloppy Seconds. What the actual fuck. But then I thought: Maybe Mo really was happy for me. Maybe she didn't want to interfere, knowing I might end it with Graham once I learned that she'd spent a summer rolling around with him in the great green yonder. I might have. But I might not. And wasn't that for me to decide?

And *then* I thought: Graham! I knew it. I *knew* there was more. But a whole summer? A romance, maybe? A relationship, maybe even love? Maybe he had always loved her! Why hadn't he come clean when he had the chance? What was that about? Maybe it was too painful. Maybe he'd been devastated, shattered after she'd broken it off. A shag. Hah! *It meant nothing to either of us.* Had it meant nothing? And did it matter, given that he hadn't known me at the time? It was an innocent lie, and not a total one. A teensy lie that you tell in a marriage, an omission maybe, knowing that on balance you're doing less harm than good. That, in fact, you're preventing harm. So the lie doesn't matter.

When does a lie matter?

Before I fell asleep, my final thought—an image, really—of Graham at the luncheon where we first met, and Mo. I remembered how their eyes met, a knowing look, something passing between them, a secret, a feeling forever unresolved, or a resolution itself, a pledge or an oath. Maybe I was imagining it. But all the old questions, the hurt and insecurity, appeared bolded in my brain, in caps.

TWENTY-FOUR

In the blackness there was knocking. And I rose up, as if I had been drowning, a full-body pull to the surface from the dreamless depths of sleep. As if I were gasping for breath, I woke.

"Liv?" Ben's whispered voice from outside. Another soft knock.

Ben.

"Yep, thanks," I called quietly. Before I'd left his room last night—not even last night, a few hours ago—I'd kissed the creased space between his sleeping eyes. With tenderness. Gratitude. I was grateful for his kindness, this man, his generosity. His gentle heart. He was a good man.

Okay, maybe not *that* good. I mean, he'd cheated on his wife.

I heard Ben's steps retreat and moments later the muffled clink of a door's hinges as it closed.

Sitting up, I felt around the inside of my sleeping bag for my headlamp. The light, once on, made the room seem darker, less friendly, and I dressed hurriedly in the relative warmth of my sleeping bag. Over long underwear I pulled on a pair of waterproof trekking pants and on top I added a fleece and a down vest. I had worn my puffy jacket, hood on, while I slept, but I chucked that aside and stood to put on the trekking company's large down parka. Plus ski mittens and a wool hat.

My pack was ready. I hadn't refilled my CamelBak — what little water remained seemed frozen — but I took it anyway, hoping there'd be sun later to melt it. I could refill when I returned. I added Mo's ashes in its Ziploc to the main zippered compartment, along with extra batteries for my headlamp. We had an hour or more before it got light and I wasn't taking any chances.

Once again I wished I'd brought a little poem, pithy or profound, an excerpt of an essay or an account of a climb written by a mountaineer Mo admired. Something I could use to express her spirit, her essence, without having to find the words myself. Because somehow I couldn't — or hadn't yet — unearthed them. At the time I didn't stop to wonder why that was.

I stood in the cold, dim room. All at once I unzipped my duffel and plowed my hands inside, groping past wool and synthetic, my book, extra socks, toiletries. I hadn't even thought to brush my teeth.

A knock on the door.

"Coming!"

I rummaged through the duffel, searching, trying not to wreck the neatly rolled and folded items of clothing, to maintain their deliberate organization, picturing Ben and Rick waiting for me outside, wishing Joshi was there with his patient perspective.

Where was his Ganesh? That little fellow of good fortune—I needed him.

"Liv?" It was Ben's voice, so I opened the door.

There the two of them stood, gigantic in their parkas, white halos of light shining from their headlamps.

Ben and I looked at each other, smiled, then looked away. I wanted to touch him, to say something, but didn't dare. Did he regret last night?

Did I?

I stepped outside. The frozen air sliced at my nostrils.

"I'm sorry," I said. "I always think I'm so organized, but then forget the thing I need the most." I rubbed my mittened hands together. "Wow, it's cold."

"The ashes?" Rick said.

"Oh. Hah," I said. "No, I didn't forget those."

We began walking in the darkness.

Machhapuchhre was behind us, I knew, and the trail from there which had led us to base camp. We headed in the opposite direction, toward Annapurna I. I couldn't see it. But it was there, shadowed rock against black sky.

The snow crunched under our feet.

My trekking poles shushed in and out of the snow, their clicking sound muffled, occasionally striking a rock hidden under the mounds of white. After a short while, we could hear prayer flags snapping in the wind. Rows and rows of them hung together from giant boulders, like a curtain almost, their colors grayed by the dark. We stopped as we came near, watched them stir and flap, listened to the hollow soft of cloth on air. Nearby was a little platform with a spire coming from a stone wall with a plaque on it. From the spire more flags were strung.

Ben went to the platform and cleared the snow from the plaque.

"*Mountains are not stadiums where I satisfy my ambition to achieve. They are the cathedrals where I practice my religion,*" he read.

Wow. Talk about words capturing Mo's spirit.

"Who said that?" I asked.

"Anatoli Boukreev," Ben said. "Did you ever read *Into Thin Air*? He was that Russian guy in the Everest disaster who wound up saving a bunch of people."

"And he died here?"

"In an avalanche. A year later. I remember reading about it—he was attempting a winter ascent just weeks after winning an award for his rescue efforts on Everest."

"That's so sad," I said.

"At least he died doing what he loved," Ben said. "He was who he was to the end."

And it felt strange to be standing there, looking at this memorial, talking about Boukreev's death and his mountains, when we were supposed to be talking about Mo's death and her mountains.

"Should we keep going?" I said, motioning forward with my head. "The glacier's on the right here—you can't really see it yet, it's still too dark—but Sagar said if we just keep hugging to the left and up," I pointed with my trekking pole toward the shadow of Annapurna I, "we'll steer clear of it and have a great view of the sunrise. There's some ledge we should get to in about an hour."

We started walking. Rick was in front, with me following and Ben last. At the time, I didn't think it odd that Ben was behind me; I just worried that I'd slow him down. The trail had begun to rise and narrow, the incline so steep I was already panting.

"It's so dark," I said. "Even with this headlamp, I can barely see."

"Yeah, I always wondered," Rick said, "why Mo would leave in the middle of the night. Why wouldn't she wait until morning?"

It was a shock to hear him say her name. I was expecting, from his drone, another story about the time he led an expedition of ill-prepared *ladies* to the summit of some hill or another where they expected to be served tea and crumpets instead of the Cliff bars and water they should have hoofed to the top themselves.

I hoisted myself up between two boulders. "I know," I said slowly, needing a moment to catch my breath. "It made no sense to me either. But that was Mo. Impulsive. Once she got an idea she just kind of flew with it. Plus, you know, we were so young. Who took the time to consider risks? Did we even know what that word meant? I mean, did you?" I had thought I'd known. But Mo?

"But what was the hurry?" Rick said. "I could never understand. And you girls were such good friends. Why would she leave without telling you? Sneak away like that? Never made any sense."

I shook my head sadly, as if I, too, couldn't comprehend such bizarre behavior and it wounded me. Not that Rick could see me, of course, but it was an instinctive response, born of many practiced years, and I went through the motions regardless.

"And there was the whole thing about that porter. Tika." I was, grossly, good at this. "He disappeared too. I mean, maybe they went together, right? He couldn't have left in the morning—he would've gotten in trouble for that, someone would've seen him—and then who knows what happened."

"Maybe he fell, like Mo," Rick said.

"But his body was never found."

"That can happen, up here," Rick said, ever the expert. "I was talking to Naba about it yesterday, and that's what he said."

"He said he knew Tika? That he had died?"

"No," Rick said. "Just that it could happen." He stopped, breathing hard.

"Not to change the subject," I said. "But have you heard of a Momo Herzog? Ben?"

I turned to look at him; he had been quiet this whole time. "How are you doing?" I said. "You okay?" I'd been surprised to learn that Ben reminded Mo of Graham, though that surprise vaporized in the wake of the other, bigger surprise, which still (unfortunately) rankled me. And not that it mattered, not that it would mean anything, but I couldn't help wondering if she'd been with Ben. I mean, sloppy seconds all over again.

"Yep," Ben said. "Just a little out of breath."

"Let's rest," I said. And to Rick, who'd already started up again, "Hang on a sec!"

"I'll be okay," Ben said. "No need."

ANNAPURNA

"Are you sure?" I asked. Ben was the only one among us who had actually climbed mountains, using crampons and ice axes and doing the whole dangle-by-your-fingertip bit from a tiny crack in an otherwise smooth surface that happened to be thousands of feet in the air. So hearing he was out of breath didn't exactly fill my world with sunshine and roses. But maybe it wasn't that at all. Maybe it was what he knew and couldn't say. About last night. About Mo. "You know me," I said. "I'm always more than happy to take a break."

Rick was far ahead, plodding along. Going up.

Ben took a step toward me, indicating he was ready to go. I touched his mitten with mine and smiled. He smiled back. We started up.

TWENTY-FIVE

It was harder to breathe now, from the elevation but also because of the steep climb, mostly over and in between large boulders. No one spoke. I scrambled in the snow as best I could, often on all fours, trekking poles dangling from my wrists. Graceful, I was not.

Rick was still too far ahead for me to see, but I could hear his grunts—from frustration, maybe, or effort—and hoped he knew where he was going.

And then I don't know what made me turn around. I don't remember a sound or a word or anything in particular, but for some reason, my hands clutching at the slick rock above, I turned to look at Ben, who at that moment was staggering. Backward.

The light from his headlamp veered crazily, first up and then down and I called *BEN!* over and over as I twisted, trying to reach him, to go down, but he was just a blur of lamp in snow and I couldn't look up to find him and at the same time watch where I was putting my own feet and suddenly there was a yell, from farther up and then a *whooshing* sound and a light flew by. A thud. *RICK?* I called, terrified—what was happening?—and I heard a groan, a low one; it was Rick, and I saw his light below me. *Hang on,* I called to them both. *I'm coming. Don't move.* And I got to Ben first, who was crumpled in a ball and I knelt down, asking him what had happened and what hurt and how I could help.

His face was the bluest white, his hand pressed to his chest.

I leaned over, brushing snow from his forehead with my mittened thumb.

Is it altitude sickness? I asked.

Don't think so, he said.

Then what?

Heart.

His heart?

A heart attack? I asked. His lips were dry and cracked.

He made a noise in the back of his throat. A year ago. I didn't want to stop.

And so this was, what, like your goal? To come here?

To try again. And to see you. What that felt like.

I shone my headlamp away from his eyes but I could still see his expression. That yearning. And suddenly I understood—his determination to carry on, his teary eyes when he reached base camp, his silence—he was thinking of his own life, his own trajectory. His ability to do what he loved where he loved it. To be who he was, like that climber Boukreev.

And those knowing looks; maybe all he knew about Mo was her soul. I had been so focused on my own fucked-up thoughts I assumed he'd been thinking about Mo too.

Are you in pain now? I asked.

Some.

Do you have aspirin?

He pointed to his pack.

I removed my mittens and dug around. In his first aid kit were some Band-Aids, a tube of Neosporin, and a vial of aspirin. He packed light. My own kit, though lacking aspirin, had a full array of gauze and surgical tape and bandages, in addition to Pepto Bismol and Imodium and antibiotics and Advil.

Are you taking Diamox? I said.

He nodded and I wondered if it was okay to take aspirin at the same time, but he opened his mouth, like a baby bird, and I dropped in an aspirin, gently. He chewed it.

Can you breathe all right? I asked.

I heard another groan from below.

Oh God, I said, remembering Rick. Are you okay for a minute? Rick fell somewhere and I think he's hurt.

I'll be fine, Ben said. Which seemed doubtful to me, given how white he looked, how pinched, and the fact that he was curled up somewhere above 14,000 feet in the middle of a mountain, having suffered a possible heart attack. With no one to help but me.

Wait, did you bring your phone? I said.

He motioned to his coat pocket.

Please Please Please.

But no, of course not, the gods were still asleep or too busy fucking around with someone else to care and the tiny gleam of hope I had was doused. Angry tears pricked my eyes. I brushed them away.

I'll be right back, I said, not wanting to leave.

My headlamp dimmed and I smacked my mittens against it, as if that would help, before I put them on.

The light flickered but then steadied, and I swallowed in relief.

I followed Rick's groaning, which was more frequent now, and louder, which I took as a good sign. At least he could make noise. Sitting down, I scooted over the snow-covered rocks, holding on as I moved away from the path we had made and over toward the glacier, the thought of which made my heart knock hard against my chest. I stood. One misstep could send me over the edge. My knees shook.

It had happened before, I knew.

I kept my eyes locked on the inches in front of me, the next step. Kicking down with my heel, making sure I wouldn't slip.

I slipped.

And it was a sudden stomach lurch, the way you feel when you're on a roller coaster at the very top and it plummets straight down and there's that impossible instant when you wonder if you'll survive, that wonder snatching at your throat, which was where mine was until I jammed one of my trekking poles into the snow, turning on my belly so I could use both hands, and stopped myself.

Sweat poured down the inside of my down parka, my fleece, my layers of wool.

What was Sagar thinking, allowing us to go up here by ourselves?

He had asked, Livy! He had asked and you said NO.

My eyes searched the darkness below me.

There, a glimmer of light, just a few feet away and to the left.

A few feet closer to the glacier.

I called to Rick: I see you! I'll be there in a sec!

It was more than a sec, but when I saw him, splayed out, eyes closed, his huge belly to the sky, I dropped to my knees.

The snow around his head was stained with blood.

Rick? I touched his shoulder. Oh my God.

He opened his eyes.

Don't move, I said.

My head.

I know.

His headlamp was twisted around his neck and I moved it so that it shone away from me. His hat was gone and I could see a huge gash running from his left temple to behind his ear. Or it looked huge, but it was hard to tell because of all the blood.

What else hurts? I asked.

Chest. Can't breathe.

His voice sounded strained, strangled.

Can you move? I mean, fingers and toes?

I saw him lift his arms like a robot, bent at the elbow, one hand bare, fingers wiggling.

Okay, good, but where's your glove? I said, looking around.

He made sounds like he was sipping air.

The blood flowed from his head.

What's in your pack? I asked. It was underneath him, I thought, since I couldn't see it anywhere. And where's your cell?

It turned out his pack had gone the way of his glove — missing — and though his phone was in his coat, it had no service. Of course.

I took off my own pack and mittens and started rummaging through. Mo's ashes, extra batteries. Where the hell was my first aid kit? And then suddenly I saw it, a zippered yellow pouch with blue lettering, nestled not in my pack but in my duffel, back in the room. Where it would be, in all of its abundance, completely useless.

Fuck, I said. Fuck fuck FUCK.

I sat down in the snow and pulled everything out of my pack. At the very bottom was a large Ziploc of tampons and pads. I chose two heavy-flow pads.

But what to use to secure it to his head, to staunch the flow? The duct tape was gone, used to repair Joshi's boot. For a brief moment I thought of the tampons, and considered tying them together and then around his head, like a daisy chain.

But then I remembered my bandana, and with frozen fingers untied it from around my neck, which seemed to take forever, and then set about applying the maxi pads to Rick's head.

Unnnnhhhhh, he brayed.

I pulled off the protective strip covering the sticky side of the pad so that the bandana might adhere better and pressed down hard, but not too hard, hoping that would slow the bleeding. If nothing else, the pads were super absorbent and would sop it all up.

I tied the bandana around his big head, and it was tight, and he kept groaning, and even though I told him not to, he sat up, but then felt dizzy so he laid back down.

I called out to Ben, to check on him.

At first there was no answer; frantic, I called his name again, louder, asking if he was all right. Finally, I heard an *I'm okay.*

I'm going to get help, I said, first to Rick and then louder, shouting, to Ben.

I figured Sagar would come looking for us if we waited. But it was freezing, and Ben needed emergency medical assistance, and probably so did Rick. I could see the lights of base camp below us and to the right, away from the glacier. Normally going down would take half that of going up, but it was still dark, and I knew the very real possibility that I might slip if I hurried. I wasn't sure how long it had taken us to get to where we were but at least an hour, maybe longer. It didn't matter. I knew I had to go. At the very least, I'd meet Sagar on the way up. They'd be okay for forty-five minutes.

It won't take me long, I said to Rick.

You'll come back? he said.

Of course.

You'll be okay?

Yes, I said. I'll be fine. And then I smiled, and patted his shoulder, thinking maybe he wasn't so bad after all, lying there with his head split open, worrying about me.

Because I'm not gonna last, he said. My head is pounding. And this blood.

Of course. Still, I couldn't blame him, given the circumstances.

ANNAPURNA

Look, I said. Keep that hand covered. Stick it down your pants or something. You don't want to get frostbite. And I'll be right back, I promise. I'm coming back. Just hang tight for a little. And don't move. Don't try to come down on your own. We're really close to the glacier here.

I collected the contents of my pack, put on my mittens, looped my trekking poles around my wrists and stood.

Check in with Ben from time to time, I said. If you can.

And I started down.

TWENTY-SIX

T he cold settled around my shoulders.
Moisture from my breath clung to my lips and
cheeks, my chin, freezing on contact. The wind
whipped at my hat, tugging at it, as if it were trying to pull
it from my head and fling it against the mountain.

But down I went, using my poles for balance as I
found my way back to our trail and retraced our steps,
each step tentative, and then as I continued, more confident, more secure, until I was stepping down hard and
fast, digging in with my heels, finding a rhythm, my eyes
focused on the circle of snow illuminated ahead, every
now and again pausing to look up and assess how much
farther I had to go.

It was easier than I thought, faster, the path already
made, and on the steeper sections I just sat and scooted,
planting my poles below me. Going down, I could breathe.
I could do this. I *was* doing it.

The lights from base camp, though distant, burned brighter, beckoning.

And my heart surged a little, lifted.

Ben would be okay. Maybe Sagar could get a helicopter up to base camp as soon as it got light. Fly Ben straight to Kathmandu. What irony, I thought angrily, the one time the phone worked without a hitch was when I called to cancel the helicopter. I pictured Ben lying in the snow, and last night. God, his face. And Rick's—though his was just a flash—what had I done?

And then with a flicker, my headlamp died.

And I stopped. All was black.

There was a clanging in my head, like a siren, and I held onto my poles, leaning into them, too terrified to move. To take another step.

There was no moon, no wash of light from above.

Bent at the waist, head facing down the mountain, I waited, knees trembling.

For what?

For nothing. For no one.

My eyes screamed in the darkness.

Batteries. Extra batteries! Those, at least, I'd remembered. I sat in the snow and pulled off my mittens, fumbling with stiff fingers through my pack for the cold cylinders. It took forever to open the battery case to my headlamp in the dark—hours and hours it seemed—and to put new batteries in properly felt impossible. Twice I dropped one in the snow. Whoever said to bring extra batteries had it only partly right. What was needed was an extra headlamp with new ones already in it.

I clicked the case closed and switched it on.

Nothing.

Again I tried. And again.

I removed the batteries, unzipped my coat to dry them on my fleece, switched them around. Tried again.

Nothing. Batteries drained quickly in the cold. But this quickly?

Tears filled my eyes and my nose began to run.

Fine. *Fine!* Nothing to do but go. *Carry on.*

I sat for a few more minutes, wiping my eyes, waiting for them to adjust. Finally, I was able to pick out shades of darkness in the snow, dips and rises, and as I looked at the sky, begging, it became a paler shade of black, less dense and fearsome, a softening, as if someone had added more water to a brush while painting.

I stood and took a step forward. And another. I began to walk, halting at first, unsure, and then with a bit more conviction. A surer step.

And then suddenly I was sliding, my hands clawing, everywhere, the air, and in my head I heard the words *This is it* as if spoken aloud by a teacher or preacher, solemn and steady, everything else silenced, the sound turned off; I was tunneling in a vacuum, a blank whoosh, scrabbling, banging into the frozen earth, my knees, and then abruptly stopping; slamming into a snow-covered rock.

And then sound returned. My knees howled in pain. I could hear from above, Rick's voice, but couldn't make out what he was saying.

I'm okay, I said shakily, uncertain if he even knew I had fallen, less certain that I was okay. Knowing, regardless, he wouldn't be able to hear me.

I rolled over and lay on my back; I sat up.

ANNAPURNA

Okay. Yes, I was okay. Everything hurt, but I was intact and my poles, mercifully, still hung from my wrists. My slide had been just that: a slide. It had taken me down a steep stretch, but one that sloped instead of dropped and had, in fact, made my descent in the dark perhaps quicker. Using my poles to heave myself up, I stood.

There, below me, were the lights of base camp. I had avoided the black abyss of the glacier that loomed to my left; the dark holes of our footsteps lay just to my right.

The wind returned, savagely, but at my back now as if driving me on.

On I went.

I thought of the silence as I had fallen, the hush. It made me think of another silence, another fall from the sky. Sophomore year at school, winter, cold. Not cold like here, with this serrated air, but cold. Mo had come back to our room from a frat party, trashed, smelling of cigarettes and sweat. I had been at the same party but had left earlier. Shots of vodka, of Jägermeister, one after the other, made the floor of the room slant and sway. I had held on to the keg next to me, trying to signal to Mo that I needed to leave, but she was backed against a wall, arms circling the neck of a guy named Skip, a senior who wore round glasses and headed the Outdoor Club. They weren't grinding away, or even kissing; instead, it looked like they were talking, their foreheads almost touching, lips moving, Mo's eyes half-closed. I stumbled out the door, weaving down the hill and to our room, where I lay on the floor, miserable, trying to focus on the ceiling that refused to stop moving.

By the time Mo came in, possibly hours later, possibly minutes, I had moved to the bed, the room having stopped its carousel swish.

"Let's go to the diner," she said.

The diner, open twenty-four hours, was no more than a ten-minute drive from campus and, since Mo's grandmother had gifted her with a white Subaru wagon that year, had become a late-night/early-morning ritual. Nothing like a two a.m. study break of fried eggs and toast with a side of hash browns and bacon. Which was what Mo would eat. I'd have a toasted bagel, plain, and if I were feeling really decadent, I'd get it with butter. If I'd been drinking, which was often, it was a chocolate chip muffin or a glazed donut. Or both. With a side of fries, salty and greasy and perfect.

I didn't respond.

Mo opened the drawers of her desk, her bureau, leaving them wide-mouthed gaping. Bras and underwear, socks, camisoles flew to her bed and the floor.

"Aha!" She held up her keys, jangling them.

"I don't think I can."

"Oh come on, you'll feel better if you eat."

"You mean, you'll feel better."

"Up we go." She yanked me to my feet. Unsteady, I allowed her to pull me along by my outstretched arm: a wayward child being dragged by a parent.

Outside, fog hung in the chill air. Our breath glowed in white puffs.

"I forgot my coat," she said. "I'm freezing."

I let go of her hand and unzipped the sweatshirt I was wearing. "Here." I wrapped it around her shoulders, help-ing her arms into the sleeves. "Are you okay to drive?"

But it was too late. Mo ran to her car, which was parked in the lot just ahead, clutching her arms, her keys, laughing maniacally.

I reached the car and slid-fell into the passenger seat. Mo had turned the heat on full blast. The air in there smelled of Mo, musky and warm, but green, too, fresh. Like cut grass. Like earth.

Put your seatbelt on, I told myself. *You'll probably get in an accident.* I clicked the cold metal of the belt into place. This was how drunk I still was. How stupid.

The car had a stick shift. The fact that Mo could drive it—on the wrong side of the road for her and with such ease, such grace—always struck me as the definition of cool. She had tried to teach me but I never got the whole press-and-release thing with the gas pedal and clutch. *Like a seesaw*, Mo would say. *You have to feel it.* And though I felt something—left foot down, right up, shift, right foot down, left up—it wasn't the right thing, and the car would stall.

Mo never stalled, and she drove fast, feeling whatever it was you were supposed to be feeling. That night was no different.

As we raced downhill, fog settled in the valley the way water rushes to fill nooks and crannies. We were in a cranny. The road, deserted, twisted in a series of sharp turns, and I saw the *25 mph* sign blur by as Mo swung the car first to the left, then right. The black asphalt gleamed in the headlights.

I looked at the speedometer: *80 mph*.

She turned left again and there was that silence.

A lift, a weightlessness, and in slow motion, without gravity it seemed, the car flipped with us in it, astronauts strapped in for flight, and there was the groan and creak of metal as we flipped, again and again.

But Mo hadn't been strapped in. And when the car stopped, she was gone. The windshield was shattered, glass everywhere. I opened the door and crawled out. I called her name. Blood covered my palms.

Mo was lying on the ground, several feet away. On her back, her golden hair blooming red with blood.

I ran, sober now, to a neighboring farmhouse and pounded on the door, heedless of the time or my bloody appearance. When the ambulance arrived, the paramedic said Mo was lucky to be alive.

Her lucky angel, I remembered thinking, *to the rescue again*.

But luck is nothing more than a collision of circumstances gone right—a string of unrelated choices that create a fortunate event. Cause and effect ignored in the favor of fate, or chance. And chance can go either way. A flip of a coin.

No one is lucky forever.

I looked up at the sky now and could see the watery light had filtered through the black. Ahead, I could just make out the toss and flip of prayer flags, straining in the wind, their colors still muted in the gray light.

I was almost there. Thank God. Each step brought me closer, and again I thought of Ben. Of him lying there, curled, in the snow. Waiting.

For me.

Faster, faster, I told myself. *Go.*

I was still a bit above and to the right of base camp, though separated from the rise on which Boukreev's memorial rested by only four or five hundred feet. I could see more clearly now, and the relief and excitement of nearing base camp and knowing help would be on its way to Ben and Rick warmed me as if the sun were already shining.

Suddenly, I saw a figure walking from base camp up the hill. And I started waving like crazy, flailing my poles, yelling HELLO, not quite jumping up and down but bending and stretching as much as I could without causing myself to go hurtling from my little perch on the mountain.

The figure stopped.

Cheered, I waved some more.

The figure started walking again, and I could tell it was Sagar, even at this distance, from his steady, deliberate stride, the way he kept his hands on the straps of his pack at his chest.

Sagar! I could have kissed him.

Walking was easy now, the slope gradual. I hurried down the trail, loping (but carefully), trying to imagine, for the first time, how to get both men back down. We would need someone, several porters maybe, to carry Ben, and what about Rick? Would they find them more quickly on their own, following our tracks? They were so much faster than me. No. No, I needed to go back. But what would be best?

I looked up from the pitted snow and saw Sagar raise his head at the same time. He opened his mouth.

And that was what I would remember, his open mouth, his raised head, that image, as a wave of snow crashed over him, a surge of sea and foam. Its spray wet my face, my hair, covered my body in a fine dusting of snow and ice. From far off I could hear a growling, that rumble, and the wave tore down the mountain, ripping into and over the blue roofs of base camp and beyond, carrying Sagar with it. Burying him, and how many others. Burying any hope of saving Ben and Rick.

TWENTY-SEVEN

I sat in the snow. My whole body shook. I was making a low, dull sound in the back of my throat. All I saw was snow, heavy and final and suffocating and white. A shifting river of white. Whatever else was there, was there no longer.

Sagar was gone; base camp, gone. And all the people in it.

The porters, the cook, people I'd seen but hadn't noticed, not really, too consumed with getting home to Paul or getting up the mountain for Mo. With myself and my stupid, petty worries. And what about Ben? And Rick?

I squeezed myself into a ball, tried to control the shaking. I would have to go back up, tell Ben and Rick what happened, help them down to Deurali. But how was that possible? Should I go right now, on my own? Get help and bring them to Ben and Rick? I would be faster; I could make it in maybe three hours. It was early enough that there'd be time for strong climbers to get back before dark.

Who was I kidding?

I covered my face with my mittened hands and rocked back and forth.

I knew it was useless. I was too slow — Mo had been the goddamn mountain goat — I was clumsy. I would get lost.

But more than that, or besides that, and more importantly, there was no way a man who had a heart attack, lying in the snow, would survive without medical attention. In all that cold. And what about Rick? It looked like just a head wound but what if it was something worse? What about his breathing?

I had promised. I had promised I'd return with help.

Too many people had died already. I thought of Sagar's open mouth and pressed my forehead hard against my knees. I couldn't let Ben and Rick die. I couldn't make a mistake. I had to do things right and not fuck up and not be the idiot I had been the first time around. With Mo.

We wouldn't have been here if it weren't for you, I shouted silently at Mo. *I never would have come in the first place, and I never would have come back. It's all your fault. Your goddamn fucking fault!*

But it wasn't true and I knew it and I hated myself for it.

Hot tears wet my face and then froze against my cheeks.

I was wasting time. I pushed Mo away, her name, shoved her out of my head.

I stood, brushed the snow from my coat, shaking my head so snow spilled from my hat, my hair, stamping the ground to loosen the clumps that had formed in the creases of my pants. I glanced up, stricken. Would stomping cause another avalanche?

The air was still. So now: what to do. Go down? It might take more time, I reasoned, to get to Deurali and have porters go back up to get Ben and Rick, but maybe not. Trying to help both men by myself would take forever. If that were even possible. I was unsure I could get even one of them down. Could Ben walk? Would that be safe? And what if Rick fell again? Both men were much taller and bigger than I—Rick might have weighed twice what I did—and I could barely get myself down without careening off the mountain.

But Ben and Rick were waiting. They would think I had gotten lost or maybe didn't care or wasn't hurrying. And wouldn't it be safer for them to be moving, albeit slowly, than lying in the snow waiting for frostbite to set in?

I looked at the sky, as if the answer would appear among the clouds.

Please, I begged. *What should I do?*

Exertion couldn't be good for someone who just suffered a heart attack. Right? Better to have frostbite and live.

Right.

I started slogging through the snow, heading not toward base camp but around it, to the right and away from the avalanche track and the glacier beyond. Our path was gone; the snow deep, up to my hips, in some places to my waist, and I thought how hard it must have been for Rick to break the trail earlier that morning, going up the mountain. He was stronger than I gave him credit for, and I wondered if I should have at least gone back to get him.

As cold as it was, I started sweating. Every step as I punched through the soft snow made my lungs burn. I could feel rivulets of sweat drip from under my arms, down my sides, between my breasts. And yet my legs were numb with cold. I was wearing that huge down parka but only a pair of long underwear and trekking pants. Although waterproof, they weren't warm. My body was divided into two separate, opposite, temperature zones: tropical and arctic.

I reached base camp. Or what I thought must be base camp. I couldn't see it, not really, but knew it must be underneath those huge chunks and humps of white. It was impossible to be sure; the blue roofs were gone and the flags and even the sign. Gone. The avalanche had walled off that part of the mountain from where I stood, I couldn't get to it, but everything that had been there had disappeared. It was as if a volcano had erupted and buried an entire city in molten lava. As if it never existed.

I bit my mitten to stop myself from crying.

And then I saw the sun rising. A splash of fiery orange, terrible and beautiful, flared across the mountain. Like someone had struck a match, it burned; the mountain shivered in its brilliance.

I turned back, in the direction of Machhapuchhre, its massive peak bathed in the reflected light.

I wiped my nose with the back of my mitten, tightened my grip on my trekking poles.

"Go," I said aloud.

I went.

TWENTY-EIGHT

The avalanche had wiped clean our trail. Not that I could've reached it, given the amount of snow and ice that had poured into the valley, but it meant I'd have to continue to make my own path, at least for a while. I thought of how Ben and I had stood just below base camp when we arrived, feeling the earth tremble and hearing the crush and tumble of an avalanche somewhere else on the mountain. It could have been us. It would have been, if it had been today.

The thought of another avalanche, one that could occur at any moment, made me twitchy. I tried to move lightly, but it was impossible, floundering as I was. It was a gentle slope down, but I was in a narrow valley at the base of all these mountains, and though I couldn't get lost and eventually would arrive somewhere near Machhapuchhre Base Camp, it also meant I was in a particularly vulnerable spot when it came to avalanches.

All rivers lead to the ocean, I thought. Was that even true? Where did I hear that? From Mo, probably. She had been the source of any lore regarding nature and the outdoors. She *was* nature and the outdoors. And I thought of her smell, earthy and sweaty and the dust of vanilla, and I hated her.

I plowed on.

She was selfish, that's what she was. Selfish.

That night, her last night. After she had fucked Ben. Not that I knew that at the time. Or did I? Didn't I know *something*? It was so obvious now: the flush on her face, the way she was sitting on her bed, all rumpled, her braid a mess. When I walked into the room, Tika was there and Mo was saying something, reeling him in, as if Ben weren't enough. But Tika backed out of the doorway, shamefaced, fast. So shy, dipping his head, eyes averted. Mo had been teasing him. Of course. As if that kid could even speak English.

And she looked at me so smug; so satisfied. With that cool air of certainty, of assurance, so pointed. A push, as if she were shoving me hard and away, away from her.

I knew. And maybe she'd wanted me to know. Maybe that's why we fought. Maybe that's why I'd turned to her as I organized my belongings, not thinking but cruelly saying, "You're going to torture that poor boy, the way you did Skip."

Poor Skip was what we called him—rarely just *Skip*— because after the night of our car accident, Mo seemed to take on some mythic quality for him, some mysterious splendor of heroic fragility that made the guy salivate with desire. Yet she was neither heroic nor fragile, and he was not one to salivate. He typically had some tiny thing trailing after him with long dark hair and small breasts — ballerinas who someday would teach yoga — pretending to want to sleep outside without a tent, and not just for one night.

But Mo loved sleeping outside without a tent and once Skip realized that, in addition to the fact that she could fly through a car windshield relatively unscathed, he decided they were meant for one another. He had been in a number of accidents, not all of them in cars.

And Mo?

She went from, *It's like he and I are the same person, we both love eating cold tofu dogs!* and *We're going to spend the summer in Alaska, climbing Denali!* to *I can't spend all summer with a guy who thinks Virginia Woolf and Tobias Wolff are related* and *It's like all he can talk about is where we're going next, which big mountain or trek.* Which was weird of course because that's what Mo liked to talk about, too. But she had started referring to him as *Poor Skip*, and so did I, because no matter how gently or plainly or harshly she tried to put him off, he stuck around. Kind of like the long-haired chicks that trailed after him. Until the day he tried to solo a particularly dangerous pitch along a cliff near school, notorious for kicking climbers from its jagged edges, causing broken ribs and wrists and legs, shattered knees, and several severe head injuries. And those occurred in summer.

Poor Skip tried to climb it in winter, hoping to impress Mo.

He had asked her to come along and she had refused. So off he went, alone, with ice axes and crampons but without ropes — free soloing — dangerous even for an accomplished climber, which he might have been, in his own mind at least, but not accomplished enough. Not to climb without the safety of ropes. Maybe the ice was too brittle, too thin. Maybe it was too cold or too dark or just too difficult. Maybe his legs gave out, or his arms, trembling with tension. Maybe he clung to the cliff, until his strength gave way, until he hurtled into nothingness. Maybe he just slipped.

Mo blamed herself for Skip's death. Or not blame, not exactly. More like considered it a shame that he hadn't gotten the message that they were over. That he had involved her by inviting her along. Like she was part of it, somehow, despite not being there.

Poor Skip, I thought now. And *Poor Liv*? Poor me?

No, I thought. Not anymore.

I unzipped my parka, but not all the way. Cold air lifted strands of damp hair from my neck.

We said some terrible things to each other her last night. Or I had. Unforgivable things.

If I could have closed my eyes against the shame. But no. No. I needed to keep walking, as fast as possible, so I had to keep my eyes open. Even if I didn't want to see, I had to look.

Mo hadn't said anything. She let the name "Skip" hang in the air like a piece of soiled laundry, too filthy to touch. She pulled out her journal, bent her head, started writing.

But I. I couldn't stop myself.

"So, it's Tika now, huh?"

Nothing.

I turned my back, pretending to sort my gear for the next day.

"Gonna play around with him for a while? He next on your list?"

The air seethed.

"I get it," I said. "Although Ben's more your type. Done with him already? Does he know it yet?"

"Shut up."

I turned to face her. She wasn't looking at me but at her journal, sitting cross-legged on her bed, hunched over, braid resting on one shoulder, touching her cheek.

I was holding a pair of socks, hers, that had somehow found its way among my things. It was rolled into a tight ball. And smelled.

A small flick of my wrist and the sock-ball bounced against the side of her head.

She looked up.

I grinned, but I had nothing. Only the desperate glint of fear.

"What's wrong with you?" she said.

"I could ask the same of you."

She put her journal down and stood.

"I'm leaving tomorrow," she said.

"Obviously," I said. "So am I. We all are."

"No." She hesitated. And maybe, I would always wonder, that was the moment. Maybe if I'd reacted differently. If I was different—less of, or more. Maybe that hesitation would have turned into something else. Something less final.

"I mean, not with you," she said.

"Believe me," I said. "It's not like I want to walk with you either." And yet the truth was that's all I wanted.

"I don't want to fight."

"I don't care what you want," I spat. "I'm not one of your little groupies."

"Why are you being so hateful?" Her voice was quiet. Mine, I was sure, was shrill. "It's not like any of this is my fault. *I* didn't do anything. *I* wasn't the one who, who—" She looked around the room, arms open, fingers spread as if hoping to grasp something. "Why couldn't you leave it alone? Why'd you have to get so *weird*, so—"

I pushed her. Not hard, just a quick shove to the center of her breastbone. So I could walk away, walk past her, out the door. But she lost her balance—who knew she was so unsteady, so easily undone—and wound up on the floor, caught between two beds. Instinctively I reached to help her up, an apology already forming in my mouth, the taste of regret, the desire to soothe.

"Don't touch me," she said, pulling away.

And I saw that, the recoil. Her arm moving so fast it hit the side of the bed.

I drew back, silenced.

She stood, and I could see she was shaking. "Don't you ever touch me again," she said. "Ever." She started shoving things into her pack: the balled-up socks I had thrown, a fleece, her water bottle. "I'm not finishing the trek, not with you. It's ruined—everything is ruined—"

"And that's my fault?"

Her pack was overflowing; she could barely fasten the clips. But she hoisted it over one shoulder and pushed past me out the door.

I followed.

It was getting dark. Lights shone from the communal building, which was crowded with trekkers and porters, their breath and body heat fogging the windows. Outside, it was freezing, empty. A cold, bitter smell clung to the air.

As Mo walked, she pulled up her hood, tucking in her braid.

"Where are you going?" I called after her.

She turned.

And her face. Such a look. I had seen it before, just not directed at me. Disgust, pity. Or pitiless, as if she'd left already and I alone refused to believe it. Her eyes brittle. Her mouth, those lips, a thin line.

Maybe if I had looked harder, or longer, I would have seen something else. Sadness, maybe. Hurt. Confusion. Maybe not.

But I didn't look. Instead, I laughed.

It was a fake laugh, and loud. Probably more like a cackle than a laugh. A sneer. "Go then, why don't you? You're such an expert mountain climber, right? Why don't you just go now? I bet you could skip right down, with one eye closed." Somewhere, I heard the sound of spitting, that hawk and smack, but I ignored it, so far gone was I, and just carried on, out of my body, without a mind. "GO," I said. I waved her away, dismissing her.

I wanted to cry.

"I'm gone." She turned and started walking.

"Good," I said, laughing again. "Hope you fall off a cliff and die."

I reached Machhapuchhre Base Camp, where the slope flattened, making it easier to regain our original trail. Our footprints had melted and froze and were now covered in snow, but they were ours, stretching in a line as far as I could see. Filled with hope, I followed them down. Everything was easier now, faster, and in my head I told Ben and Rick that help would be there soon.

The sun shone from a bright blue sky, sparkling the white around me. When the wind blew, snow rose like glitter from the ground.

It was warmer now, and I was getting thirsty. I usually carried about three liters of water but I hadn't refilled my CamelBak. In the preceding days, I'd drank all three liters by the time we reached our teahouse.

I took an exploratory sip: a weak burble of water moved through the tube. Almost gone, but no longer frozen. I wasn't worried. I'd be at Deurali soon and the headache that nagged at the base of my skull and brow was hardly a big deal. And I was going down to a lower elevation. I was fine. But what about Ben. And Rick?

I pictured the sun warming them, creeping over their faces, thawing their fingers, their toes. But would the sun even reach them? Were they shadowed by the angle of the mountain, freezing to death? And how much water did they have? Was it enough?

I thought of them lying there: Ben, calm and gray; Rick, spattered in blood, probably cursing my name.

Every step now became a step for their survival. That's all I wanted, for them to survive. And every minute that ticked by—gone, wasted, who knew how many—was a minute that might save them. Life and death were separated by seconds. I had seen it, on Sagar's face.

Lengthening my stride, I used my poles to force myself forward, swinging my arms as if I were cross-country skiing. Bounding, almost at a run, I made my way down the mountain.

This time, I thought, *would be different.* This time, of course, *was* different. I was there. When Mo fell, when she died, I wasn't.

But it was my fault she had left that night, instead of waiting till the morning, just as it was my fault that Ben and Rick were stuck on the slopes of Annapurna.

My big idea. I should have known better. Both times. I should have known.

So consumed with anger, so thick in my swirl of hurt and humiliation, I had thought Mo went to find Tika that night. She'd stayed with him before. I had gone to dinner, sitting next to Joshi. What he said when he spoke that night made little impression on me. It was his tone. Like the sound of bathwater, that soothing *slipslap*, a musical hush and rock. I felt my anger dissolve.

Not completely, though, so when Rishi came to ask where Mo was and did I know what she wanted for dinner, I told him she was in our room but she'd come when she got hungry. And then I ordered for her. Everything I could think of. A veg omelet and stir-fried noodles and boiled potatoes and a high-altitude apple pie, for which the Annapurna Base Camp was famous. Just hearing her name stirred something in me, murky and viscous, and I tried to listen to Joshi again, to feel his windless voice.

Instead, I pictured Mo with Tika. He wasn't at dinner either, which seemed to prove my theory. And I saw them laughing. Laughing at me, *Poor Liv*, sharing Mo's derision.

When the food arrived, and Mo didn't, I ate it all, in addition to my own dinner. I stuffed myself, trying to fill an emptiness that couldn't be filled. Joshi, if he noticed, didn't say anything. Except after we were done, zipping up our coats, he asked me if Mo was feeling okay. She's fine, I told him. Don't worry about her.

And you, he asked. What about you?

TWENTY-NINE

Now the trail became steeper. The snow less deep but glazed in ice, like the soft center of a candy encased in a sugary shell. I could punch through if I stomped down hard. I sat down and slid over the larger boulders and rocks, using my poles for purchase. Nestled in the crux of several snow-covered mounds, I hurriedly slurped at my water, disappointed to find only a few drops. My mouth was dry. And I was boiling. I took off my pack and then shimmied out of my coat, keeping it zipped at the bottom and tying the sleeves around my waist. Immediately I felt a chill. My many sweat-wicking layers needed to start wicking or breathing or whatever it was they were supposed to be doing to keep me from freezing my ass off. I put my pack back on. If I remembered right, I was almost there.

Clouds were beginning to form. I could see them racing from one side of the sky to the other, jamming together like cars on a busy highway.

What time was it? I thought of my phone, wanting that connection, missing it, missing it so much I took off my mitten and drew it out of my pocket, willing it to come to life, which, of course, it didn't, which made me mad that I'd even wasted those ten seconds trying. Stupid. *But what about Paul?* I thought. What if Graham was trying to reach me?

Paul was with Graham and Graham was a good father. Responsible. Smart. He could take care of him. Fiercely I loved Paul. But Graham loved him too. He would know what to do.

He certainly knew enough not to get himself stranded on some horrible mountain in the middle of winter. A mountain of death and destruction. Of desperation.

Suddenly, I missed Graham. Our simple life, the way it was in the beginning. When we first moved to our little house near the lake. Only an hour from the depressed mill town where I'd grown up, but far enough in expanse of sky and piney woods and rolling fields of corn. In the blue-black depth of the lake. The clean-swept sidewalks of Main Street with its coffee shop that served pancakes at the counter to college students swiveling on its cracked-vinyl stools. The red-and-white striped awnings. The burnt-sugar smell of waffle cones made at the ice cream shop. The neat rows of preserves, the glint of glass, at Sienna's gift shop, where I worked.

I remembered Graham when we renovated our house. Living among plastic sheeting and cans of joint compound and the fresh smell of wood shavings. Whistling as he sanded or painted or spackled. And he danced. Loved to dance, whether there was music or not, and he'd grab my hand and twirl me around and dip me, dimple laughing, or pull me in, hand on the small of my back, reaching down to grab my ass, his knee between mine, swaying lightly or crushing into me, skin gritty with sweat and dust, a sweet green breeze floating from the open window, carried in by the yellow sun.

One time he brought a picnic upstairs to what would be Paul's room, where I was painting the walls a pale lemon. It was a month after my second miscarriage. The first had brought me to my knees, weeping; the second, to a state of open-mouthed disbelief, dizzying in its nothingness. I was touched by his effort. His very British idea of a picnic: tinned sardines, Carr's water crackers, a bottle of sparkling white. A beautiful, ripe pear. A small chunk of Stilton. The latter of which was a luxury and, I knew, not easy to find in Upstate New York.

He put down my paint roller and wiped my hands on his pants, already splattered with paint, and pulled me to the floor. We sat in a square of sunshine that slanted from the window. He poured the bubbly wine into plastic cups and touched his against mine, saying, *To my Livy*, and I smiled, though I didn't feel like it. I was still numb from the miscarriage. But there he was, trying so hard. So when he kissed me, mouth cold from the wine, I let him. And I let him, not wanting to, move on top of me, my spine pressed into the bruise of wood floor, the back of my head against its hard surface. I let him unzip my jeans, slip them from my ankles, my bare feet, peel my underwear from my hips. I let him kiss me. Kiss my thighs. Between my legs. Open me up with his mouth and his tongue. And then I was crying, and he was inside me, kissing my face, and I was kissing him too, desperately, wanting him then. Wanting.

Later, my head propped on his chest as we lay on the floor, I thought how much I loved him.

Much later—nine months later—we had our son. We had Paul.

I thought now of Ben, of last night. Of having sex with him. Dear Ben. How different it had been, despite all that want. With Graham, it was want coupled with love, and that was more.

When I saw the blue roof of the teahouse below, I remembered seeing Sagar waiting for us, probably getting nervous—though he'd never seemed nervous about anything, not even avalanches—and how relieved he must have been to see me. Or possibly not, given that I was alone, without Ben or Rick. And then what? Did he see the avalanche coming, that wave of snow, his mouth open in wonder? In horror.

I thought of my own relief when I saw him.

Now, as I stepped down to the teahouse, again that relief. I'd made it. I'd made it! And it was still earlyish (hopefully, I didn't really know), and thank God, thank God, someone would be there to help.

But the door, when I went to open it, was locked. Urgently I tried again, knocking, calling. Rattling the doorknob, stepping back, looking around, I called *Hello* again and again.

Walking the length of the teahouse, knocking on windows that I now saw were shuttered, I realized that without trekkers there was no reason for these teahouses to remain open. It would only cost them money. In the middle of winter and avalanche season, the few trekkers who passed through probably booked ahead. We were meant to stay in Bamboo that night, not Deurali.

I would have to go to Bamboo. Impossible. I wanted to cry. I turned around, in a circle, looking for someone, anyone, who might help. *Help!* I wanted to shout.

Instead, I shouted. *HELLO?* Over and over, my voice ragged.

And my words echoed empty, and I knew I'd have to walk fast, across the glacier—another major avalanche track—and even as I wondered if I'd be able to do it, if I could make it, I knew it didn't matter. I had no choice.

THIRTY

The trail descended sharply but I didn't pause, just slipped and slid my way down, keeping low to the ground, using my poles for balance, looking up every now and again, hoping to see a villager or child or porter or goat or *something*, any sign of life that might point the way to help. To someone who would increase the odds of Ben and Rick surviving. I refused to think; I just went.

Until the glacier appeared, and I could hear its low hum as it waited for me, crooning its indifference.

I wiped my dripping nose with my mitten. Wet now from all that drip.

Stopping at the glacier's edge, my eyes scanned its expanse, its bumps and dips, looking for our previous path across. But it was hopeless. I'd have to forge my own way.

The sky was the color of bone.

From somewhere below, the sound of burbling water.

I began to scrabble across, stabbing my poles into the snow to make sure I would step on solid ground. My whole body, knees bent, eyes focused on the next step. Every step.

With a jolt my right pole sunk in the snow to my fist and I was thrown forward, my left arm swinging wildly, my legs staggering in every direction so that I almost fell.

If I'd been watching myself, maybe I would've laughed to see the lunatic that I was, lunging around in the snow. But I wasn't laughing.

I finally found my balance and stopped, panting. My head bowed. I pulled my pole from the snow. I was trembling all over. I could have plunged right through the crust of snow, into what? And to what end? No one knew where I was. And no one would be coming to rescue me. I swallowed hard, tried to quiet the frantic clatter of my heart.

Still trembling, I started walking again. I took smaller steps, lighter. One foot directly in front of the other. Fast.

And then suddenly, leaning into my right pole, I punched through the ice—*again!*—but this time my left foot plowed through too, my whole body flung forward, wrenching my leg, arms splayed, the right pole wedged under my wrist.

My leg. My left leg.

The red scorch of pain.

On my elbows now, saliva and mucous leaking onto the ice.

I tried to sit up, to push myself up and back so I could pull my leg out, my wrist throbbing, and my chin, where it must have hit a rock hidden in the snow, and I grunted, turning, using my hands to walk myself around, moving my right leg up and out of the way, leaning hard to the right so I could draw my left leg out.

Instead, I felt my left leg drop, the snow collapsing around it to my thigh.

I leaned back, pushing down and away with my hands. The shift in weight made my bottom start to sink and it struck me that I was going to fall again, this time through the hole I'd made, but I managed to slide back, pulling my left leg out, and I sat there and sobbed.

Little ragged edges of panic were coming loose in my throat, crumbling like bits of rock and soft earth, cascading down, causing more and more bits to break free. And then I started laughing. There was nothing funny and I knew this and what was frightening, among other things, was that I couldn't stop.

My tears froze and I laughed.

My leg was sopping wet. I laughed.

I was sitting on a glacier while two men, injured and ill, were waiting for me to bring back help.

I laughed. My stomach hurt I laughed so hard. Tears streamed from my eyes.

And people—porters and guides—had died. Died. Because I had brought them there.

My laughter stopped.

Get up, I screamed silently. And then aloud. "Get up and get moving before you freeze to death. Before Ben and Rick freeze to death. Get up. Get UP."

Before an avalanche came thundering through.

But I remained motionless, too frozen in some part of my brain to know what to do, to make my body move. I couldn't do this.

And then I thought of the Ganesh that Joshi had given me. I tore off my pack and pawed through the contents like a wild dog, grasping and then discarding every item, frantic, because now I *needed* that Ganesh. That Ganesh was going to protect me. It would remove obstacles, right? And I had obstacles. I had lots of obstacles.

It wasn't there. Had I lost it? I tried to think back to when I was with Rick, looking through my pack, unloading its contents and then repacking them. Had I left the Ganesh—*Joshi's Ganesh*—somewhere in the snow?

I bit down on my tongue, trying to stifle the hysteria that threatened to run naked and screaming in my head. My eyes moved across the white slopes surrounding me, mottled with gray. Gashes of black.

"Help," I said aloud. To no one. And then with more force. "Help!"

I hated myself. My weak self.

I patted the pockets of my parka, hoping to discover something useful. I felt a lump. A whistle! But no, no, I'd tossed that from my pack before I'd left home, because, what, I thought it too silly? Too ridiculous? Certainly not that it could save lives and that I might need it. No. I simply hadn't thought. Or I was thinking other things.

I pulled out the lump: my Snickers.

I ripped the wrapper open and took a bite. My teeth slid off the surface, grazing the chocolate, a nut. Frozen, but who cared. Little confetti explosions. I let the sweetness dissolve in my mouth without tasting it, without pleasure.

I ate half of it and pocketed the rest.

Okay. Now go.

But my left leg, every time I tried to stand, to put any weight on that foot, made me shudder with pain. When I scrunched up my pants and long underwear, I could see a sickening bulge beneath the skin above the ankle. Red and purple bruises already blossomed along my shin. Was it broken? My hiking boot was snug around my ankle and could serve as a brace. If the swelling got too bad later, I could loosen it.

I reached for the bandana around my neck, remembering at the same time that I had used it to secure the sanitary pads to Rick's head. *Damn him*, I thought, *the fool*. And then, just as quickly, *Shut up, Liv. It's not his fault. Look at you: You fell too*. Pulling off my hat, I tied it around my shin, tight, hoping the pressure might make it feel better. But when I got on all fours and then attempted to stand, keeping my weight on my right leg, I almost fell over. The hat did nothing, of course, and would probably come untied in a matter of seconds.

I sat down and picked up my pack. I didn't need it anymore, not really, and I tugged at its straps, wondering if I could use them. *Of course* I didn't have a knife, like any prepared trekker might. Inside were my headlamp and the Ziploc containing Mo's ashes. I held the Ziploc in my hands, its weight, bits of bone and grit; I stared at it. Should I scatter her ashes here, on the glacier? Leave her among the cruel clods of ice, the vicious rush of water?

Mo wouldn't have seen it like that, I realized; she would have seen its beauty. There was movement in a glacier. There was drama and mystery and the breadth and breath of space, of excitement. The presence of all that she found so alluring in the mountains.

I opened the Ziploc. The wind dove in, its fingers rifling through the ashes, lifting them. With a twist and swirl the ashes spun through the air, aloft. Gone. What remained, I cast onto the crystalline ice.

"Thank you," I said aloud. "For being with me."

And then, "I love you."

And finally, "I'm sorry."

In my head I said, *May you rest in peace.* For a moment, I hugged the empty Ziploc to my chest.

And then I stuffed it into my coat pocket and turned to my pack.

I had to hurry.

I pulled the CamelBak reservoir out of the inside pocket and ripped out the internal pad used for lumbar support. It was stiff but bendable. I wrapped it around my shin and then doubled the stretchy band of my headlamp, which was still attached, over my leg to secure it. But the pad gaped at the bottom and would slide off. Knowing me, I'd probably trip over it. I disconnected the tube from the reservoir and lashed the bottom of the pad tight against my leg, bracing it.

Propping myself up with my poles, I stood, shaking. A cold wind blew against my face. On a ledge above the other side of the glacier I saw Mo, her hair whipping in the wind. She beckoned to me.

THIRTY-ONE

Every step, an inch, seemed to take an hour. My trekking poles became crutches and I dragged myself like a crippled drunk, staggering across the glacier and up the ledge. What mattered narrowed to a speck at the same time it intensified; became magnified; a closing of a camera's aperture. To keep moving. That was it.

And maybe that's what happens in times of crisis: You stop thinking and something else kicks in, a bright beam that focuses you on a single goal. The chatter falls away, like a row of dominoes, until you're left with one vital, elemental thing. At least that's what happened to me. I thought *GO*. I thought *DOWN*.

Time passed. I didn't know how long. It didn't matter, except it did.

When I reached the cave I paused, panting and sweating, my left leg numb with wet and cold. Maybe that was good, I thought, like a perpetual ice pack.

From there on, it would be mostly downhill to Bamboo, but I'd have to cross a stream, I knew, and I'd pass at least two more teahouses. Two more chances to find help.

I might make it. Ben and Rick might make it.

Where was that Korean woman who had reapplied her lipstick here? At home, in bed maybe, safe? *We will all be safe*, I told myself, knowing simultaneously that I couldn't know that.

Tears swarmed behind my eyes. *You are a fraud*, I thought, *in every sense of the word*.

And now other thoughts clamored for attention. Leaving the cave, I sat and scooted down a boulder glossed with ice, trying not to bang my left leg. And I thought of that last night at base camp, twenty years ago. I had gone back to my room after dinner, only to find the two women who were sharing our room already in their sleeping bags, headlamps on. No sign of Mo. We murmured our introductions as I peeled off my outer layers, keeping a fleece on over my long underwear. I could see my breath when I spoke.

I was surprised not to see Mo, even though I assumed she was with Tika. He hadn't come to dinner either, so yes, confirmed, they were somewhere together, snickering.

I lay in my sleeping bag that night, staring into the inky chill, and wondered for a moment—the briefest, most slender hair of a breath—if I should say something to Rishi, tell him I hadn't seen her. But then I thought—and quickly, so quick—*no*. No. She'd stayed the night with Tika before, with all the porters at Bamboo, and no one seemed to care. And she was fine. And maybe if I said something, Tika would get in trouble.

That one moment. I would think of it in the years to come.

And if I was really being honest, deep down, way way down where I'd always refused to go, there was a flicker, even then, that maybe she wasn't okay, that something had happened to her, or that it might. And it felt mean, but also thrilling, that I could think that and not care. And do nothing.

So I'd turned to face the wall, curling into myself. Closed my eyes and fell into a thick, uneasy sleep. Unaware that my best friend had decided to leave that night. Alone, or perhaps with Tika, we would never know. Her body was found crumpled at the bottom of a rocky ledge three days later.

By that time, I was in Pokhara. I had decided not to continue along the circuit trek.

By that time, I had showered.

No one had been looking for Mo. When she didn't show up for breakfast the next morning, I told Rishi that she had planned to go off on her own. Tika was gone too, so obviously he had left with her. I had swallowed my porridge, drank my coffee, smiled to Ben and Joshi and Rick that I didn't care, I wished her well, that we had parted friends. That Mo was just a free spirit, jonesing for her wings.

And somewhere down the trail, to Deurali and Bamboo and beyond, I had started believing it. I told myself that in a couple of weeks, a month, okay, maybe longer, I'd hear from her. A postcard of some toothless ancient Nepali woman carrying ten thousand logs on her back. A postcard of a mule. A packet of chai tea, even though I didn't care for it. Something, at some point. I told myself she was fine.

Until a young Israeli guy, on a three-week trek with his two brothers, spotted her while taking pictures of the glacier. He spotted her body.

And then it was hard for me to believe anything I told myself again.

Movement became a blur. The sky was heavy; slate. I no longer pictured Ben or Rick. I didn't want to think about what might be happening to them. I didn't think of Graham; I didn't think of Paul. I am ashamed to admit that now, that I didn't think of my son. But my mind was empty. And full.

Nor did I think of Mo, though sometimes I thought I heard her, whispering in my ear.

I tried to conjure up Joshi's Ganesh. Tried to feel its presence with me, next to me, Joshi's lullaby voice, his wisdom and perspective.

Nothing.

The wind blew harder, and with it came snow.

Just a few small flakes at first, impossible to see against all that white and gray. I felt prickles of wet against my cheeks, small stings that I didn't bother to wipe away. But then the flakes became larger: fat dollops of fluff. They clung to my eyelashes and snagged in my throat as I breathed. The sky heaved snow; outside was the inside of a snow globe, swirling with white. Wind flung it from the ground, up my nose, down my neck and fleece.

I stopped to put my arms into the sleeves of my parka, zipping it to my chin.

Squinting, I tried to make out the trail.

I hobbled forward, but couldn't see. The snow felt like sand in my eyes. I knew the path wound its way down, over and around boulders along twisty and often narrow ledges that dropped precipitously from either side. How grateful I'd been on the way up, imagining a helicopter ride, instead of retracing our steps. Because without seeing where to step, it would be easy to slip and fall. So maybe I should wait. And hope the snow would stop.

But hope, I realized, was nothing more than a refusal to accept what was true. And what was true was that if I waited too long, snow would only cover the trail more deeply, making it easier for me to get lost. Or to fall.

And I couldn't wait because Ben and Rick couldn't wait.

And I couldn't afford to waste any more time thinking about it. Or hoping.

Something shifted in me then. Maybe it was the cold nudging me on, making it more appealing to keep moving; maybe it was something deeper, some inner voice, a reserve of strength, of resiliency.

Head bowed, I started again. Step after halting step.

Now I thought of Paul. What if I died? What if I fell off the mountain, trying to get to Bamboo in the storm? How could I do that to him?

But what if I didn't try, do everything I could to get help. How could I live with that?

I knew how that felt.

Chin tucked, I tottered forward. There were humps in the snow made by rocks and boulders, just visible in the fading light. Shielding my face with my hands against the blinding snow, I lurched and hopped, jerking my body awkwardly. But without the use of my poles, I was—if possible—even slower. I pulled my hood down over my forehead as far as it would go and tightened the cord to make it stay. Screwing my eyes into tiny slits, I pressed on. Over and over and over again, I'd plant my poles and then hop forward with my right leg, dragging my left behind, sometimes thumping it against a hidden rock. When that happened, I felt it in my stomach. But when it was very narrow or steep, I could lean against a boulder or the mountain itself, plant my poles, and lower myself down.

The wet snow fell in thick white sheets.

When the wind screamed in, snow came sideways, forcing me to keep my mouth closed, to breathe through my nose, which ran constantly. Snow and snot clung to my nostrils. My eyes burned. Icy bits shot into my hood and down the back of my neck. I could no longer feel my toes.

But none of that mattered. Because now my brace was coming undone. I could feel it loosening, the grip expansive, unable to keep my lower leg from moving.

I lowered myself into the snow. And it felt good to sit, even for a moment. Even with the snow slamming down. Even with my leg on fire. I let my eyes close for a moment. *So good.*

PART
TWO

THIRTY-TWO

B
ut no. I open my eyes, reluctantly, a stubborn child forced to do her homework. I check the reservoir tube that I used to lash the pad around my shin; it's coming undone. Taking off my mittens, I pull it tight, securing it as best I can.

Get up, I tell myself. *Get up and get going.*

My mouth is so dry. Opening it wide, I stick out my tongue, but the flakes fly all over and my tongue hangs there, frustrated, an ineffective target.

Snow is *blanketing* my coat, though, and I start licking it, little nips, and then long, satisfying gobs as if I were covered in vanilla ice cream. With my mittened hands I scoop mounds of fresh snow from the ground and eat them, delighting in the wet that dribbles from my mouth.

So here I am, sitting on my ass, frolicking in the snow like some sort of deranged toddler, when in the distance, from where I came—although it's hard to tell, my sense of direction lost in the blaze of white—something moves toward me, a figure, dark and plodding, but moving—

yes—making its way, and I try to stand, managing a wave, picking up my poles from the ground and waving those, yelling, and in all my commotion, waving around, I lose my balance and fall—not hard, in a pile of soft snow—but I'm on my back, scrabbling like a turtle, trying to get my legs in a good position to right myself, so by the time I stand again, the figure is closer, and I wave some more, but supported now with one hand on a pole, steadying myself, and now I call out, over and over, until finally, the wind and snow bearing down, the sky and earth merged in a mass of white, he appears.

His huge, puffed parka; his red face. Rick.

I grab his arms. "My God," I shout. "Where's Ben? What happened?"

His hood is up but I can see my bandana across his forehead, the sanitary pads, black with blood and speckled with snow, frozen, probably, but in place.

"He's coming." He looks over his shoulder, as if expecting Ben to be there. "He's fine, he can follow my tracks."

Holding onto Rick, I squint through the snow. "Are you sure?" Already snow is filling his footprints. How can something so light, so fluffy, have so much weight? "I don't know—"

"After you left, for a while, we called back and forth. It got lighter and warmer and my back hurt lying there, so finally I sat up. And it hurt to breathe, you know, my ribs, but I wanted to try going down—we'd heard the avalanche and you weren't back—"

"I was there, I saw it. Sagar—"

"I know."

"I should have gone back up," I say. "Right then."

"Ben was helping me, he let me lean on him—it hurt to walk. To go down. But he found my pack, carried it, got me down that mountain."

"Wait, where is he?" I am scanning the blinding whiteness more frantically now, shuffling in a circle where I stand.

"We thought maybe you'd gotten caught in the avalanche. But then we saw a trail. And it was fresh, easy to follow, so we decided to keep going. We didn't know if a porter or a guide had survived, or if it was you. We moved pretty quick. But after a little way—not even to Machhapuchhre, he collapsed. He just fell over."

"You left him?" I cry. "What the fuck are you even saying?"

Rick is breathing hard, bent at the waist. He coughs. Spit hangs from his open mouth. "We should keep moving," he says. "Get to Bamboo."

I tell him to sit and wait but he doesn't want to.

"Jesus fucking Christ just stay here," I say. "I'm going to find Ben."

Gripping my poles, I start my hop and hobble, cursing Rick, cursing every globule of fat in his fat fucking body, shuffling through the heavy wet, the wind bitter, eyes locked on the ground ahead, the dips and hollows and imprints, looking up from time to time, blinking through eyelashes caked in snow, trying to discern a silhouette, a shadow, anything in the distance, calling out, yelling *Ben* over and over, my voice lost in the sound of the wind, useless, but maybe not, maybe he'll hear and follow the sound, knowing *No*, no fucking way is that possible, how will I ever find him, I won't, but still, pressing on, forcing myself to go faster, I don't feel anything at all now, numb with terror, and then suddenly, something ahead, a mound, just a few feet away and I can see, yes, my God, Ben, thank the fucking lord it's Ben.

And I'm there, crouching down, hugging him.

THIRTY-
THREE

He's alive.

He opens his eyes, as if he's been sleeping, which maybe he was.

"Ben." My eyes blur with tears. "Are you okay?"

He tries to smile. "I can't believe you found me."

I try to smile too. "Can you stand?"

"Where's Rick?"

"He's fine," I say. "He's waiting for us." The motherfucker. "Here." I offer my arm for him to grasp as I hang onto my other pole. "What's hurting?"

"I'm okay," he says. "Just tired." He looks beyond tired, the skin around his mouth white. Taking my arm, he lifts himself, and for a moment it seems that he is standing, a hummingbird motionless in the air, until my arm gives way and I stagger back, and he flumps down into the snow.

"You're hurt." He looks up at me, worried. "What happened to your leg?"

"I'm fine," I say. "I mean, maybe not, but I can walk, sort of, and we need to keep moving." *And I'm not going to be any good goddamn help*, I think. I want to cry with frustration. What are we going to do? "We're just going to have to help each other," I say, answering myself. "Is that okay?"

I plant my other pole firmly into the snow and tell him to use the shaft to pull himself up. Once he stands, I take Rick's pack and give the pole to him, as his are gone, lost somewhere above the glacier, and we wrap an arm around one another while each using a pole in our other hand for balance. We move forward in this way, leaning against each other, as if we're in a three-legged race, but with less unity in our stride, and with less speed. The disparity in our height makes our rhythm awkward, although my hop and hobble don't help much either. I can hear Ben panting over the sound of the wind. And despite the cold, and an evil inner chill, I am sweating inside my parka.

It occurs to me that Rick might not be there when we return. *Who cares*, I think. Good riddance.

Whenever the sound of Ben's panting grows weak or ragged, we stop. We don't sit, though. We tried that once, sitting, but getting back up was too much of an effort for both of us. Better to stand, and breathe, and rest.

I am panting myself when we get to a spot where the snow looks bumpy and irregular. It must be where I'd been, where Rick was supposed to stay. But where is he? Before I can start cursing him (yet again), I see a huddled figure not far from where we stand. Far enough, though, that I can't tell whether he's moving or standing or what.

Ben and I hang onto each other and head toward him. Which doesn't take long, as it turns out Rick's been standing still, unsure of what direction to go in. I decide not to berate him for not staying put, though I very much want to. I decide to dismiss his selfishness. To dismiss everything, everything. Except the one thing that matters: getting down. Maybe Ben decides the same, because when we reach Rick, he just raises his pole in greeting.

But then I notice Rick's hand.

Still missing a glove, it is red, the fingers swollen, the tips, his entire pinky, an inhuman shade of white. Opaque and mottled, like marble.

"Rick, my God." I try to stuff his hand in his pocket.

"It doesn't really fit," he says. "And it makes it harder to walk."

"What happened to the socks?" Ben asks. Of course Ben would bring an extra pair. Of course he'd give them to Rick.

"I chucked them a while ago," Rick says. "They were soaked."

"What about your pack?" I ask. "Is there something you could use?"

"I don't think so." Rick looks uncertain.

"Let me see." I pull off his pack. Inside is a first aid kit with Band-Aids and blister ointment and alcohol swabs — too late for that, but good to have — a Ziploc of cashews, one of extra batteries — hah! — an empty CamelBak reservoir, and a fleece.

A fleece. One big enough to fit me as a dress, which I would love, given the full-body chill I'm experiencing, possibly-probably due to my snow-eating extravaganza, one that I now deeply regret. (How is it that everything is so obvious looking back? Of course, you say, you shouldn't have done that. *Of course*. But is it only doing the thing you shouldn't that makes it so obvious?)

"Here." I take out the fleece and wrap his hand with it. "Wait a sec." His reservoir is tucked into a neoprene sleeve. "Maybe this can fit over, keep it dry." Rick keeps his arm stiff, hand outstretched, while I tug the sleeve over the fleece. "There." I pat it.

It looks ridiculous, a bulbous black thing hanging from his wrist, his body already so large, the sanitary pads plastered to his head. Normally, I would laugh. Now, I just ask him if he's all set and help him with his pack, adjusting the shoulder straps that I had tightened.

He nods. "To Bamboo."

"You good to go?" I ask Ben.

"To Bamboo," he echoes.

THIRTY-FOUR

B ut *To Bamboo* isn't happening.
The wind has swept clean any trace of a trail,
and we have no way of knowing if we're going in
the right direction. We don't know if our course leads to
Bamboo or off the nearest cliff. The snow is a wall of white.

Rick and I take turns leading. Although Ben's able to
walk alone, supported by one of my poles, he's too weak
to break a trail. He's so grateful, thanking us. He never
complains.

When I'm in front, the itch and burn of ice needles my
face. I blunder forward, willing my feet—well, my right
foot, really—to find solid ground. Using both hands, I
stab my one pole into the snow. My left leg flumps behind.
Rick hasn't mentioned my odd way of walking, though at
this point, talking is impossible anyway.

When Rick takes the lead, I shrink to my smallest size,
let his bulk take the brunt of the wind and snow.

I'm not proud of my smallness, in stature or in soul, but it matters little. Pride isn't going to get me to safety. I am a self-absorbed, lying, shell of a woman, but I want to live.

I think of Paul, my life at home. It doesn't seem real—any of it—where I am or what I'm doing or where I'm going.

Where *are* we going?

Rick stops. Bends over. When I come alongside, I can see his mouth open, snot or wet hanging from his nose as he gulps and wheezes. He shakes his head before I can ask if he's okay.

"Sit down," I say instead. "Come on, sit." I motion to Ben to do the same.

Rick puts his arm around my shoulder and leans in. I almost fall over. But we shamble sideways to a large boulder, and he sits, putting all of his weight on me with his enormous fleece-paw, causing me to sink in the snow as well. Shards of glass rip through my leg. I close my eyes, hold onto my breath.

When I open them I look at Rick. His entire face is wet with snow—mine must be too, I realize—and he is panting unevenly. He looks gray, without his usual ruddy flush, and as I begin to speak, to ask him how he feels, he turns to the side and vomits.

Coughing, he sits back. With one arm he clutches his chest.

"Is it your ribs?" I say. "Or—"

"Ribs."

"What about your head?" I reach up to touch the bandana. It's frozen to the pads, which I try to peel away to have a look, but there's a mass of blood making it stick; a large hump of purple swells from his forehead.

"Not good," he says.

"Okay, well, I think we should stay here, wait it out." I turn to Ben, who is sitting beside me, eyes closed. His breath comes slowly, as if he's measuring it out by the spoonful. "Hey," I say, touching his gloved hand, squeezing it gently. "How're you doing?"

He gives me a thumbs up.

Rick starts to stand, using the boulder to lean against.

"Rick, hang on—"

Holding the arm with its fleece-paw across his middle, as if he's trying to hold his body together, to prevent it from scattering into pieces all over the snow, he starts walking again. Not walking, exactly, but tottering.

"Rick," I shout, getting to my feet with some difficulty. "Wait! Seriously, don't go!"

The sky is dark now, from the lateness of the hour or the worsening weather, I can't tell, but it is impossible to see more than a few inches ahead.

"Rick! Please! Wait!" I feel desperate. Desperate and wretched, but determined, too, I stumble after him, into the relentless wind, sweating. "Rick." I grab the back of his coat. His arm. "Hey, listen, it's not safe. I know you need medical attention, but let's wait. Just for a little. We're not going to make it right now. Neither of us have working headlamps—not that they'd do much good in this, but still—and Ben needs to rest." I motion to the right, where the side of a cliff juts out at an angle, offering the slightest protection from the wind. "Come on."

He lets me lead him, hanging onto my shoulder, his other arm still wrapped around his body. It's only a few steps, but we are both gasping when we reach the shelter, such as it is. I call to Ben, but he doesn't hear or can't respond—I can't, won't think about the latter possibility—and so I go back to where he sits, snow sifted over his dark parka like confectioner's sugar. I get him to stand, and we make our way slowly to Rick and the sort-of shelter.

We slump down, backs against the cliff. I draw my right knee in and hug my forehead to it, tuck my left arm into the crook of Ben's right, cinching us close. I'm so cold. Part of me wants to curl against Rick's warmth (horrifyingly), burrow into his bulk and lap at his heat. The other part wants to flee.

But Rick looks bad and I'm worried. He squints against the wind and snow without expression. There is a dullness, and it's that dullness that worries me. It makes me want to rub my hand against his cheek, bring some warmth to it, some life. I want him to live. I need to keep him alive.

Ben, too. His eyes are closed again, those steady breaths. *Ben, too.*

We won't get to Bamboo before nightfall; I know that now. And no one is looking for us. Joshi will assume we're with our guides. We'll have to wait until daybreak or for better weather and a full moon.

Who am I kidding? We'll wait until daybreak.

"Please don't try to leave again," I say to Rick. "It's not safe. We need to stick together."

"Pot calling kettle black," he says.

"What?"

"She shouldn't have left that night. You shouldn't have let her."

"Mo?"

"You were her friend."

"Of course I was her friend. My God. Of course I wouldn't have let her go. I didn't know." I spit out this last, my heart thundering in my chest. *I should've let YOU go, right off the edge of the goddamn mountain.* "You have no idea—how close we were—"

"Hunh," Rick snorts. "What, were you girls doing it? I always wondered. Even said to Ben—"

"What is your problem?" I hiss.

He shrugs, his parka and hood moving in unison. "Is that a no?"

"NO." I turn my head away. *Coward.*

"If recollection serves, things got weird toward the end, that whole last bit—you two girls fighting, you know, like a normal couple, girlfriend and boyfriend type—"

"Shut up," I say. "I mean, Jesus, Rick, just shut the fuck up."

He draws into himself. "Boy oh boy am I glad I came."

"No one forced you."

"It was her dying wish. What was I going to do?"

"Please. Like you had no choice? Bullshit. Everyone has a choice, even when you think you don't." My voice was getting louder. Shrill. "You wanted to come, for whatever reason, so you came. Your choice!"

"Oh yeah?" he says. "Tell that to Ben. Who, in case you forgot, tried to warn you about the weather back in Kathmandu. Remember that?"

I remember.

I turn to Ben, whose eyes are open now. He's looking at me, but I can't meet his gaze. "I'm just saying—" and then I stop, too ashamed to say anything.

"Yeah, try telling that to Sagar and Naba and Pradip and Kewal and Sabin," Rick continues. "Tell that to their families, their parents. Tell that to their wives."

Snow clings coldly to my eyelashes.

"Tell that to Ben's wife," Rick says. And then turning his head so I can barely hear, "I'm not as dumb as you think."

My mouth opens (dumbly), but then I say, "Sagar, the porters, all of them, they've done this a thousand times, it's what they do, how they support their families. They know the risk."

"And you think *I'm* a pig." It isn't a question, and it makes me close my still-open mouth.

"I never said that." And then I don't know what to say.

I want to say: I lied. I lied to you and Ben and Joshi and Graham and Paul and every porter and cook and guide whose name I don't know. Because we weren't all here for Mo, not really. We're here for me. And I want to say: Yes. Yes I did think you were a pig and maybe you are a pig but I'm a pig, too. A worse pig.

And I want to say: It's my fault. All of it. Every death. Every single one.

And how will I live, knowing that?

Rick's eyes are closed. "I had a good year—sales were up—I had put in the miles, you know, kicked some ass. But I couldn't seem to get a group together. A trip. To hike, I mean. No one seemed, well, no one was willing to go. I thought of doing a segment of the Appalachian Trail this summer but couldn't make it happen. The wife, even she didn't want to go. Then this came along."

"Where did you want to go?"

He opens his eyes but he isn't looking at me. "Anywhere. I would've gone anywhere."

"You'll put something together," I say. "I bet once this summer rolls around, you'll be leading a group up a mountain for sure."

Rick coughs, wincing.

The three of us huddle together, our heads bowed against the snow.

The wind wails around us.

Rick twists to pull off his pack, unzipping pockets and, with his teeth, removes his one mitten, hugging it under his arm. He puts something into his mouth and chews. "Cashews," he says, offering his open hand. "Go ahead."

I remove a mitten and with icy fingers take some for Ben, who nods his thanks, and holds the nuts in his hand, not eating.

"Try to eat," I say.

He puts a cashew in his mouth, chews slowly. He is trying. I want to hug him.

Rick pushes his open hand again toward mine, motioning for me to take some.

I hesitate.

"Stop feeling sorry for yourself," he says.

"I'm not," I say. And then more quietly, "I just feel guilty."

"Same thing," he says. "And it won't change anything. It just makes you feel better to know you feel bad." He licks the salt from his fingers before putting his mitten back on. "The question is, will you do better?"

This coming from Rick? He doesn't even know what he's saying and yet he's right, goddammit. Which pisses me off. Which, I have to admit, isn't the strongest sign of doing better. But do better I will.

Or at least, I'll try.

THIRTY-FIVE

Night presses in, cold and black. There is a ghostly silence; the sound of snow falling; the brilliance. I look at Ben. His eyes are closed; clumps of snow cover his lashes. I nudge him, once, then again, until his eyelids flutter open. We don't speak. I punch my thighs, thump at my arms, try to keep warm. Try to stay awake.

Rick does the same.

Ben is so still, though. I rub his arms, his shins, gently pummel his shoulders. What if he doesn't make it? No, no. *No*. That can't happen. It won't.

I take off a mitten to dust the snow from Ben's cheeks. Immediately my fingers are freezing, and I think of the hand warmers I ditched while I was packing at home.

Home. What will that mean, when I return? If I return. When.

I think of Paul. What if I freeze at the foot of this wall, covered in snow, my last minutes on earth suctioned to Rick, of all people? But to Ben, too.

My throat closes. Paul.

Is it dangerous? he had asked. *I don't want anything bad to happen to you.*

I think of Graham. His open face. His dimple.

Graham, I know, will be there. Not just at the airport, for my return, but for what's to come. Or will he? I just want to go back to what was normal, when everything seemed right: our lives together, in our little house, dancing and eating kippers and drinking red wine. But nothing, it seems, will ever be normal again. And what does that even mean, normal?

Graham was normal. Graham was sporty. He was a natural teacher too, and loved showing me new things: how to fish, how to sail, how to ski. And I was a good learner, trained under Mo's sparkly tutelage. And like Mo, Graham sparkled. At parties before we married — never the one telling stories, entertaining groupies with an inebriated baritone — no, his was a muted force; compelling. You were special when he singled you out. You were chosen. At faculty meetings, eating those little cubes of orange cheese, he'd make the otherwise-morose chair of the anthropology department chuckle, his bald head shining, his gigantic glasses sliding down his nose. Even chilly Sienna, whose husband Allan was a philosophy professor at the college (and who had, as one does, gone with Graham in the separation), became a sleeker, smoother version of herself around him. Silky as she spoke. As she touched his sleeve.

And Graham's students loved him. Before Paul was born, sometimes I'd go to one of his classes, sit in back. I'd watch his students lean in, pens poised. Their eager heads nodding; the way they asked questions; the way they laughed. I'd listen to his voice, that accent, watch him smile or frown. He'd sit on the edge of his desk, legs stretched out in front of him, ankles crossed, turning a piece of chalk between thumb and forefinger. That quiet attention.

I loved him, too.

It stops snowing. Not all at once, as if someone has turned off a faucet, but a lessening, almost imperceptible at first, and then smaller flakes, lighter. The sky is a different kind of darkness now, shifting, a torment of clouds, roiling and thrashing, soundless, and I sit there, my eyes alight, watching the stage above. Below and all around us, the snow is the purple of night.

Time expands. Retracts.

Ben's eyes are open now; Rick's too. Together we sit and wait for dawn.

Finally, the sky begins to brighten. We can't see the sun yet but we can *see*, and that is something.

"How are you doing?" I ask Ben, trying to turn to look at him. Everything is stiff and sore, chilled and wet in a way I've never felt before. My blood feels cold, my belly.

"Better," he says, though he doesn't look it. The flesh on his face is gray. His cheeks sag.

"I need water," Rick says. Indeed, his voice sounds cracked and desert-dry, as if we are surrounded by drifts of sand instead of snow. He lifts his ice-crusted fleece paw and licks it.

"Yeah, don't have too much of that," I say. "It'll just make you colder."

He looks at me. The bandana on his forehead is entirely black with blood — so much for super-absorbent menstrual pads — his tongue hanging from his mouth. I almost laugh: that wide mouth, broad face. A gorilla.

And then, as if to apologize for my bitchy thoughts, I take out my half-eaten Snickers. "Here. This'll get the juices flowing." I offer it to Ben.

He shakes his head. "You first."

"Please." I push it into his mittened hand and help him unwrap it.

"Do you remember the cake?" Rick asks. He plucks the Snickers from the palm of Ben's outstretched mitten.

"What cake?" I ask.

"The chocolate cake."

And at first I don't know what Rick means, and then I do: the chocolate cake at Chhomrong on our first trek. How Joshi had treated us all to coffee and cake at the pocket-sized bakery that miraculously existed there, how the crumbs clung to Rick's chin — he had licked his plate, literally, clean — how Mo and I had tried (not tried) not to laugh, disgusted, revolted really, giggling away even as we started down the seemingly unending steps of stone. We thought him so ridiculous; so oblivious. "Yes," I say. "I remember." I remember how easy it was, how innocent we were.

Now we sit, not moving, nibbling away at the Snickers, a flicker of warmth between us, not speaking, watching the sky and air lighten, until the Snickers is gone and I fold the wrapper and tuck it back in my pocket, ready now to try and stand, when Rick says, in that dull annoying voice of his, "You are the best, Livy*est.*"

I set about tightening the tubing and brace around my leg.

"Livy*est* is the B*est.*"

My fingers move with difficulty, fumbling with the knot.

"You don't like it when I call you that."

I am surprised into speaking. "No," I say. "I don't."

"Why not?"

Ben rises. His tall frame sways just the slightest bit against the flat expanse of sky.

I give up on the knot and put my mittens back on. "Let's go."

Rick leans against the snow and rock behind him, using it for leverage to stand. "I thought Mo used to call you that."

"Exactly." I busy myself with my trekking pole.

"Sorry."

And I know he thinks I meant it's because those memories are still too painful to bear. Which is true, but not in the way he imagines.

"Do you need a hand?" Ben says to me.

"Oh, no, thanks." I'm stabbing at the ground with my pole, trying to stand without putting weight on my left foot.

"Seriously." He holds out his hand.

The pole skitters out from under me and I thump down hard. I'm not hurt, but I feel the burn of tears in my eyes.

"Liv."

Letting my pole dangle from my wrist, I grasp his hand and pull myself up. "Thanks. You okay?"

He takes a few experimental steps and gives me a thumbs up. "You?"

I hop after him; everything hurts but I do the same.

"Let's get a move on," Rick says, having not moved an inch from the wall where we've been sitting. "The faster we get out of here, the better."

Just then, from above, from somewhere, comes the sound of a stampede, a million hooves beating the ground, that thunder. The earth shudders under our feet.

And it's a split-second, slow-motion tackle, Ben's arms around me, my back flung against the wall, his body on top of mine, just as several slabs of ice fall from the sky, landing only inches from where we stood. Snow sifts down, great swaths and chunks of it, until the sound of hoofbeats quiets, as if whatever animals they belong to have finally passed, on their way to some far-off destination.

"We need to go," Rick says, using his fleece paw to dust the accumulated snow from his parka.

"Did you see? Where those rocks came down? That ice?" I say. "My God, that could've been us. You saved me, Ben, seriously. Thank you." I am babbling.

Ben rolls to the side, but not without hugging me first. He sits up.

"We've got to get down before the sun comes up and warms all this new snow," Rick says. He's still standing, though he now holds his fleece paw arm close to his body. His voice sounds strained, as if he's holding not just his side but his breath, too.

I touch the tip of his paw. "Are you okay?" I ask.

"I'll live."

ANNAPURNA

And though I believe we'll live—of course we will, we've made it through the night in the middle of a snow-storm with nothing but a couple of cashews and each other, it is unbelievable to think any one of us will now die—I also think, *maybe not*.

Because with so many people already dead, the unbelievable can happen.

THIRTY-SIX

My body feels as if it's been beaten with a wooden baseball bat, like in some gangster movie, the kind that Graham weirdly (and inexplicably) loves: *The Godfather* and *Goodfellas* and *The Departed*. All that violence and blood.

But I'm not bloody, Rick is, so I lead the way down, punching through the crust of snow, each step an effort. Ben follows Rick. If I can make it easier for them, I am determined to do it.

My pace is painfully slow, though, as I still use my hop-and-drag method of walking, and I worry that I'm holding them back, making things, in fact, worse, by forcing them to follow.

"Feel free to pass," I keep saying. "I don't want to slow you down."

"It's fine," Rick says. "You're doing fine. Keep it up."

But Ben is not doing fine, and the distance between him and Rick is growing.

I stop. "Hang on a sec," I say to Rick. "Let Ben catch up."

"He's not going to want you to wait."

"How do you know?" I say.

Rick kicks at the snow impatiently.

When Ben gets close, he motions with his hand for us to keep going and Rick glares at me.

I ask Ben if he's okay and he tells me he's fine, we can keep going, and Rick shakes his head at me in a giant "I told you so" gesture.

So on we go like that, stopping several more times to wait for Ben, as the sun rises in the sky.

Sweat begins to form above my chapped upper lip, at the base of my neck, under my arms. When we've stopped again, I unzip my parka and take my arms out of the sleeves, tying them above my waist.

"Aren't you hot?" I ask Rick. His face, I'm glad to see, is back to its normal ruddy hue.

His coat is unzipped and I can smell his unwashed body, his sweat, from where I stand several feet away. Not that I smell any better. He begins to shrug one arm out of his parka but it won't go over his hand-paw.

"Hang on," I say. The neoprene liner is snug over the fleece, stuck almost, and I worry that I've cut off his circulation. It comes off as if I'm peeling a banana, the fleece unraveling almost without effort. Carefully, I hold his outstretched arm and remove the makeshift mitten.

Once exposed, we both look at his hand. Red in places, swollen, with patches of blistered, yellowy-white on the tips of two fingers. His pinky is still marble to the first knuckle.

"Can you move it okay?"

He curls his fingers inward, as if he's holding a tennis ball.

"Could've been worse," he says.

I agree.

He takes off his coat and I help him wrap it around his waist, the sleeves just tying under his (big) belly.

"Let me put this back on." I hold up the fleece. "It's still cold, even though we're not feeling it right now."

He nods and holds his hand out again. A little boy getting a boo-boo bandaged. For a moment, I think of Paul and the flap of skin on his chin, the hospital, the stitches. I touch my own chin, still raw from its slam on the glacier. But no. I direct my attention back to Rick and his paw.

When I'm finished, I turn, tightening my own parka around my waist.

Ben is approaching. I can hear his breath matched with every step, deep and effortful. He reaches us and stands very straight. His chest rises and falls.

For the thousandth time, and though I know his answer, I ask if he's okay. As if "okay" even applies.

"Onward?" Rick asks.

"Onward," Ben says, though with less gusto. "Which way?"

I stand there, suddenly unsure. Below, I can see trees, and I'm glad, as I remember on the way up that we climbed through forest before the trail opened above the tree line. Except looking down, the path isn't clear. Or really, there isn't a path. We can either descend following the edge of the mountain, clearly visible, or we can work our way a little more to its interior, avoiding the cliff's steep drop but with less of a discernible route.

"Any thoughts?" I ask, motioning with my hand ahead of us.

The sun is silver on the snow. Far below, a tangled froth of green.

"I think it's safer that way." Rick points away from the mountain edge.

I nod. I do too.

Still, I hesitate. "But don't you remember, on the way up, the path always seeming to fall away on our right? I mean, I actually fell down it at one point trying to pee." Which part of the trail was that? Desperately, I try to remember. "I'm just worried if we can't see where we're going, we'll get lost."

"But if we slip, we're done. We have zero chance."

He's right. And the chance of slipping, in all that snow, isn't teeny-tiny.

"Okay," I say.

But I don't go. I stand there, thinking back to the trek up from Bamboo. We had stopped above the forest, and I had peed behind a boulder. Joshi wasn't there, so it wasn't the time I had fallen. Peeing, oddly, had marked my territory.

"The river!" I say suddenly. "Ben was taking pictures of it. I think if we can see the river, we'll be okay."

I turn to Ben. His eyes are closed, and though he's still standing, he's holding on to his trekking pole with both hands, hunched over, as if he's been punched in the chest.

"Ben, oh my God." I reach for him, dropping my own pole, and we stagger together to the ground. I shift his body so he's lying on his back. His face is a terrible color, the thin gray of dusk, and I touch his cheek. It's dry and cold. "Can you breathe?" I ask. "Do you need water?" Which is stupid, of course, since we have none, but he grunts in a way that sounds like yes, so I scoop some snow on my mitten and hold it to his lips. He'll be cold, but there's nothing else. "What about aspirin," I say. I wrestle his pack from his back (gently, gently) but when I look inside, the vial is empty. "Are you okay on your back like that?" I ask. "What do you need?"

"We need to go," Rick says.

I look up. "What?"

Rick's huge form, his red face, stands above us. The sky behind him has flattened into white, the sun gone. "It's going to snow again."

"Okay," I say slowly, like I'm explaining why you don't touch a hot stove. "But Ben is not okay. This is not okay," I say again. "We need to wait here, let him rest."

"Look, he's not going to make it," Rick says.

"How do you know?" Who made him doctor? "You don't know. And we can't leave him." As I'm saying the words, I'm worried what Ben will think; I mean, he's lying right here, and I take his mittened hand, hold it to my chest.

"I'm just being practical," Rick says. That dull, monotonous voice. "We should go."

"Yes." A whisper, from Ben.

"See!" Rick says. "He wants us to go! Even *he* knows that staying won't help. There's nothing we can do for him."

"For fuck's sake, we're not leaving," I say.

"It's okay," Ben says. "You can come back."

"Fine," I say, turning to Rick. "Why don't you go? You've been dying to ditch us anyway. I mean, you already left Ben stranded in the snow once." My jaw clenches around every word. And suddenly, I am back at base camp twenty years ago, telling Mo to leave, cursing her existence, condemning her to death. My self-righteous fury.

And I won't do that, not again.

"See if you can spot the river." I keep my voice even, measured. "It'll be a safer way down, I think. And when you get back, maybe Ben will be better. Rested. And then we can all go." I look at Ben. I'm still holding his mittened hand, and I give it a little squeeze. He's looking at me, too, but he doesn't squeeze back.

"When I get back, he'll be gone," Rick says.

"What?" I say sharply.

"When I get back, I'm gone. I'm leaving."

And this time, I don't argue.

I sit next to Ben, holding his hand in my lap, until I see Rick's spaceman-like figure disappear. He probably won't return. Rick is concerned with Rick.

Fine. I wish him well.

Leaning over Ben, I brush a few flakes of snow from his cheeks. Rick was right, goddammit, it's started snowing again. I zip Ben's parka all the way to his chin, snug his hat down over his ears before lifting his head to pull up his hood. "Are you warm enough?" I ask.

His eyes are closed but he opens them. "Thank you," he says.

"Pshaw," I say. "You'd do the same."

"I mean for everything."

"Yeah, right. Just rainbows and butterflies all the way." I lean closer, touching my cheek against his. "You're too nice."

"I cheated on my wife."

Valid point, but still. Given all the shit I've done, who am I to judge?

"I lied to you." The words burst out of me, though quietly, as if I've been kicked in the back and whatever was in my mouth just tumbles free.

Ben breathes in, long and slow.

"I lied to all of you." To Graham, too. "Mo never said she wanted her ashes scattered here when she died. Neither did Hugh. I made that up. It was a total lie. A total, complete lie. I'm not even sure Mo ever talked about dying. Like, that never entered the equation."

I'm looking at the ground, all the white, and then to the sky, the flakes of snow stinging my eyes. My heart thumps thickly. I pat the ground, as if I'm trying to soothe it. "I'm sorry," I say. I close my eyes. I listen to the rustle of my parka, the slight lift of my hood in a gust of wind, the snowflakes falling, the nothingness. My stomach churns. I wait.

And then Ben says, "I wanted to come. I would've come regardless."

And I look up, into his eyes, and what I see is compassion, and forgiveness. Two things I don't deserve.

"I meant what I said," he says. "I'm grateful. It was my choice to come; I wanted to. It doesn't matter your reasons."

"Ben—"

"We came for our own reasons. Think about it, Liv. It's too big a trip to make for a twenty-year-old memory. Even a tragic one."

He is shivering. I lie down next to him, press my body against his. I don't want to make it harder for him to breathe, but I don't want him to be cold, either. I rub his arms, dust the snow from his face. He blinks away a flake that lands on an eyelash.

"Hey," I say. "When Rick gets back, we'll get you to a more protected place, wait out the snow again. Or start moving a little if it stays like this." It isn't snowing hard, just an intermittent wafting, the way fake snow floats down in movies. "Actually, do you think you could sit up, if I helped?" As much as lying down seems ideal, Ben must be freezing, the cold from the ground leeching through the warmth of his parka. "We won't try to walk yet, but sitting might be warmer, and you can lean on me." From the way Ben is lying, though, so still, not to mention his shallow breathing, walking is out of the question. And so is sitting.

He closes his eyes.

"Hey," I say again. "Don't fall asleep on me." *Please don't fall asleep*, I think. I beg. *Please be okay.* And what's happened to Rick? Not that I expected him to return, not really, but where is he? Is he safe? I try not to picture him falling off a cliff.

What looks like beads of sweat—impossible—have formed on Ben's upper lip.

"I don't want to die," he whispers.

"Of course not," I say, shocked. "You're not going to die. Okay? You're not."

He doesn't say anything.

And then I realize, yes. He is. He is dying.

I hold him close.

"Ben." My mouth is dry. "It's okay. It's going to be okay, no matter what happens. This is just a trek, a trip, and maybe we don't know exactly where we're going." I don't know what I'm saying; the words just kind of tumbling out, an unchecked current, and I worry that I'm not making sense, or the sense I'm making is too trite, too cliché, worthless words that I hope will comfort him nonetheless, give him some peace or reassurance, goodness, anything that might help. I want to help. "It's like you said back at base camp, you never know what's coming next. Right? You never know, even when you think you do, what a trip's going to be like. Where you might end up, how it'll be. But that's okay. It's going to be okay. You've got this. And I'm here with you; I'm not going anywhere." Which is true. And who knows, who knows, he might make it. Somehow. "Your boys are with you, too. And Nancy. Everyone."

Which, of course, isn't true: We are alone, on the side of a mountain. Ben's wife and boys on the other side of the globe.

The snow floats down from a white sky. Ben's lips are tinged with blue.

I hold him. I press my cheek against his. I listen to the sound of his uneven rasp. Until it stops. And there is silence.

THIRTY-SEVEN

I don't think of our night together. I don't think of Ben's sweet, stale breath, the salt smell of his skin, his mouth or his hands or the way his hair stood in tufts on his head. I don't think of the way he kissed me, his hand still circling my wrist. Or of his concern, his kindness, or of the guilt I know we shared.

I think of his boys, home now, with his wife. There is a terrible pain in my throat, and I try to swallow to make it go away.

Snow slams silently to the ground.

They don't know yet, his boys. They are sleeping or eating or skiing or watching TV, alive with the assumption of living. Their world still intact, even when it isn't.

Shaking with cold, or from something else, I cinch his hood more snugly under his chin. Just because. Or because I want to do something. To dignify him, to offer the grace he deserves. I brush the snow from his cheeks.

I jam the trekking pole he was using upright in the snow next to him and prop his backpack against it. I will make sure someone returns for his body. I want to cover him, but of course the snow will do that. And the thought is biting, and sharp.

What had Ben said about Boukreev, the climber who died trying to summit Annapurna? *He was who he was to the end*. I wonder if Ben would say that about himself. I hope so. I believe so.

I want to stay with him. To make him comfortable, oddly, to protect him. But I get up, I do it, my body rising even as I'm thinking of his boys, because I'm thinking of my boy, too, Paul, and yes, even Graham. Because what matters in the wake of a death? Life. And how you're going to live it.

I never thought about that after Mo died. It was more like a wild body scream that quieted only with the passage of time.

And so I steady myself. I move forward. I'll find Rick. We'll get to Bamboo. There is horror in my body, my bones. But there is hope, too.

I follow Rick's path behind the snow-humped boulders and there he is, not far below. I am relieved, and disgusted.

When I reach him, he says Ben's name and I shake my head, a tight, quick shake, my lips pursed together. I look away, before anything spills from me.

I don't ask him why he hasn't gone farther, and he doesn't tell me. Instead, I shuffle over to the edge of the mountain and peer down. That opaque gush of green-gray ribbon, twining below.

"There." I use my elbow to point. My hands are glued to my pole, which is glued to the ground. At least I hope it is.

"I don't know," Rick says. And his stubborn doubt, his slack insistence, itches between my shoulder blades.

We turn our heads, this way, and that, considering. And then the sun elbows the clouds away, and gradually, it stops snowing. We look out across the shining mountains, the limitless sky, squinting in the sun's glare.

Finally, I start moving forward.

And Rick, after a moment, follows.

I pick my way among the rocks and ruts, steeply angled, regretting my choice almost immediately. One misstep and I'll be flying over the edge, limbs flailing, a heap of crushed bone and oozing brain where I land. Or Rick — it could be Rick winging over the side, bashing his skull in — no. Already it is too much.

The sun stabs the snow, metallic and mean. My eyes ache. My whole body seems to be sweating. I can hear Rick behind me, his breathing loud. A burble of hysteria wells in my throat. I might be wrong: The way we're going might lead nowhere or maybe right off the edge. Maybe we'll have to climb back up, try again. Can I even do that? Can Rick?

It doesn't matter. I made this choice, and though it doesn't feel good, in fact it feels pretty shitty — why oh why didn't I go a different way? —there is nothing to do but keep going.

I stab the ground with my pole. Slide down a boulder. An exploratory step. Nope. Again. There. No rhythm, no rest, just breath. Just *breathe in*. Just *breathe out*.

A shivering wind; the constant chatter in my leg.

Lean in, stay low, hold on; step down. Just down. *Go down.* Just Down.

I bang my foot on a rock and waves of red hot flood my belly, making me wretch.

Once, glancing up, the lace of green below appears closer, and denser.

I won't, can't think about it. Won't.

Think of nothing. Think of nobody.

From behind, Rick's uneven breath, his lumbering weight.

THIRTY-
EIGHT

We reach the trees, which turn out to be masses of giant rhododendrons.

The trail is more visible here, the snow not as deep.

I stop and turn to Rick. He thumps my arm with the back of his hand. "Come on, we did it. How about that?" His voice beams with pride.

Instantly I think of Ben. Of Sagar. Of the porters and workers at the teahouse who died. I can't speak. Instead, I touch Rick's sleeve, then give a little tug in the direction of the trail.

We walk silently, though it's easier now and we can move more quickly despite our injuries. We don't need to stomp through thigh-high snow and the trail is wider and less steep. And we can see the damn thing.

Suddenly I can picture myself going home. Seeing Paul and Graham. What will they think of me? I picture

Ben's wife, his boys. The cook's face when he brought us our popcorn and tea.

And Mo. I picture her, too. I wonder what she would say if she were here.

She's *dead*, I tell myself; she's been dead for twenty years. And yet I can feel her breath on my neck, a flicker in my ear.

Below a steep ravine, I can see the river and a pair of logs lashed together to form a bridge. Beyond that, the stem-like trunks of bamboo, a blur of green.

I look back at Rick.

"I wish we didn't have to cross that thing," I say. I am not much for heights and though the log-as-a-bridge is not particularly high, the river below foams and churns, choked with rocks and shallow enough, I am sure, to guarantee a bone-breaking fall. Even Mo, on the first trek, had tried, wherever possible, to skirt around those bridges made of logs.

And there she is again. In every aspect of my current life, even at home. Even as I'd constructed a life so conventional, so average, a life she never would have lived.

Even as I had married Graham.

How do you exorcise a person who lives inside your head? How can I ask her about Graham? About me? How will I know if she loved me the way I'd loved her?

I won't. And it strikes me: Maybe it doesn't matter. Maybe rectifying it—*putting it to rights*, as Graham would say—means learning what matters. To me.

And what matters now is crossing that river.

I slither and bump my way down the ravine and stand at the river's edge. It is a chalky, green tumble of water. Rocks glazed with ice. A rushing sound; the wind is very cold.

I crossed that bridge on the way up, so I can do it again. I have to.

"Want me to go first?" Rick says from behind.

Surprised, I say, "Do you *want* to go first?"

"You can if you want."

Where is this generosity coming from? Is he channeling Ben somehow? Or is it a renewed confidence, having made it this far?

"No, I mean, I don't care, truly, if you want to, go ahead, but if you don't, that's okay —"

"I'll go," he says. And he moves past me and starts across. How will I navigate those ice-slicked logs with my bad leg? It looks too narrow and slippery to use a pole.

Rick stops. Slowly he turns to me, stretches out his good hand. "Come on."

I shake my head. "No, no, no, you go. I'll drag you down."

"Come on."

"Thank you, but no."

He waggles his mitten at me. "You can't hop across. And forget about your pole."

And somewhere, I can hear Mo chortling, *Really? Rick? Of all people?* She'd tried to avoid him as much as possible, positioning herself at meals between Joshi or Ben on one side, me on the other. On the trail, he was dust to her. She was faster and more fit, and she found her own rhythm and pace, far from his swagger and gloat. He was, as she liked to say — with his loud shirts and loud laugh and loud boasting — the *very worst kind of American*. His large frame didn't help.

"Okay," I say. "Thanks." Why *not* Rick? "But if it looks like I'm headed for the drink, just let me go."

"That's not the point, now, is it?"

I hold his mittened hand, grateful, and then, for better grip, his forearm. I can't hop, it's true, so I have to put weight on my left foot. The pain is shattering. Blue shards in my brain. Gasping, I take a step. I can feel my parka slipping from my waist. But I can't let go of Rick, his meaty arm. Another step.

The river heaves below, its white fingers snatching at our ankles.

My parka skitters to my knees. I freeze, trapped in its tangle.

And then suddenly, a shout, not Rick's, not mine—of that I'm sure—and I look up, still holding on, and there is Naba—*Naba, who is dead*. Or isn't he?—running toward us from the opposite bank, dropping his pack, stepping onto the log, his thin frame graceful, his movements effortless. He could've been jogging in a garden filled with sunshine and glory.

"Naba!" Rick shouts. I'm afraid he'll start hooting. I'm afraid I might, too.

"Fuck," I say, as my parka slides to my ankles. I widen my knees, trying to stop its journey, causing it to unzip so that it tumbles to the water below, sleeves untied and flapping. It dances among the rapids, a bodiless figure, before being sucked under; the river's triumph.

Naba reaches Rick and takes his arm.

Hanging on, steady now, we move together, step by step, the three of us, one united being.

On the other side, in his halting English, Naba tells us what happened. Yesterday morning—was it really only yesterday?—Sagar told the porters to leave early, just before sunrise. They'd be descending about eight thousand vertical feet to Bamboo, and it was preferable to do it before the sun heated the snow and caused avalanches. Or before it began to snow later in the afternoon. "We eat and go," he says. "We go quickly. Many avalanches."

"But what about the workers in the teahouse," I say. "The cook?"

"They are there," he says. "They stay."

God, how pointless, such death.

"And where were you going now?"

"To find you," he says. "No one hear from Sagar."

Now it is our turn to tell him what happened.

Stricken, Naba decides to return to Bamboo with us, where he'll rally the porters and go back to base camp, find Ben, and check the teahouse if they can. I try to explain that it had sunk, like a giant ship, under a sea of snow. He nods, his face drawn, his eyes unreadable.

It is less than an hour to Bamboo, he says, but I doubt he knows how slow we are. He gives us water from a bottle in his pack. It tastes fresh and cold and clean: gallons of ice cream on a burning hot day. I stop myself from drinking it all and hand it back, reluctantly, wiping my chin. Naba points to my leg but has nothing in his first aid kit other than Band-Aids and a used, less-than-snappy Ace bandage. I take the latter and use it to shore up my brace. Anything is better than a CamelBak tube.

Naba takes from his pack a pair of gloves and hands them to Rick. I unwind his makeshift mitten and help him with the gloves. Naba points to the fleece and to me. I look at Rick and he nods.

I hold the fleece in my hands, swallow its sour smell, and put it on. It's my smell, too.

The trail descends darkly, deeper into the forest. It winds through stands of tall bamboo, the pale sun filtering through no longer a source of warmth. They clack and cackle, the dry leaves swishing, rustling as we walk.

I shiver and keep moving.

Rick plods ahead. Naba is patient, walking at my maddening pace, and quiet.

The bamboo rises in a wall from either side of the trail.

There is a loud cry and Rick's arms are windmilling, toes pointed to the sky as he slides, jerking his heavy body in one direction and another.

Naba rushes forward and steadies him. "Careful, is very slippery."

I tighten my grip on my pole.

Naba holds on to Rick. "Bamboo is under snow." He points to the snow on the ground and then twirls his finger in the air, to signify the bamboo all around us. At least, that's how I understand it. "Uses for roofs and mats. Baskets."

And so we continue, the three of us, stepping with care down the unpredictable path, through the shaded light of the bamboo, until there, finally, ahead of us in a narrow valley, is the teahouse where we left Joshi only days earlier.

As we approach, we see him, his tall figure; he is in the doorway of the common room. His face is calm.

THIRTY-NINE

We sit. We have tea. Cup after cup. I swallow the heat, feel it slide down my throat, spread through my chest and belly. Joshi brings us food: fried eggs in blue bowls with white rice, plates of noodles, garlic soup. I tell Naba where Ben's body is, how I used a trekking pole and his pack to mark the place. Naba and the porters leave.

We eat.

Afterward, we rummage through the teahouse's first aid supplies and I ask for some boiled warm water. Sitting astride the bench as best I can to face Rick, I strip the bandana from his head and then gently, using warm water and cotton balls from the kit, begin to pull the pads away.

Joshi listens as Rick tells him of our last few days. Of last night. Of Ben. His voice drones on, without emotion, and I think how differently I would've told it. How differently, perhaps, I lived it.

Finally, the pads fall away. Across his forehead, slicing toward his left ear, is a gash, black with blood, almost eight inches long.

I sip my breath in, my lips pressing together.

"That bad?" Rick says.

"You should've had stitches," I say. "Though maybe it's not too late? How soon do you have to get them?"

Joshi hands me some alcohol pads. I look at them and then at Rick. These will hurt.

Which they do, of course, but Rick grunts his way through, sweat running down his forehead, making me swab again with the alcohol. Joshi finds some nonstick pads (not as thick and cushy as maxi pads, but, to their credit, sterile) and using some Band-Aids (there's no tape), I stick them to his head and cheek. They fall right off. Joshi produces a pair of clean socks and I tie them together and around Rick's head. Who has clean socks?

"What about your ribs?" I ask. "How's your breathing? And your hand?" I lean over to examine it. "I think you should soak that thing in warm water." Fluid-filled blisters have begun to form on his pinky. "You really need a doctor."

Rick grunts again, still sweating. "I'll live."

And I think, *Yes, that's what it's come down to*. And the dearness of that.

Joshi turns to me. "How can I help?"

"Is there a phone somewhere?" I am desperate to check on Paul. Ben's wife will need to be called, too, and I resolve to do that as soon as Naba returns.

"In my room," he says. "I will get it."

"That's okay, I'll come. I want to change out of these clothes, anyway. Wash my face."

Outside, the sky is white, the sun gone. It is warmer here but still cool enough for me to shiver in my damp clothes.

Joshi stops outside a door. "This is your room, where your duffel is. Would you like to change first?"

"That's okay," I say again and follow Joshi a few doors down, hopping and dragging, still using my pole. My arms, even my wrists ache. I have blisters on my palms.

Inside his room, his duffel is neatly stored underneath his cot.

"So how was it here?" I ask. "Were you alone?"

"It was peaceful. I had no idea, of course, what was happening. I am sorry. For me, I meditated. I read. I spoke with my wife and daughter. I heard my grandson laugh. To be here was a gift. I never felt alone." He reaches into the side pocket of his duffel and pulls out his phone. "We can talk more tonight," he says, handing it to me. "We can honor Ben."

"Thank you." The sound of Ben's name. "Joshi, I—I'm so sorry, I feel terrible—but I lost your Ganesh. I brought it with me, in my pack, when we climbed up to see the sunrise, to scatter Mo's ashes. But after Ben, after Rick fell, I don't know, I took everything out and later I couldn't find it and it was gone. I lost it." I start crying. Giant, heaving sobs. I am making grotesque sounds, snot and tears running down my face.

"In all that was lost, it is so little," Joshi says, not moving. "And even without the Ganesh, you found your way."

But have I?

He pats my back and leaves, closing the door behind him. I sit on the bare mattress, a sleeping bag rolled in one corner, and call Graham.

When he answers, I think I might start bawling again but I swallow hard. My voice is steady as I speak. I think of Rick and his monotone. I sound just like him.

Graham listens. I can picture him standing in the kitchen, a hand on his hip, the phone to his ear. Legs spread a little, feet planted. Looking out the window above the sink, maybe. At the snow, or maybe the frozen trees, their black trunks shiny with ice, their branches brittle. What time is it there? Or here? I have no idea.

"I'm glad you're safe," he says. "We've been thinking of you, Paul and I." He gives the phone to Paul then, so he can start researching how to get us down the mountain and to a hospital. But before he does, he adds, softly, "We want you home, Liv. Come home."

It feels like months have passed, years since I've been home.

I remember how I felt when I first arrived here, that grim excitement, that resolve. That stupid lie, the one I'd told myself, that if I just went to Nepal, did this thing for Mo, that I'd be done.

"Mama?"

And then, yes, the tears. This time they slide down my cheeks unchecked. I cover my mouth with my hand, squeezing hard.

"Honey," I say, removing my hand. "How're you feeling?"

"I'm good." And yes, he is everything good, even when he isn't. "When are you coming home?"

"Do you still have a fever? And what's happening with your cough?"

"It's good, I'm fine," he says. "But what's it like there?"

"Okay, well, you *sound* good." And he does. His voice is clear and strong. But I want to see him. For myself. To touch his forehead, brush his skin with my lips, press my cheek against his.

I tell him I hurt my leg but I'm fine, glossing over the details of what's happened, not wanting to worry him while I'm still away. There will be plenty of time for truth at home.

After we hang up, I leave the phone on Joshi's cot and stagger to my room. Graham said he would call the main office in Kathmandu with information about how we'd get out of here, but in the meantime I need to get out of Rick's fleece, my long underwear, clammy with sweat, my soggy boots and socks. In a daze, I unzip my duffel and dig through, pulling out my first aid kit (my *fucking* first aid kit) and toss it angrily aside as if it's to blame for not having made it into my pack. Snatching it up again, I take out the Advil and pop four in my mouth, swallowing, swallowing. I sit on the edge of the cot and lean forward, my hands feeling through the contents of my duffel, and finally, having found what I want, I lean back. Toothbrush, toothpaste, and soap. I haven't showered since I'm not sure when and couldn't care less. But I want to brush my teeth at least, wash my face.

I sit there, holding my toothbrush, not moving.

What I really want is to rest. Just a little. Just for a sec. Then I'll go to the sink outside. Brush my teeth. I scootch back on the cot and lean against the cold wall. A weak light shines through the single window and onto the floor.

I close my eyes.

FORTY

When I wake, I'm still holding my toothbrush. The room is dark. From outside, the sound of rain. I flick the switch and a dim yellow light burns from the single bare bulb overhead. I pull off Rick's fleece, followed by layer after sticky layer of rancid clothing. I unwrap the ace bandage, untie the reservoir tube and remove my headlamp and its band, still miraculously attached, from the makeshift brace. It is impossible to take off my left boot. I untie it, loosen the laces, but tugging it makes me wretch. My foot is so swollen. Should I ask Joshi to help? No. I tug again, tears running down my face, tug again and again. It comes off. Off comes my right boot and pants, my socks. Still on the cot, I survey my leg.

A storm of bruises below my knee, which I can't bend. My shin is the size of my thigh, my ankle the size of my shin. What the fuck. I look down at my foot, also swollen, and at an odd angle, toes pointing out. They feel numb.

I am shivering, naked on the cot, maybe from the cold.

I dress in clothes that if not clean, exactly, are clean enough, and smell faintly of a fabric softener sheet meant for dryers that I had packed to keep the stench of dirty laundry from overpowering my duffel. It's amazing what I had remembered. And what I had not.

I put two socks on my left foot to keep it warm — I can't put it back in that boot — and refasten my brace, ditching everything but the ace bandage. Pocketing my toiletries so I can still use my pole, I hop-drag myself outside to the sink.

The night air is cool and dry; it isn't raining. The sound of rushing water is from the river nearby, and I can picture its riotous journey, its clap and splash, high-fiving in celebration past the stolid of rock and tree, the snag of ice and mud.

The stars shine mercilessly above.

At the cracked basin, I wash my face. The water is so cold it burns my skin. I think of Ben at Deurali and brushing our teeth together outside by the river. Not touching, not speaking. In the glistening darkness. That closeness I had felt, that unspoken connection. He always appeared so calm to me, so certain. Yet he had climbed to base camp not knowing if he'd make it. He had chosen that uncertainty, that risk.

But had he? Had Sagar? The cook? A choice isn't a choice when you have none. What was it I'd said to Rick the other night? *Everyone has a choice, even when you think you don't.* And maybe that sounds good, in theory. Empowering. One of those *rah-rah* bumper stickers. But in practice? In real life? It's bullshit, and wrong, and I knew that at the time.

Mouth full of toothpaste and water, I remember too late not to use tap water to rinse. I spit. "Fuck it," I say aloud. "What's a few microbes at this point." Face dripping—I've also forgotten a towel—I shake out my toothbrush and chuck it onto the cot back in my room.

Rick and Joshi sit on the bench inside the common room. They are drinking tea.

"I fell asleep," I say. "What time is it?"

Joshi checks his watch. "Nine-twenty."

"Oh my God, I must've been out for hours."

"I just woke up, too," Rick says. "I don't know where the cook's gone, but we missed dinner."

"I'm starving." I sit down next to Joshi, who stands.

"I will find him," he says.

After Joshi leaves, Rick turns to me. He isn't sweating anymore, and he's changed clothes as well, but they hang on his large frame as if they belong to someone else. He seems shrunken, somehow. Deflated. "He told me to thank you," he says. His boom is gone. To my surprise, I miss it.

"Joshi?"

"Ben."

"Ben?" I stupidly repeat. "When?" For a crazy moment I think he somehow just spoke with Ben. That he's here.

"On our way down from base camp."

"But you were so far ahead."

"Not the whole time," he says. "And we talked, about a bunch of stuff. Like how he knew he wasn't going to make it. And about his wife, his boys. How much he loved them. And he said to thank you, to tell you—" his eyes go to the empty kitchen door into which Joshi disappeared. "Well, that it wasn't your fault. And Mo didn't blame you."

What? "Did he say anything else?"

"Just stuff to tell his wife, how he was sorry. And —" Rick stops.

Joshi is carrying two bowls of porridge, which he places in front of us. He goes back to the kitchen and reappears with another bowl, three spoons, and a glass jar of honey.

Gone again, I hear Joshi speaking in Hindi or Nepali, presumably to the cook.

He comes back with a mug of tea for me.

"Thank you." I try to smile. "Where'd you find the cook?"

"He was asleep," Joshi says. "There is a cot behind the kitchen."

I wait, as if it matters, for Rick to begin eating, and then Joshi.

The tea and porridge are hot and I drink and eat without tasting.

Afterward, Joshi carries the empty dishes to the kitchen and the three of us sit, not knowing what to do. Retiring to our rooms to sleep seems out of the question. What if Naba and the porters return with news? What if they found someone alive?

The lightbulb blazes above.

"Do you think they'll come down in the dark?" I ask.

"They might," Rick says.

For a while, no one says anything. And then, from his pocket, Rick takes out a deck of cards. Wordlessly he deals them.

Wordlessly we play.

FORTY-ONE

A
t some point in the night we stretch out on the padded benches that the porters use when they sleep, covering ourselves in blankets Joshi finds stacked on shelves near the kitchen. We leave the light on.

And there I lie, wondering about Ben. His frozen body. The skin I touched. If they find him, how will the porters get him down? Slide him in the snow like a sled? Carry him down the steeper, rockier parts? Or lower him with ropes? These are low-altitude porters, not trained, I imagine, in climbing and rescue techniques, unskilled in things like ropes and knots. And yet, their strength is astounding, the relentless up and down, the huge loads, how many times in a season? And wearing only flip-flops in good weather, or sneakers. Now, at least, they are wearing boots. But I know how slippery it is and though none of them are injured, carrying Ben and descending in the dark seems impossible.

And then there are Ben's words. Thanking me, saying it wasn't my fault, that Mo didn't blame me. His last real conversation, maybe, with Rick. Freeing me from guilt. Talk about impossible.

Once, in our freshman year, early in my thrall of Mo, we were walking together across campus. It was spring and damp and the ground was muddy from melted snow and rain earlier in the day. We passed two bikes leaning against the broad trunk of a leafless tree. Mo stopped.

"Wanna ride down to Jessie's for cinnamon rolls?" she said. Her eyes laughed.

I eyed the bikes. "Walk, you mean?"

"We'll just borrow these for a sec." She took one by the handlebars. "See? They're not even locked. They won't care; we'll bring them right back."

"What if the *owners* are coming right back? What if they see us? What if they see us cruising across campus on their bikes? Do you even know who these belong to?"

"It's fine. We'll be gone all of twenty minutes." She held onto the bike, started wheeling it away. "Are you with me?" she called over her shoulder. Not even looking.

And yes, dammit, I was. I took the other bike and followed. Hopped on and rode downhill, the wind whooshing, not thinking of what it would be like to pedal back up. And I was thrilled, watching her. Her freedom. And I was afraid, too. Not about the bikes, not really, though that was part of it. It was also about Mo, about the fear of her leaving me, losing interest. Finding someone or something more exciting or adventurous. Someone not just game but gallivanting. Someone not me. Someone else.

We parked "our" bikes outside Jessie's, a tiny bakery selling blueberry muffins and oatmeal scones and giant chocolate chip cookies. We shared an enormous cinnamon roll, warm, dripping with cream cheese frosting, our mouths melting with the buttery sweetness. I was happy.

When we stood to leave, Mo bought one more, to go.

It started raining again as we walked the bikes back up the steepest part of the hill. Or rather, as I walked — Mo continued to ride, albeit slowly, standing up, her backpack protecting the cinnamon roll from getting wet — and I became less certain that our little adventure had been worth it. I was convinced we'd return only to find the bike owners standing under the leafless tree, sopping wet, pissed as hell.

Could you get arrested for stealing a bike that you returned? *Was* it stealing, I'd wondered, if you really were just borrowing it?

When we got to the tree, the owners weren't there but a note was, stabbed through the heart by a spindly branch.

It said: WE KNOW WHO YOU ARE AND YOU WILL GET IT.

"I knew it," I said. "I knew we shouldn't have taken them."

"Then why did you?"

"Don't you feel bad?" I said. "They probably had somewhere they needed to go. Plans. Maybe someone was waiting for them."

"All good points, but too late." Mo leaned her bike against the tree and balanced the paper bag with the cinnamon roll between the tree and bike. It would get wet regardless. "And no, I don't feel bad. Why should I? Bad is when you let things happen that you regret—" she wasn't looking at me, but I felt her eyes anyway "—and I make choices. They may not be perfect but at least I know what I'm doing at the time. I don't twaddle about them later."

Mo plucked the note from the tree and, using a pen from her backpack, scrawled a large and loopy THANK YOU on its back and repositioned it on the branch. We went to our rooms to dry off and change, and I spent the rest of the afternoon in the library doing the reading I had been avoiding for my English lit class. Penance.

I wonder now if I only understood part of what Mo said. At the time, I thought it some great rationalization of her actions, some hollow claim to owning your own shit while refusing to admit when you're wrong. Maybe it was. But maybe all I've done is let things happen, and then feel sorry for myself after. And as Rick pointed out, that helps no one. Maybe I haven't been willing to own my shit, not really. Because if you own it, if you accept it for what it is, then there's nothing to do but do better (again, yes, Rick). Maybe it's a choice not to spend your life wallowing in the muck of guilt. Or regret. Mo would want me to regret nothing. And that, I realize, includes not only our moment of lust (my lust) but the last words I ever spoke to her.

Hope you fall off a cliff and die.

What was said could never be unsaid.

Ben understood. Maybe Mo had confided in him, maybe she'd told him that I had attacked her, a wild-haired lesbo, that I'd been stalking her my whole wasted, pathetic life. Maybe not. Maybe he was talking about what happened on this trek, the senseless tragedies, and

ANNAPURNA

what Mo would've said. I'll never know. But maybe it doesn't matter because Ben understood. He understood Mo—her freedom, her decisiveness, her religion that was the mountains—and he understood me—my guilt and worry and shame—and he had thought of that somehow; it was important to him, knowing that he wouldn't live, for others to continue. To live.

Much later, I will wonder if I am misinterpreting his words, or hers, but I don't think so. Ben and Mo looked at life through the same lens. And though it's not my lens, I can appreciate it; I can see its prismatic light. It is my choice now. And I can do better.

I must have slept, though I thought myself awake all night, my leg sending its now familiar stab of fury every time I shifted. A thin light leaks from the windows that line one side of the room.

I sit up. From the other end of the bench, I hear a loud snore. Rick's body rises and falls, a bear in hibernation, not to be disturbed. I stand carefully and my blanket slips to the floor. Picking it up, I fold and then place it on the shelf where it belongs.

Where is Joshi?

I find him outside, standing in a cluster of men, all speaking at the same time, none of it in English. Naba is at the center, and when he sees me, he bows his head but continues without pause.

Positioning myself next to Joshi, I wait. Presumably, Naba is telling his story. And I am so relieved that he and the porters have made it back safely, I can listen to the men's urgent voices, watch their hands move through the air, console myself that I will know soon enough what has happened on the mountain above.

There is no sign of Ben or a body.

One of the porters leaves, returning moments later with tea. He makes several trips, handing the cups around. It is milk tea, hot, and I drink it gratefully.

Finally, Naba begins in English. His mastery of the language is not as varied or polished as Sagar's—possibly the reason Naba is assistant, not head guide—and he stops to confer with the porters, who speak even less English, and with Joshi, who often explains more fully what has happened.

This is Naba's story.

With no loads to carry, the porters went up quickly, following our trail. They found Ben, covered in snow, the trekking pole still upright. After covering him with a blanket they had brought, they continued, reaching Machhapuchhre Base Camp before dark. Once there, though, they could hear avalanches farther up the mountain. The porters refused to go any farther. After much back-and-forth negotiation, one porter, Amrit, agreed to accompany Naba to ABC to look for survivors.

Naba and Amrit headed up at once. They had little more than an hour or two of daylight remaining and the weather might turn at any moment. It was getting colder, which made the snow more stable, but it also meant the porters waiting at Machhapuchhre would be getting colder as well.

They went all the way to ABC without finding anyone. They circled around what remained of the base camp, the teahouses buried in snow, their blue roofs smothered. In some places, just a floating scrap of color on a sea of white. The snow was too deep to approach any of the buildings—up to their shoulders; in places, above their heads—but they called and called, hoping and searching for some sign of life.

It was getting dark as they started back down; the trip had been in vain. Base camp had seemed a place of death to them, impenetrable, unforgiving.

When they reached the Machhapuchhre Base Camp, it looked as if the porters were gone. But they had broken into the teahouse—without causing any damage, Joshi stresses, after Naba speaks to him in a firm, pressing voice—and lit a fire and made some tea. There weren't any other provisions there, but they were warm. Naba and Amrit joined them, drinking tea and resting, waiting for the darkest hours of the night to pass. It was still dark when they left Machhapuchhre.

By this time, Rick has joined us. I can hear his breath, heavy, uneven. My leg hurts; I need to sit.

Naba and Joshi continue: On their way down, they retrieved Ben's body, wrapping it with the blanket and tying each end with a rope. At first, they descended with the body sliding in the snow between them. But the porters were young and inexperienced. As the trail became steeper and more narrow, rockier, the body needed to be carried. There was much stopping and arguing, until finally Naba and Amrit took control of the body, making their way down more slowly than they otherwise might if more porters had helped.

Twice the body twisted from their hands. But they were able to hang on by the ropes that were still lashed around the blanket, and the body was saved from being lost forever.

"Where is he?" asks Rick. "Ben, I mean. His body."

Joshi looks at Naba, who gestures behind him, up a steep incline. "It is just there," Joshi says. "We cannot bring him to the teahouse. A matter of respect."

"Thank you, Naba," I say. "And Amrit." I look at each of them in turn. "All of you. I know Ben's family will be incredibly grateful."

Another porter, one whose name I don't know, steps forward. He looks first at me, then Rick, uncertain, as if trying to decide something. He bends down and pulls a black case from his pack.

Ben's camera.

I hold my hands out to accept it, making the decision for the porter, so that Rick won't have to carry anything in his damaged hand. "That's wonderful. I forgot about his camera. Thank you."

The porter bows. We both smile solemnly.

I ask Naba if I can call Ben's wife, if there's a way to get her number, and he tells me that someone in Kathmandu has already called. So they know. His family knows. His wife, his boys.

I go back into the common room, my leg too painful to remain standing. The rest of them follow. Preparations to leave start as soon as we're inside. The cook makes breakfast—more porridge and hard-boiled eggs—and Naba gets on the phone to the office in Kathmandu. Rick borrows Joshi's phone and goes outside to call his wife.

Joshi goes to check on Ben's body. To offer whatever he can in the way of care. "In the Hindu religion, death is a part of life. It is a natural process," he explains. "The body alone dies, and the soul is reborn, in a different form. We cremate the dead; we have our own rituals. But I imagine Ben's family will want his body returned to them. He needs to be looked after."

And I?

I sit at the table; I look out at the brightening day, a vibrant blue sky; around me, the confusion, the chatter of porters, Naba's murmuring. Someone coughs; the wind scrapes a dusting of snow from the ground and it rises in a mist, and then falls. I hold Ben's camera.

I am going home.

FORTY-
TWO

The helicopter will pick us up at Chhomrong and transport us to Kathmandu via Pokhara. To get there is a trek of several hours, including a climb of 2,500 stone steps to the village where the helicopter can land.

Our porters shoulder double loads so that Naba and Amrit can carry Ben's body. Joshi helps me along the trail. Kaji, a porter who spits incessantly but has a beautiful smile and is very strong, helps Rick down the steeper sections; on the way up the steps, he becomes his crutch.

This is what I remember of that trek: sweat.

Sweat stinging my eyes, wetting my lips; the salt of sweat; the sun. Going up. More sweat. Sun pouring down. I steady my breath, I'm so close, not looking up, not wanting to know how much farther, just one step at a time, my right leg first, pulling myself up, blowing out with my breath, panting, and the sun. The sweat. Another step.

Joshi's graceful strength, his silent support. His careful hand at my waist.

I think of the first day of our trek—years ago, it seems—and the steady Left-Right rhythm I'd found climbing the stairs that led to Ghandruk. I want to go back, shake myself, tell that woman that the cost is too great, the loss too bitter; that what she's searching for isn't what she thinks and won't be there, anyway.

Another step. Breathe. Another.

At the top, in the tiny cluster of buildings that make up the village, we are here. We sit on a stone ledge outside the now-closed bakery of the famed chocolate cake, waiting for the helicopter. And for a moment we are all there, the past and the present, I can see us, the rich coffee aroma, the taste of chocolate, even as the bitter wind chills the sun on my skin. Rick is eating the cake, those chocolate crumbs. He licks his fork when he finishes. His head tilts back when he drinks the last of his coffee.

Naba offers us cups of tea from a tray he is carrying, a bowl of popcorn.

My stomach clenches; I can't eat. I can't drink.

It's not from the tap water I used while brushing my teeth the night before; it seems I've been spared. It's just, if I open my mouth I'm afraid everything I'm holding inside will come vomiting out in one hideous torrent.

FORTY-THREE

The sound of the helicopter. The cut of blades ablaze in the yellow sun.

Thock thock thock thock thock thock thock thock and the churning air lifts my hair, and there is dust, everywhere, in our eyes, our nostrils, the corners of our mouths, and we blink; we rub away the grit, and we are lifted; the earth tilts beneath us as we rise into the incessant blue, forward then, swooping. Outside, inside our heads there is too much noise to speak and there is nothing to say, and one of us can no longer speak, anyway. The juddering of the helicopter hammers at our hearts, shakes our shoulders, makes our fingertips tremble. We look down, out the window, straight ahead. We can see the curving horizon, the roundness of the earth, spinning on its axis in the blue; and the people, scurrying to work or just waking up, going to school or eating oatmeal or sleeping in a king-sized bed in an apartment or in a tent or under the stars. The stars! They are there somewhere; somewhere it is night, and dark, and someone, a small child perhaps, an old woman, is making a wish. Below us now, there are neat rows of green; there is green everywhere, with narrow ribbons of brown and black, and, in the distance, grand and shining, the crystalline white of the mountains. Everything (life) is before us.

But for one.

From the helicopter we are separated; we leave the rooftop of the hospital, the air sliced by the whir of blades, in different directions.

We wave; we call to each other; we say that before we leave Nepal we will regroup, catch up, reconnect. We will meet again, one last time.

Except one of us, who will make his way home. Alone and silent. Unaware of the cold in his body, the way his skin isn't skin. The pain of his arrival, the grief that awaits him.

FORTY-FOUR

Rick and I are taken on gurneys into an elevator. Nurses or doctors—I'm not sure which—talk above us in muted voices. It is crowded and hot and I itch and my leg throbs. Although I haven't spoken to Graham again, I know he's made these arrangements and will book my flight home as soon as I'm able to leave. My eyes are dry but inside I am crying, grateful.

The doors open.

When they roll Rick into a separate curtained cubicle, I want to climb onto his gurney, hang on to his beefy arms. For all his sweat stains and foul breath and annoying drone, for all his grossness and girth, I want him to stay.

But the nurse flicks the curtain closed and he is gone.

She must be a nurse—taking my temperature and blood pressure and speaking in sort-of English, a small barrage of questions in a soft voice that I answer by saying, Excuse me and I'm sorry and Might you say that again please? She is short and dark-skinned with a thin gold ring in her delicate right nostril. Her movements are quick and efficient. Her green scrubs give me comfort.

An interpreter arrives, along with a doctor, I think, who takes off my brace and examines my leg and tells me that I need X-rays. I am rolled down hallways and into a small room and hoisted from the gurney to a cold table where I'm told to lie down and hold still and my leg is positioned at different angles and I want to hold still but when the technician touches my leg I also want to scream so I keep my lips closed and scream inside my mouth.

I am rolled down more hallways and I close my eyes against the bright lights that flash from above. The insides of my eyelids bloom orange as they pass. Back in my curtained cubicle, I wait. I say Rick's name a few times, tentatively, each time louder, with a question mark, wondering if he's still in the cubicle next to me. I look at the pale-yellow walls, the white curtain, hoping for an answer. When the nurse comes in to check on me, I ask where Rick's gone. She tells me, I think, that he's in X-ray. Did we pass each other along the halls? Is he there now? Will he come back?

The doctor returns with the interpreter, who tells me I've suffered an ankle fracture involving both the tibia and fibula. It will need to be put back in place, and I will have a cast. Most likely I will need surgery, but that can wait. I'm not happy about the surgery but the fact that it can be done at home — *I'm going home* — is a relief.

I ask the interpreter to please find out about Rick and to contact Graham, if he can, to give him an update. The nurse in her green scrubs bustles about. She gives me pain meds so the doctor can "reduce the fracture" and I swallow them, greedily.

I let my head rest against the pillow. My eyes close. I sleep.

When I wake, Joshi is there. Now I'm in a bed instead of a gurney, and though a curtain surrounds us, I can tell from the chair where Joshi sits and the absence of medical equipment that I no longer am in the examination area where we arrived. Plus, the walls are white.

Joshi stands. "You are well?" he says.

I sit up, propping the pillows behind me. "I am," I say. A white cast (a plaster splint, I'm told later) encases my left foot and leg to the knee. My toes, no longer numb, poke out the front as if I'm wearing a sandal. Experimentally, I lift my leg with its cast. It feels heavy, and it hurts, but in a different way. Gone is the shriek that blasted through my body. In its place is a bruising ache, almost pleasant. "Where's Rick?"

"He is upstairs. Some broken ribs, a collapsed lung."

"Oh my God."

"He is lucky. The doctor said it could have been much worse."

"And his head? His hand?"

"They are tending to him now."

"And, what about—" I look away. "Ben?"

"His family made arrangements for his body to be transported back to Ohio."

His body. That's what it is, after all. But it's so much more, too.

I return my gaze to Joshi. "When do you go home?"

"I leave tomorrow night." Joshi's thin face breaks into a smile. I can see his rabbity teeth.

"I bet you're looking forward to seeing your wife," I say. "Your daughter, and grandson."

"I am pleased to go home. It is the final part of this journey. But of course, all journeys, eventually, and in their own way, are a journey home." His voice lifts and lowers, a boat bobbing along, but the words feel anchored in my heart.

They are in me still.

Joshi leaves to get an update on Rick just as the interpreter arrives. He looks so young and innocent, his skin smooth and unblemished. A boy. Nineteen, maybe twenty. He reminds me (surprisingly, startlingly) of Tika, whose face is a blurred image of youth and strength. And innocence.

He tells me that he was able to reach Graham. I will be flying home the following day as the doctor will discharge me in the morning. "Do you need anything?" he asks.

"I'm better than I have been for a long time," I say. "Thank you." And though it's true, there is something else, too, something nameless, tugging, an insistent yank.

"I am here this evening until eight." He stands formally at the bottom of my bed, hands at his sides, as if he's a server at a restaurant. "Please call on me for anything. You can ask a nurse to find me. I am Kush."

After he leaves, I lie back, staring at the white ceiling. From the hall, smells of disinfectant, that sharp slice in your nostril, but also of warmth, and spice. Curry. Am I imagining it? I can hear the echo of steps, a throat clearing, the buzz and strum of wheels on a smooth floor.

A short while later a nurse comes in with tea. This one is older, with less bustle, but her brown hair is clipped from her face with a pink barrette so that her eyes appear huge. They are long-lashed. A doe's eyes. She moves silently as she enters, places the tea next to me on a little table, a thermometer under my tongue, two fingers at my wrist. Those doe eyes fixed on her watch; after several moments, or minutes, she lowers my wrist, removes the thermometer, and leaves.

I drink my tea and wait, for what I'm not sure.

Joshi returns with news of Rick. Too much time has passed for his head wound to be stitched; it was cleaned and he was started on a course of antibiotics for infection. His ribs will heal without treatment but it's his collapsed lung that is worrying. He's receiving one hundred percent oxygen to re-expand the collapsed lung segment; if that doesn't work, he'll need a chest tube to suction the air between his chest wall and lung. Regardless, it will be at least two weeks before Rick can fly home.

"The poor guy," I say. "He must be so bummed."

"He has talked someone into bringing him food—he is eating—chicken and rice and dal. He is happy now."

I laugh. "Of course." Maybe that's the spice I smelled.

"I thought tonight we can all have dinner together," Joshi says.

I gesture to the bed.

"You can go by wheelchair to Rick's room. I have asked. And Naba will bring food."

"I would love that." A flood of genuine appreciation, of indebtedness, washes over me. I want to reach out, grasp his hand, hug him. But his tall, thin frame remains by the curtain, his hands clasped behind his back. "Thank you," I say. "For helping me—for everything."

"It is what anyone would do." And while I know that's not true, I also know it is true for him.

He leaves and I finish my tea, which has cooled. In my mind, images flash of Joshi and Rick. Of Ben. Of Sagar and Naba. And then Paul. I can see him, his eager eyes, his wild blond curls. I picture him sailing—the both of us—the wind as it streams through his hair. I watch him take the slim tiller in his sun-browned hand; the angle of his elbow, the jut of his knees. I feel the boat lift and together we lean back, keeping it down, and he turns to me, eyes shining.

And I see Graham on the shore, eyes shining, too.

Graham at home, both of them, home. I imagine what it will be like when I first see them. The *kaboom* of it. But after that, the hugs and tears (my tears), the happy laughter, then what?

What will happen then?

FORTY-FIVE

The doe-eyed nurse wheels me into Rick's room, where he is sitting up in bed, wearing a blue hospital gown with a bright-orange marigold garland hanging from his neck. Joshi is there, wearing a garland, too, and when I enter the room he places one around my neck. The smell reminds me of death, but I don't want to hurt Joshi's feelings. I keep it on.

The wheelchair is cumbersome and my leg in its cast sticks straight out, but I move as close to Rick as I can. His head is bandaged and his face is its normal red color, which I take as a good sign. He looks cleaner, too, and smells, if not fresh, fresh*er*.

For the first time I realize how badly I must look. How filthy. Over the cloying smell of the marigolds, I can smell myself—at least I think I can—and I reach up to touch my hair, which is pulled back with an elastic. Its mess of tangles is greasy, gritty. Lovely. I pull my hand away.

"How are you?" I ask Rick.

"I am A-OK," he says. His boom is back and I'm glad. "The docs here are patching me right up." He lifts his hand and waggles his pinky, a sausage swathed in white. "Called the wife and told her I'd be resting here awhile before heading home and it looks like she might take a little vacay in Nepal, come to Kathmandu. Keep me company."

"That's wonderful," I say, trying not to let the term "the wife" work like sandpaper against my skin. "How'd you call her?"

"There's a phone you can use, they just charge you for it. Per minute," he says.

"Hunh." I think about that. I can call home.

"Would you like me to ask?" Joshi moves toward the door.

"Oh no, stay," I say. "No, thanks. I mean, not right now."

This distance I have from home suddenly seems necessary to me. Precious.

"I asked Naba to bring a deck of cards," Rick says.

I laugh. "Of course you did."

"I brought Nepali peda," Joshi says, picking up a bakery box from the chair next to him. "Milk candy. For dessert."

"I've never tried it," I say. "But it sounds perfect." Milk candy. The name itself soothes.

And then, awkwardly, there is a pause, a silence that becomes larger and then gaping, loose and wobbly, as if a giant whale has swum in and swallowed our words, leaving nothing but a vast expanse of water.

I shift in my wheelchair. "So, what're they saying about your lung? Did that oxygen-breathing thing work?"

"Like a charm," Rick says. "But we have to wait and see. It could happen again."

We lapse back into silence.

There is a knock at the door, although the door is open. It is Naba.

He holds up bags of food, which Joshi takes from him, making room on the chair and the little table next to Rick's bed. I smell garlic, and cumin maybe, cinnamon — and my stomach aches with hunger.

"What've we got here?" Rick thunders. He is pulling one of the bags onto the bed next to him.

And then another man, older, appears in the doorway. He is fit, not old-man skinny or sinewy, but like a retired tennis player. Small-boned and lean. He is looking down at the floor.

I am starving. I watch Rick paw through the bag of food.

Naba steps to the side and motions the older man forward. "This is Tika," he says.

And Tika looks up.

My hunger vanishes.

"Tika, my man!" Rick practically whinnies. "How are you?" He holds out his good hand and Tika shakes it, bowing his head a little.

Joshi steps around my wheelchair to greet him. "It is a pleasure to see you again," he says.

"Wow," I say, turning to Naba. And then to Tika, "Wow, I mean, hello."

Tika bows his head and murmurs, his eyes again on the floor.

"You all speak of Tika," Naba says to me, "and I ask friends, I say is important, that you wish to see him after what happens. And one knows from a village, who knows more, and so on. I meet him and bring him here."

And I'm not even listening, my mind ablaze, a scream of wonder and worry because this is the man whom I blamed, at least publicly, to others, for Mo's disappearance, and yet here he is, in his quiet way, listening to Rick bellow and bark, smiling even, and someone will ask, for sure, where he went that night, what he knew, and he might know everything and, in fact — suddenly I remember that sound of spitting, I heard it that night, standing there with Mo as I spewed poison all over her. I heard it and hadn't cared — and as I look at Tika now, watching him, he raises his eyes to mine and I know he knows what I said, how I practically tossed Mo off the cliff with my words, how it's all my fault that she left. He heard.

Joshi is pulling food from the bags, passing plastic utensils, while Rick makes room on the bed for others to sit. Naba goes to find another chair.

I sit in my wheelchair, a container of hot food on my lap, fork in hand, not eating.

Cumin and garlic curl in the air and knot in my gut.

Naba returns with a chair that barely fits in the room and which nobody sits in.

"Please eat with us," Joshi says, and I make similar noises. "There is too much for us."

But Naba and Tika remain near the door, standing. Joshi sits, eating and speaking amiably, sometimes breaking into Nepali but mostly in English. Rick is perched on his bed like a king on his throne, surrounded by food, by all of us, his wide mouth busy, merry.

Tika goes to find tea for everyone. I stare down at my food, poke at it with my plastic fork.

"It is wonderful you were able to locate him," Joshi says to Naba.

Naba smiles at me. "You think he dies, you worry. And now is good."

And then Tika reappears, holding a tray of tea things, passing out cups and serving us, as if he is still our porter. Joshi opens the bakery box he brought and begins to offer it around. I take one of the candies: pale like shortbread and round, but soft, not crumbly. It has a pistachio in its center. I take a bite; my mouth is too dry to swallow.

"So, Tika, you were the mystery man," Rick says, helping himself to several candies. "We always wondered where you ran off to." He pops one in his mouth and chews noisily. "Where'd you go? Why'd you leave?"

Joshi turns his face to Tika, open with peaceful curiosity.

My body is wood; the milk candy sweats in my blistered palm.

FORTY-SIX

Tika clears his throat. He stands close to the doorway, as if he might turn and run, and I remember
him in the doorway of our room at the base camp
with Mo, the way he stood, so shy and sweet and uncom-
fortable. He was just a boy.

I feel sweat dripping from everywhere. My leg inside
its cast, even. Hot with misery. And then, though I'm
not looking at him, I feel his eyes on me, the side of my
neck, and maybe I'm imagining it, but the heat is searing,
and I look at the candy in my hand, wondering what to
do with it.

"That night," Tika begins, his voice soft, "I hear you,
both angry. Saying bad things maybe, but I don't know
English good then so maybe I don't know."

I force my eyes away from the candy. I look at Tika,
who is, indeed, looking at me.

Tika turns to Rick. "Mo walk away, and I follow her. She does not see me, I go very quiet, and she is noisy, crying, but she go fast, going away from teahouse, from base camp, and so I call to her because I know is dangerous to go at night."

I watch his face as he speaks. His expression never changes; his mouth moves only a little. His eyes see things only he can see.

He tells us that she turned, finally, after he'd called her name several times, and waited while he caught up to her. She was still crying. I try to picture this—the darkness, Mo's face wet, her tears, nose running—but she wasn't much of a crier, and except for when her grandmother died, and barely then, I hadn't seen her cry.

Tika tried to persuade her to go back with him, but she wouldn't, so they started walking together, not down the mountain, the direction she was heading, but back up and away from the teahouse, toward Annapurna's peak, toward the glacier. Mo was speaking, clearly upset, and he let her talk without understanding much of what she said. When they climbed up to where the flags were strung—about where Anatoli Boukreev's memorial is now—they stopped and sat down. It was cold and Mo huddled into him. They were at the edge of the glacier. Empty space below, and blackness. Blank.

She stopped crying. And she was trying to make him understand something, so she said it again and again, *I hate her.*

And he nodded, but she shook her head, saying it again, pointing back to the teahouse.

No, really. Really. I hate her.

And she stood, upset, so he rose too, pulling her close, hugging her, not sure what she was saying, but he knew that word, hate, and he kissed her, trying to make her feel better, and I see him pressing his mouth to hers, and I can taste her even, all these years later, the sweet salt of her, and she was kissing him too, until she pulled back, shook her head.

Livy, she said. *I hate her.* She pointed to her chest, and then to the teahouse.

But he kissed her again, maybe her jawline, her neck, and her head went back, to the sky, and he grabbed her hard so she wouldn't fall or lose her balance but she must have misunderstood, because she looked at him, shocked, and she was reeling, but he held on, harder now, his hand squeezing her wrist, and he stumbled toward her as she wrenched free, running in the darkness, away from him, and he started after her, terrified that she'd fall, not know-ing what to do. He stopped. He didn't want to scare her; he knew what she must have thought, but he didn't want her out there alone, in the dark.

He called to her. Louder. But she seemed only more determined to run — he could see her golden braid jounc-ing in the black, moving farther away from him — and suddenly he was frightened. What if someone from below heard him call her? What if she said he attacked her? Who would believe him? It would be her word against his. A white woman, British. And who was he? No one. Nothing. He would be ruined. His mother and sisters still lived in Asrang, a remote mountain village in Gorkha, and they relied on the money he sent them. His future was their future.

He fled.

She would feel safer if he left her alone, he reasoned. His presence was only making things worse. She would calm down once he was gone and find her way back to the teahouse. It wasn't far and the lights of the building were bright. But when she returned, what then? She would tell everyone. And he would be fired. He would be disgraced. His family would be disgraced.

Without a headlamp, his ability to see would depend on the moon. He looked up. Dark clouds skittered across the sweeping stretch of sky. From behind, thin shafts of moonlight.

Panic seized him.

He crept down to the teahouse, watching for any movement outside the common room, where people would stay until they went to bed. His thought—which filled him with shame, even then—was to steal a headlamp from a trekker's room. His gear was stuffed under a bench in the common room, where he and all the other porters slept. He waited, humiliated, watching below, looking up from time to time to see if maybe Mo was on her way down. But from his perch it was impossible, the wrong angle, and he knew that every moment he waited was another one wasted. And how would he steal a headlamp anyway? Everyone wore theirs to and from the common room; none would be left behind.

And so he left. Without a headlamp. Without his gear, which was minimal, but would cost him to replace. Without food or water. Without any idea of where he was going or what he would do. Without telling anyone.

"I know maybe I die," Tika says. "I don't care. But Mo—I never think—I think she is safe."

"You were young," Joshi says.

"But what happened?" Rick's hinged jaw hangs open. "Where'd you go?"

"I walk all night," Tika says. "I go slow. I keep warm moving and it not so cold. Sometimes the moon come out and I go faster then. When is light there are many people on the trail and I go a different way, your group will not go. Far into the mountains."

"You disappeared," Rick says with admiration.

"But your family?" Joshi says. "Were you able to continue to porter?"

"It is busy season then for trekking. I stay in different region, in Manaslu."

That poor boy, carrying so much weight up and down mountains, more than most.

"Did you know?" I say. It is all I can manage.

He shakes his head. "I find out a long time later. Many months. I work as porter in Annapurna region in April, May, and I hear someone talking about girl who die in October and porter disappear and I think, I know is Mo."

It's not what I meant but I nod.

Tika takes a step forward. "It is too late maybe, but I want to ask you—all of you—to tell you I am sorry." He looks at me, and I can still see that young face of his, that innocence. "All these years I live with this. Now you are here and Naba brings me. Please." He says again, "Please."

"It wasn't your fault," I say, with some difficulty. "I'm to blame. You were right—we fought, Mo and I—and I said some terrible things to her, things I'll never be able to forget. And it was me, those words, that made her leave that night." I look at Rick and say, "I told her I hoped she'd fall that night. That she'd die." I say it plainly. And then to Tika, "It wasn't you, or anything you did or didn't do." I want to hug him, collapse his stiffly held frame against my own, offer him comfort. Instead, I drop the half-eaten candy I've been holding into the container on my lap, wipe my hand on my hospital gown and reach for his. I hold it for a moment. It is dry and calloused. I think of Ben. "It wasn't your fault," I repeat. "No one blames you."

Joshi rises. He places the bakery box at the foot of Rick's bed and moves around us so he can shake Tika's hand. "You are a brave man."

"I am weak."

"To say this now, you are brave," Joshi says. "You were young, you didn't know. What choice did you have? A delicate situation, yes, and difficult to navigate, even under the best of circumstances. One cannot go back and pretend it was otherwise. One cannot judge now what was true then."

I am picking at the blisters on my palms, peeling away a loose circle of skin, a flap. I pull. Underneath, it is red and raw.

I had gone back; I had judged. What had Ben said? *Maybe she was beautiful, to you.* Mo was beautiful, and to be fair, not just to me. But she was many other things, too — impulsive and selfish and heedless of danger — and she was young. I had been young, also. And maybe I needed to look back with compassion instead of regret. Forgiveness instead of longing. Had Mo hated me? Maybe, in that moment. Maybe not. I wasn't what she wanted me to be, but neither was she.

And anyway, it doesn't matter.

And then Rick is talking, reaching for the bakery box, asking Naba for the deck of cards, which he produces, and we crowd around Rick's bed as best we can, and Rick deals the cards, and though I'm playing, I'm not paying attention.

I'm thinking: I am the weak one. For after all this time, the way I treated Graham. I knew it was wrong, that I was being unreasonable. But I couldn't look at him the same way, not after I learned about him and Mo. Knowing, somehow, there was more. And he couldn't understand because he didn't know. Because I hadn't told him.

All those words, unspoken, left us speechless. Their power left us broken.

FORTY-SEVEN

If you fly business class, you might as well make the most of it.

This is what I'm telling myself as I sit on Air India's flight to Delhi, the first of four flights, to London and New York City before landing almost twenty-four hours later in Syracuse. In business class.

Except that I know we can't afford it, and Graham has booked it anyway, because of my broken ankle.

Graham.

I chew at my lips; I chew his name.

I swallow the last of the champagne I am given after boarding, the bubbles prickling my throat in the best kind of way. I adjust the reading lamp and scroll through the available movies and unzip the little striped pouch they've given me containing socks and lip balm and ear plugs and an eye mask, and I lower the seat's headrest and raise my legs.

My God, I can lie down. Flat. With a blanket and pillow. *Graham.*

Silently I thank him.

And then the flight attendant stops at my seat, collecting my glass, asking if I need anything, taking my dinner order. Someone is talking over the intercom system, and then there are safety instructions, and the plane, with a sudden jerk, moves back, and the engine, its roar, gathers in my belly, and we are racing down the airstrip with tremendous speed and that pull, forcing me back into my seat (my cushy seat) and then I feel that lightness, the lift, as we rise in the air.

Religiously I watch movies. Anything. I flip through Air India's sky magazine. Eat my dinner and the square of mango cake with vanilla frosting that is dessert. Practically lick my fork clean.

When we land, a wheelchair comes for me and I change planes.

This time, I drink several cups of chamomile tea. I try to sleep. I watch Virgin Atlantic's ambient lighting change from velvety purple to trippy lavender. I watch more movies. I drink more tea.

In London, I board the Delta flight that will carry me back to the States.

The air in the plane is cold. It will be cold at home.

I wrap myself in my business-class blanket. Try to swallow with my business-class boarding champagne the mixture of fear and anticipation and longing that clogs my throat. A solid hunk of cement.

Finally, I sleep.

FORTY-EIGHT

"I'm so sorry."

I've clonked my neighbor's arm with my crutches as I try to settle into my seat. The last flight: JFK to Syracuse. "I'm still getting used to these things." I shake my crutches, smiling, as if they are to blame. On the previous flights, my neighbors were shielded by the more spacious seat configuration and sizable barriers meant for privacy, if not physical protection.

The woman next to me doesn't smile. Her white hair is pulled into a large bun on top of her head, not tight against her skull but bouffant-like, a puff of white with tiny curls at her neck. It is an old-fashioned look. She must be in her seventies or even eighties but she wears a black turtleneck and black leggings, very cool and mod, a la Audrey Hepburn. On her feet are black, ankle-high booties with low, chunky heels.

She turns back to her phone. She's texting away, and not with her pointer finger either, like most women her age (or mine, who am I kidding), but with her thumbs. Her nails are clipped short, the skin on the back of her hands ropy with purple veins.

The flight attendant comes around offering juice or water—no champagne, I gather in faint disappointment. So spoiled am I now!—and I look at bun-woman as she politely declines a beverage, trying to catch her eye. I haven't spoken to another person in what seems like a long time, other than to say please or thank you or excuse me.

Bun-woman is having none of it.

We fasten our seatbelts and, after some waiting, the plane taxis and rises in the air. Abruptly, there is a huge bump and a drop, making my stomach sink to my thighs, and I clutch the armrests of my seat, my fingertips white. I look again at my neighbor, willing her to speak before we die.

Calmly, she looks out the window.

The seatbelt sign dings (unnecessarily, as no one is up or even thinking about it, I'm sure) and the captain comes on the intercom to let us know (in case we haven't realized) that we're going through some "light" turbulence and he hopes to get through it and above the "weather" in about ten minutes.

The plane lurches again.

Outside, dark gray gauze presses against the windows.

I remember what Graham said about turbulence: Think of it like waves, the way a boat goes up and over them. *Just ride the waves*, he'd say.

Just ride the waves.

There's a loud rattle, as if the plane's innards are coming loose, and I stare at bun-woman with desperation. All

that champagne and tea and business-class (but still dubi-
ous) airplane food is swishing inside my belly. I unglue
one hand from the armrest to root through the seat's side
pocket, which contains JetBlue's safety instructions and
a brochure of the plane's amenities, but no barf bag. Do
they even have those on planes anymore?

I wonder how bun-woman would feel if I seized one of
her ropy hands, which I might, if things get worse. There's
no way I'm going to die in a crash alone. Crazily, I wish
Rick was with me. Rick!

The plane slams down, hard, jolting me forward. The
overhead compartments shake. Everything seems plas-
ticky and rickety and fragile, as if the entire plane is a
child's toy made of Legos. Even Legos seem too substan-
tial. Popsicle sticks. Toothpicks.

And then with one last shudder, the plane lifts above
the clouds.

Immediately there is a brightening; relief. I almost
laugh.

Bun-woman sits quietly, head still turned toward the
window, hands folded in her lap. I think: *Maybe she's had
a terrible life*. Maybe she's been married to a total dick for
the last fifty years and now she's just venomous. Maybe
she missed an earlier flight or she's had some bad news. I
think: *Maybe she's just a quiet person*.

With some satisfaction I note several flakes of dan-
druff against the black of her turtleneck.

And then she plucks her phone from her lap and holds
it to the window and starts taking pictures. "Look at this,"
she says, pointing.

I lean over. Beneath us a roiling sea of clouds, humps of fluff, shine in the silvery light.

"It's beautiful," I say.

She looks at me as if I've said something stupid.

I sit back.

"Are you, do you live in Syracuse?" I ask.

"Yes." Her voice is surprisingly low, husky.

"Visiting the city?" I don't know why I'm still speaking, trying to engage her. "Or just passing through?"

She pauses, as if considering whether to respond. "I was visiting." She looks out the window again, her spine straight, her bearing regal.

"That's nice."

She doesn't reply.

"I mean, I hope it was nice."

She doesn't turn to look at me. "It wasn't."

"Oh." Her candor surprises me. "I'm sorry."

"I hardly think it was your fault."

"Well, no, I just meant—" Why did I even start talking to this woman?

"My lover died a month ago of pancreatic cancer," she says to the window, her accent clipped—not British— more like one I imagine acquiring at a finishing school. "We had planned a romantic weekend in New York— decadent food, some lovely wine, getting lost in museums. Snow in Central Park. I wanted to show him the seals, if they were there, in the zoo. Have you been?"

I shake my head. I'm still stuck on this elderly woman using the word *lover*.

"No. Well. I grew up in the city. I loved the seals. I wanted to show Miles. But he died." She turns to look at me. "And I thought I'd cancel the trip. But I kept putting it off, as one does, and before I knew it, the weekend was upon me, and I decided to go."

"That must have been really hard."

Again, that look of disdain.

"Indeed." She focuses her gaze out the window again. "I stayed in my room at the Carlyle. Ordered room service. Walked halfway to the park before turning around. I couldn't do it. I didn't want to see the seals. Not without Miles."

"I'm sorry." I'm not sure what else to say. So far, I haven't been all that successful.

"Yes. Well. Such is life." She lifts her chin. "We keep going."

"It's a terrible thing, though, to lose someone." This, at least, I know to be true.

She tilts her head toward me, raises her eyebrows. "My dear," she says, "you have no idea. As you get older, the people in your life drop off, one by one. First your neighbor, then your cousin, then your friend from the second grade. Until one day, there you are. Alone. And alone isn't such a terrible thing, you know. It's not what matters, the struggle. We all struggle. We all die. You accept that at my age, or at least you're forced to. You don't 'lose' someone—they haven't been misplaced, like a pair of glasses, you know—they're never lost, not really."

I open my mouth to speak but she continues. "We'd only been together two years, Miles and I," she says. "But two years is enough. You want more, of course, and sometimes you get lucky, but, well, you love who you love, one person and then another, and you don't stop loving the first when you start loving the next. Unless, of course, you do. Sometimes you change, sometimes they do. But it doesn't matter. All that matters is having loved. That, my dear, is the purpose of life." She pats my hand when she says this last. And winks.

I am shocked to hear her say so much, to receive a pat and a wink. She is my personal, real-life Yoda and I've met her on a plane, which seems equally bizarre and appropriate. In response, I can only smile and nod, which makes me think of Ben, which makes me think of Graham.

Graham and I had kept in touch after I returned home from Darren's funeral in London. He wrote actual letters, which I've saved in a shoe box on the top shelf of my bedroom closet. In the summer I was interning at a literary agency in the city, living in a one-bedroom sublet on the sixth floor of a walkup on the Lower East Side with two other girls. And one hot July night, coming home from work, there he was. Outside the building, looking all surfer-dude California with his tousled, dirty-blond hair and faded jeans and flip-flops. But with that British accent, that Cupid dimple. And I was sweaty, I remember, wanting to get out of my work clothes and into a shower, my hair tangled against my neck, a blister on my heel rubbed raw and bleeding.

He kissed me, his hands cupping my face.

And there was a flutter in my chest then, the merest breath of wings.

We went out that night to a Mexican place a few blocks away, and we downed shots of tequila, sipped margaritas. Ate too many chips. Slid our knees against each other. I was wearing a sundress. He rested his open hand on my bare thigh. His palm was hot against my cool skin. I felt his fingertips graze the lace edge of my underwear and I could hear myself breathing. He threw some money on the table and took my hand and we ran back to my apartment, kissing, pulling at each other, stopping on the stairs, his hand under my dress and then his fingers pressing into me.

And they took flight, those wings, over the next few days as he lay next to me in bed, and then in the following weeks and months, after he returned to London and I to school. At night, early in the morning, waking up as the other went to bed, we tiptoed and then galloped across our separation, our separateness. When I graduated and we finally moved in together, there was rhythm in the wings' movement, no longer a flutter, but a deep and steady beat.

He lay next to me in bed one rainy Sunday afternoon, reading *The New York Times*. He rubbed his bare foot against mine. I was reading one of the thousands of manuscripts from the slush pile at work, glancing through it, really, my eyes blurry, as I was nursing a minor hangover from the night before. Suddenly, he tossed the newspaper aside and leaned down to kiss my foot. Its arch. He raised his head. "I love you."

He had said it before—we both had, too many times to count—but somehow this felt different. He held my foot. Smoothed its instep with the pad of his thumb.

I let the manuscript slip from my lap.

"I don't want to live without you," he said.

I reached for him. "I love you, too."

He let go of my foot and crawled on top of me, propped on his elbows, our noses almost touching, his eyes clear and earnest. *Forthright.* "No," he said. "I mean it."

"I mean it, too." I kissed him.

"I've never felt this way before, Liv. This is it for me. All I want."

And I kissed him again, overcome, feeling that love, kissing his forehead, his face, but even in that moment, I remember a twist of something—a doubt, a thought; a memory—that clipped the wings thrumming in my chest.

A memory of Mo. Whom I had loved, too.

And as I sit next to bun-woman now, so stoic and graceful, grateful for her grief, I know that what Graham and I have is real. It is love. But I had loved Mo, too; she was a part of me. And I had lied about that by never admitting the truth—to Graham, to myself—so that the truth became the lie. I'd pretended Mo and I were best friends, always, and that was it. Yes, it was because she was a woman, because I'd crossed a line. Because I was afraid. Because Mo's disgust made me feel disgusting, because I'd ruined our friendship. Because in the end I'd been disposable, and discarded, like so many others before me. I hadn't been special; I'd been just me.

I think of Graham's face as he kissed my foot. How will he look at me now?

FORTY-NINE

I am the last one off the plane.

Bun-woman steps around me, precise and polished. I have a weird urge to hug her, to say something comforting, or hopeful, something wise that will make her remember me. What I come up with is: "Take good care."

The rest of the plane's passengers crowd the narrow aisle. One man's shoulder bag hits a middle-aged woman in the chest. She opens her pink-lipsticked mouth, sucking in wounded air, but he is facing forward, oblivious, his small, bald head shining in the cabin's bright light.

And then the plane is empty, and the flight attendant hands me my crutches and I hobble off the plane where a wheelchair waits, a snappy man in a blue uniform behind it. He rolls me into the airport, humming, down the corridors and past the stores selling magazines and neck cushions, into the baggage claim area where Graham and Paul are waiting.

ANNAPURNA

Paul runs to me.

And he is in my arms. I hold on. His hair smells of shampoo, floral and green.

He steps back and I take his hand in both of mine, surveying him — he is pale, thin too — and taller somehow, rapping his knuckles gently on my cast, asking me if I can feel that, and Graham is thanking the blue-uniformed guy, telling him we are all set, and then Graham touches my shoulder, and I look up at him, and after an awkward moment he bends down, and I raise my mouth to his but he presses his lips to my forehead, and I worry about my greasy hair, how I must smell, and I smile at him, embarrassed, and he pushes the wheelchair out of the flow of people, Paul trailing alongside, holding my hand, wanting to know what movies I watched on my flights, whether my seat had turned into a bed.

I tell him as many (and as few) details as possible, wanting only to listen to his voice, watch his face light up as he speaks. I want to know how he's feeling.

Paul coughs, as if to prove that he isn't entirely well, and I look up at Graham, who has positioned me away from the crowd. "What about that cough?" I say. "That doesn't sound good."

"The doctor said it might linger," Graham says. "It could take several weeks. Not to worry."

Worry fills my head (all kinds of worry) as Graham collects my duffel and backpack and Paul wheels me outside and we bundle ourselves into the freezing car. Syracuse in January is like a load of laundry whose colors have bled into a uniform gray. Gray and more gray. Dirty

snow piled alongside the roads. Dirty sky. Dirty buildings, empty and unused, or used and worn out. Sagging.

I think of Nepal—the green, the soaring mountains,
the limitless sky—and yes, the white of snow up above,
the darkness in it, as well as the beauty, and I know I
can never put into words all that lives in me of what happened there.

"I'm glad you're home," Paul says.

I reach into the back seat and squeeze his hand.
"Me too."

FIFTY

Graham makes dinner that night, roast chicken and vegetables. It is hot and delicious. We eat and Graham opens a bottle of cabernet and I show them pictures and try, while Paul is there, to minimize the dangers of the trip, if not the tragedy. And then Graham lights a fire and I want to stay awake, to talk to him, once Paul goes to bed, but at some point, my face warm from the fire, my belly full, my leg with its cast propped on the coffee table, I fall asleep. When I wake it is dark in the room, the fire cold, and I am stretched out on the couch, a quilt tucked around my shoulders.

It is three in the morning and I can't go back to sleep.

All I want is sleep, to fade into its nonthinking cush. I close my eyes in the stubborn darkness. It feels endless, and suffocating. I open my eyes, hoist myself from the couch, and crutch my way into the kitchen.

I will bake. Make a feast for my boys (yes, both of them); Graham has done so much for me while I was away, for Paul. I will surprise them with breakfast. It is nothing, just a gesture, but somehow it feels urgent.

I read through recipes, search the pantry for ingredients, and settle on pumpkin scones and chocolate chip muffins and yeasted cinnamon buns with cream cheese frosting. But baking with a broken ankle makes me clumsy and cleaning up becomes a study of trying to stay dry. So much hobbling around and carrying things with one hand and bumping into and knocking over, so much bumbling movement, leaning into the counter, the sink, to relieve the ache in my leg from so much standing.

But it keeps me busy, measuring flour and tracking baking times, and it makes me feel useful and productive. And when the counters are wiped clean and the cinnamon rolls finally in the oven and the whole house smells sweetly of spices, I make a pot of coffee and sit at the kitchen table, looking out the window at the rising sun. A thin line of light at the horizon. A glimmering. I think of the snowy, black night in the mountains with Rick and Ben, waiting for dawn. I remember the hush as the snow stopped falling, as the sky began to brighten; the three of us sitting silently, together, wanting the morning light.

I break off a corner of a scone and put it in my mouth. The snap of ginger, the mellow warmth of brown sugar. It makes me want to weep.

I need to write to Ben's wife. Not that I know her, but something, I feel, is appropriate. Not everything, obviously, but I was there. I owe her that. I owe her more.

And Hugh, too, I think. He should know that Mo's ashes, her remains, are on the mountain where she belonged.

ANNAPURNA

I don't want to bang my way up the stairs to get my laptop, so I rip out the back blank page of a recipe book and stay at the kitchen table, my coffee cooling, tapping a pencil against my cheek, thinking. I'll copy what I write onto a card for Ben's wife, an email to Hugh. Or maybe a card for him too.

Dear Nancy,

What can I possibly say?

If anyone understood Mo's love of the mountains, it was Ben. He showed us all what it meant to be kind and supportive and generous.

Ack. No. Too generic. Too trite. Especially after what Ben and I had done. No.

I think of Mo's memorial service in London, how I mumbled and stumbled over the most banal of platitudes to her family: *I'm so sorry* and *She was such a special person* and *I will miss her terribly.* I think of bun-woman on the plane and her derisive looks at my vapid comments. My pathetic farewell. Surely I can offer more.

The timer goes off and I take out the cinnamon buns, fat and oozing, and let them cool while I make the frosting.

"Liv?"

Graham stands in the kitchen, freshly showered but wearing his clothes from yesterday. I haven't even brushed my teeth.

"I stayed last night," he says, looking at the scones, the muffins, the electric mixer in my hand. "In case you needed anything. Hope that was all right."

"Of course," I say. "Thank you."

I bend my head and turn the mixer on high, making it impossible to speak.

Speak.

The mixer whirs in my hand.

Speak.

I turn the mixer off.

"Graham, I—there's a bunch of stuff—I need to talk to you," I start.

He rubs his stubbled chin. "Okay."

"Okay." I try to sound confident. I wipe my hands on a dishcloth. "Okay. Well."

"You've been busy." He takes a scone, smiling wide. "Brilliant."

"I couldn't sleep. Want coffee?"

OKAY ALREADY, I tell myself, *GO ON*.

He sits down, nodding, mouth full, leaning back in the chair, legs stretched out, crossed at the ankles. He swallows. "How's the leg? You all right to do all this?"

I hand him the coffee. "Believe me, after hopping halfway down a mountain, this I can do." I sip from my own cold cup. "So." Where to begin. I feel naked in the daylight, over coffee. "I guess, what I want to say, what I should have told you a long—"

And then Paul, my boy (our boy), comes into the kitchen, coughing, announcing his entrance.

"Still that cough," I say, folding him into a hug.

"Oh my God. Cinnamon rolls?" He pulls away. "What kind of muffins are those?" He loosens one from the tin. "Oh, man, chocolate chip! Can I?" He holds it aloft, his mouth open, grinning, his cheeks flushed.

I laugh. "Of course. Go for it."

"Thanks." Mouth full, crumbs on his lips. I hand him a napkin.

Graham stands. "Juice, anyone?"

"Me please," Paul says. Mumbles.

Graham fills a glass with orange juice and then reaches for a cinnamon roll.

"Hang on," I say. "Let me frost those."

I hop to the counter and find an offset spatula in one of the drawers. My heart is knocking against my chest, but not with the effort. Plopping on thick mounds of frosting, I slather and swirl, smoothing and daubing as if this alone will make things right.

"I wish," Paul says, mouth still full, "you woke me up. I wanna make them." He watches as I continue my swirl and daub.

"Next time," I say. This is what I want. This life; the three of us. A Next Time.

"Tomorrow?"

"Tomorrow." We will be rich in cinnamon rolls.

Several silent minutes go by; I focus on the frosting.

When I am finished, finally, Graham raises his eyebrows, looks at me oddly.

I select a roll for each of them and set them on plates. "Here." Triumphant.

"Wow," Paul says. "Thanks, Mama."

And that *Mama*. In the years to come, when I hear a child say that word, it will make me stop, wherever I am. It will reach inside me, grip my heart with its small hand, and squeeze. Such innocence, love without regret. The purity of it.

Graham and Paul clear away the dishes while I haul myself upstairs to shower and wash my hair while somehow keeping my cast dry. I lean on my crutches, holding a lawn-and-leaf-sized garbage bag. How will I do this? Thinking exhausts me.

There's a knock on the door. It cracks open and Graham's face appears. "You good?"

"Oh yeah, all set." I hold up the garbage bag.

"Sure?"

"Sure." With a confident smile. But maybe not, because he leaves and when he returns, I'm still standing there and he's holding a chair and a plastic lemonade pitcher from the kitchen.

"I'll do your hair," he says. "And you can have a wash with a cloth after. We'll find a better way once you've had more of a rest."

My eyes sting with grateful tears.

He positions the chair against the sink and I sit with a towel wrapped round my shoulders. I lean back. There is warm water and the clean, beautiful smell of shampoo and the feel of Graham's hands on me as he massages the suds into my scalp. My eyes are closed. I want to take those hands and kiss them.

I want to press his hands to my face, to my lips.

I feel a long pour of water and then a soft towel around my head. I want to—

I open my eyes; he is gone.

FIFTY-ONE

From downstairs, the sound of Graham whistling. Its warble breaks my heart.

I wash and put on a pair of sweats from college and a T-shirt worn almost translucent. I have never felt so clean in my life and yet I know that's not even true. I sit at the top of the stairs and lower myself down one by one, too tired to use crutches.

Graham has made a fire and is sitting on the couch, sipping tea, thumbing through his phone.

"My God," I say. "That was wonderful. Thank you." I look around. "Where's Paul?"

Graham puts his tea and phone on the coffee table. "Outside with Dill. Sledding." He stands to help me hop to the couch. "Tea?"

"No, thanks."

We sit. My hair is wet, combed back from my face, and it feels soap-scrubbed and luxurious.

"I've got some work to do tomorrow," he says. "Classes started Monday."

"Oh, I'm sorry, I've probably screwed up your whole schedule. I don't even know what day of the week it is."

"Thursday." He grins.

The fire flickers in its grate. Yellow flames skip and twirl.

I open my mouth.

I close it. There is a loud crack from the fire, a flurry of sparks.

"Graham, remember when I found out, when Hugh told me—he thought I knew—about you and Mo? And how upset I got, and—" The heat of the fire burns my cheeks. "Well, there's something else, something you don't know, that I never told you, and it hasn't been fair to you, not knowing, and it might explain, or at least help you understand, and—"

"Liv." His eyes tell me to slow down, he understands, it's okay.

Right. But it's not.

"So, well, first of all, you know that letter from Hugh? The one I got with Mo's ashes?" He nods; there is an expression of mild curiosity on his face. "Well, he didn't exactly ask me to go to Nepal, and Mo never really said anything about dying, or where she wanted her ashes scattered. I mean, I don't even think she thought about death."

"Why did you say that then?"

"I don't know," I say automatically. And then, "No. I think I wanted to go. I couldn't admit it to myself, but I wanted an excuse. I didn't want it to be up to me, a choice. And yet it was, anyway."

I look at the fire and there is the smell of wood smoke and it is so very good.

I look back at Graham, who is looking at me. "What?"

He reaches his hand toward mine, and I draw back, though just a little. I want him to take my hand, I want to feel his touch; but if I do, I won't continue.

"That's not all," I say.

"All right." He's moved his hand now, his arm resting along the back of the couch. I know he'll wait until I'm ready to speak; he won't try to get it out of me.

And so I tell him. All of it. From the moment I saw Mo in school, at that frat party. To the words I spoke, the last words I ever said to her, that sent her careening off in the night, to her death. The love and the shame. The unending guilt. The desire.

And his face, unreadable. His eyes, unmoving.

"Why didn't you ever tell me?" he finally asks.

"I could say the same to you."

He shakes his head. "How do you mean?"

"I mean, I read Mo's journal. Evidently, it wasn't 'just a shag.'" I make air quotes with my fingers. "I mean, I know you two had a whole thing, a relationship or whatever, and you chose not to tell me. So there's that. And what was that, anyway?"

"Liv, I—"

"I mean, she dumps you, breaks your heart, and I'm like, what, second string?" I can't say the words *sloppy seconds*. And I'm not even sure what they mean anymore.

"Not quite." His face is serious, his voice calm. "I broke it off with her. I didn't love her; it was a summer thing, and she was going back to the States, and that was it. And yes, it was a shag—many shags, to be sure—but that was what it meant to me. I liked her. She was fun. And shocked, too, when I told her it was over. Same look on her face as yours right now." He smiles, but it vanishes quickly. "Not telling you didn't seem to matter, because she didn't matter. As opposed to how much she mattered to you."

"It's just, she was a big part of my life."

"And you let *that* part ruin *this* part? Our life, together? Christ, Livy."

"I know—"

"No, you don't know." The words come out slowly but his voice is steady. I can't tell if he's furious or sad or disgusted. Or something else.

"I'm sorry," I say. "I'm a terrible hypocrite, getting so angry at you for not telling me about you and Mo. I'm sorry for the way I treated you—for everything." I try to get him to look at me, but he's staring at the fire.

"So now?" He turns to me finally. "What is it you want, Liv?"

I think back to Christmas night, to standing outside Graham's house, when I'd brought Paul. Telling Graham I was going to Nepal because it's what Mo had wanted. I think of Graham's words then: *And what do you want?*

A thousand years ago; a few weeks ago, that night.

"I want you," I say. "Us. I love you." And I want to reach down and hold his instep; I want him to know. But with my leg in its cast it would be too awkward, and besides, how would he remember? Instead, I reach for his hand.

ANNAPURNA

But his hand closes on my wrist. "Liv, there's something you should know."

"What?"

"I took the job. In Boulder."

"You did." I'm surprised: He was willing to go without me. Without Paul. But I'm relieved, too. Maybe I haven't ruined everything.

"I was hoping you'd come. It would've been terrible if you hadn't. If you don't," he corrects himself. "I just want to be honest. To tell the truth."

The truth.

I lower my head and close my eyes, and with my knuckles massage my forehead. Should I? "There's one more thing."

No.

Yes.

No.

"I slept with someone on the trek."

Silence flares between us.

And though he doesn't ask, I say: "Ben."

"The one who died?"

I nod.

"Is that it then, the truth?" Graham's jaw clenches. "I won't hear later there was someone else you were shagging?"

"We were separated—" I say. Not saying that it was sweet, with Ben, it was tender. And a little fierce, too, delirious. Not saying that I was glad it happened, glad for what we shared, although not for what it had cost him.

What will it cost me, the truth?

335

Boulder, Colorado. A new beginning; a new life. What might that look like? Together, starting over. In the mountains.

I remember sitting with Ben and Rick in the hotel in Kathmandu the night we'd arrived. What had Ben said? *Sometimes the way you see yourself has to change.* Maybe Ben was trying to do that. Or maybe he was hanging on to a younger version of himself, unable to make that change. But maybe it's possible for me. To change. Maybe I already have. Maybe it's not too late.

FIFTY-
TWO

Before dinner I unpack my duffel.
Graham has returned to his house—we are to
each *have a think*, as he put it—plus he needs to
prepare for his classes.

I'm not sure what there is to think about, even though
I do, but for once I know what I want. I don't need *a think*.
I've thought enough.

Paul sits on my bed, watching me pull things out and
toss them into piles on the floor.

"Dude, your stuff stinks," he says. "And you're always
telling me to change *my* socks."

"Dude?" I say. "*Have* you changed your socks?"

"You must've sweat a lot." I can hear the admiration
in his voice.

"I did." Oh, to be admired by one's child! "Even when
it was cold, sometimes. Going up."

"I'm gonna do that," he says. "But the real way, too. Like, climb mountains."

The real way. Ha. So much for admiration.

"Maybe we can do some of that next summer," I say, before I know what I'm saying. "Not climbing, but hiking maybe."

"That'd be awesome."

"On some *real* mountain."

"That'd be *really* awesome!" Paul lies back on the bed. "Which one?"

Which one indeed. Will it be in Colorado?

I shake out the empty duffel, trying to air it out. Something clatters to the floor.

Paul sits up and then he's on the floor, searching. "What's this?" He holds up a small, brown wooden carving.

The Ganesh.

"Oh my God, I thought I lost that."

"What is it?"

I tell him about Joshi and the Hindu god and the carving. "So it's not mine," I say. "I need to return it."

"But didn't the guy give it to you?"

"It was more of a lend."

Paul hefts it in his hand. "It's so cool," he says. "I'd want to keep it if I were you."

"I don't need it," I say, realizing this truth. Whatever Ganesh's protection, its power, it was with me all along. Will be with me still, wherever I go. It is in me, just like Mo.

That night I email Joshi, telling him I will return his Ganesh as soon as I can get to the post office. I also email the trekking company for a list of names and addresses of the porters and cook and all the workers who died in the avalanche. In the months to come, and with Joshi's help, we start a fund to support their families. Money isn't everything, but it is something.

I write to Hugh, and to Ben's wife, too, and though none of the words to her are pithy or profound and are instead plain and unoriginal, I mean them.

The day after I email Joshi, he responds, telling me to give the Ganesh to Paul, who immediately puts it in his backpack, and a week or so later I receive a note from Nancy, who encloses the picture of our little group, taken after our lunch on the first day.

I email Rick, and though (unsurprisingly) I don't hear from him for a couple of weeks, when I do, it is to inform me he will be our fund's first donor. Surprise, surprise.

FIFTY-THREE

Now I sit in front of the fire holding Mo's journal. I thumb the pages, so many blank and wanting, waiting for the scratch of pen on paper. And I think of the blank pages in all our lives, waiting to be filled, to be written in the squint of sunlight, beside the dry heat of a wood fire, pristine pages that might be spattered by drops of rain or smudges of tears or the rust of blood.

How would Mo have filled them? And what would she have thought, if she could have read them, so many years later.

My thumb stops on the last page on which there is writing. I haven't read this entry. And I remember, yes, I'd gotten stuck on the two paragraphs about Graham — about Mo and Graham — and that was it. I never turned the page, never checked to see if there was more.

And there is more. I read the first line:

October 25, Later

He opens the door and I pull him towards me.

And then my eyes skip down, skimming, until I see the name: *Tika*. And right, yes, he'd confessed in the hospital that he'd kissed her, and though I was surprised at the time, it really wasn't a surprise, it made perfect sense, and now I let my eyes flit along the page, not wanting to intrude, to insert myself in what happened between them.

And then I see my name, and read on:

And then Liv walks in.

Liv with her curls aflame, her cheeks flushed, her mouth open.

She stops.

Oh, she says, noticing her duffel on the bed farthest from mine. Where I had dragged it. Thank you, Tika.

What else does she notice?

Tika dips his head, says Namaste.

His eyes avoid mine and he steps out the door.

Congratulations, I say to Liv and she says the same to me. She leans down, where I am sitting, her pack still on, and hugs me.

I can smell Liv's body odor through her layers. It comes off in waves of animal heat. And I know I must smell, too, and I wonder if it's me that smells like an animal.

I know I need to tell her I'll be leaving tomorrow. We're all leaving, of course, but I won't be leaving with her. How can I tell her? It's ruined, and not just by her or by what happened.

She pulls things from her duffel; refolds; reorganizes.

I picture her face when I tell her: an inward crush. A crumple.

And then I feel sorry for her again, and disgusted. For a flash I picture Mum's face when I was five, maybe six, when I was weeping because I hadn't been invited to a birthday party. Stella's birthday party, a freckled girl who could make a clover shape with her tongue. I cried and cried, and Mum just looked at me, her eyes hard.

I'll tell her after dinner. Those other girls will be in the room and there won't be much she can say. And I'll be leaving early in the morning.

I just want this to be over.

I hug the journal to my chest. And then I toss it into the fire.

For a moment, it lies there, whole and unspoiled, untouched by the flames that surround it. I watch as orange tongues lap at it, teasing, until a corner glows red and there's a bright pop and the heat and burn spread, consuming it.

Mo was that flame. That bright pop.

I think back to that bonfire at the frat house our senior year. How Mo stood watching, alone. How her hair streamed golden in the light from the fire; how she smiled as she watched it explode. And it's her smile I consider now. Maybe it really was a smile of gratitude, for our help in building the fire. Maybe it was one of satisfaction. Or of peace. Maybe she was thinking of her boyfriend, Greg, who knows. She'd done this—roused us all to do this for her, with her—and I thought at the time there was no greater thing.

Now I wonder. Mo wasn't as glittery and innocent as I'd thought. Or if she was, that wasn't all she was.

That night, the police came. No siren to alert us, just the sudden shock of loud voices from uniformed men who were neither enthralled nor amused by our creation. They shone flashlights in our faces and halted our scrambling to hide beers and bongs and bottles of vodka and lined us up and took our names. Later, there were disciplinary board meetings and fraternity house suspensions and phone calls and letters to parents and individual probationary periods.

All fires burn out, I think now, *leaving their ashes behind*.

And the opportunity to start anew.

I keep the picture of Mo and her grandmother, saved from her journal, in the drawer of my nightstand, next to the picture of our group on the first trek to Annapurna Base Camp and the one sent by Nancy of us about to set off for our second. I see myself standing stiffly next to Rick, my tight little smile; I feel the revulsion in my belly. And I want to say to myself: *You don't know. You have no idea what's ahead of you. So think of now, and this, and know what you can. What you want. What matters.*

And regret nothing.

"There are other Annapurnas
in the lives of men."

——Maurice ('Momo') Herzog,
*Annapurna: The First Conquest
of an 8,000-Meter Peak*

"The secret of the mountains is that the
mountains simply exist, as I do myself: the
mountains exist simply, which I do not. The
mountains have no 'meaning,' they *are*. The sun
is round, I ring with life, and the mountains
ring, and when I can hear it, there is a ringing
that we share. I understand all this, not in
my mind but in my heart, knowing how
meaningless it is to try to capture what cannot
be expressed, knowing that mere words will
remain when I read it all again, another day."

——Peter Matthiessen,
The Snow Leopard

ACKNOWLEDGMENTS

Writing this book has been a journey of the very best kind: not always comfortable, but challenging and joyous in equal measure. I am indebted to those who have accompanied me along the way.

To my guides in Nepal on my (very happy and totally injury- and tragedy-free) trek to the Annapurna base camp, and to the porters, cooks, and workers in the teahouses, my deepest gratitude.

To my agent Matthew Carnicelli, thank you for never giving up on me. I'll be forever grateful to you for making my dream come true. To my endlessly supportive editor, Adriana Senior, thank you for taking a chance on me, and to Aleigha Koss, HB Steadham, Gretchen Young, and to all the people at Regalo, thank you for your wise and gentle guidance. To my brilliant publicity team, Gretchen Koss and Meg Walker, thank you for all your hard work and careful attention, and to Claudia Serino, for her keen eye and treasured insights. I am hugely grateful. For medical insights, thank you to Joe Serino. Your advice (though I'm sure I mangled it) was incredibly helpful. All mistakes are entirely mine.

To the many gifted writers, mentors, and editors who have shared with me their knowledge and inspiration on this wild writing ride—among them Lauren Groff, Pam Houston, Tom Jenks, Caroline Leavitt, Josh Mohr, John Paine, Ted Thompson, Malena Watrous, Michelle Wildgen, and all the advisers and my cohort at Bennington, most especially Amy Hempl and Jill McCorkle—thank you for making me a better writer, and this a better novel.

To my beloved and very talented writing group, Kit Smyth Basquin, Mame Ekblom Cudd, Shane Delaney, Bob Kinerk, and Catherine Purchase, thank you for your kindness, your invaluable comments, and your constant encouragement.

To my first readers, Jen Richter and Maeve Serino, massive thanks for wading through multiple drafts, and for your generous and thoughtful feedback. Your suggestions are gold. And thanks also to my dear friends who read drafts, walked and talked with me, and gave me the oomph to keep going: Sarah Bateman, Colleen Burns, Donna Jackson, Lisa Fay, Alexa Kantgias, Elizabeth Lustbader, Beth Munro, Paula Sherk and Donna Steinberg. And to my earliest cheerleaders, Andrea Chermayeff, Jane Lancellotti and Michelle McLane.

To my soulsister Amanda McKee, thank you for the adventures and the joy.

To my sister and the person I have loved the longest, Julie Shevach, thank you for believing in me when I can't, and for remembering when I forget. I would be lost without you. And to my other sister, Debbie Serino, and to Max Brenner, Tara Brenner, and Ariana and Connor Clerkin, thank you for showing up, for all the love, for being there for all of us, always.

To the person who's accompanied me on my lifetime journey, my husband Joe, thank you for your everlasting generosity, and for making me laugh. Without you, this book couldn't have been written. I fell in love with you a thousand years ago watching you walk across campus from my dorm, your head down, singing. I will love you a thousand more.

To my children, Joe, Maeve and Claudia: I dedicated this book to you because, very simply, you are everything to me. Thank you for teaching me what's important, for sharing your life with me, and for your grace.

My love for you is boundless, and beyond words. Your love is the greatest gift of my life.